The Tea-Olive Bird Watching Society

Also by Augusta Trobaugh
in Large Print:

Sophie and the Rising Sun

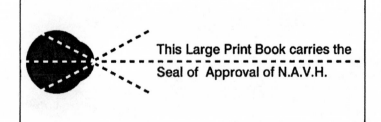

This Large Print Book carries the
Seal of Approval of N.A.V.H.

The Tea-Olive Bird Watching —Society—

AUGUSTA TROBAUGH

Thorndike Press • Waterville, Maine

L.T.E.,
Trobaugh

Published in 2005 by arrangement with Dutton, a member of Penguin Group (USA) Inc.

Thorndike Press® Large Print Americana.

The tree indicium is a trademark of Thorndike Press.

The text of this Large Print edition is unabridged. Other aspects of the book may vary from the original edition.

Set in 16 pt. Plantin.

Printed in the United States on permanent paper.

Library of Congress Cataloging-in-Publication Data

Trobaugh, Augusta.
    The Tea-Olive Bird Watching Society / by Augusta Trobaugh.
        p. cm. — (Thorndike Press large print Americana)
    ISBN 0-7862-7883-8 (lg. print : hc : alk. paper)
    1. Women — Societies and clubs — Fiction.   2. Female friendship — Fiction.   3. Bird watchers — Fiction.
    4. Older women — Fiction.   5. Revenge — Fiction.
    6. Georgia — Fiction.   7. Judges — Fiction.   8. Large type books.   I. Title.   III. Thorndike Press large print Americana series.
    PS3570.R585T43 2005b
    813'.54—dc22   2005013638

For Eric

As the Founder/CEO of NAVH, the only national health agency solely devoted to those who, although not totally blind, have an eye disease which could lead to serious visual impairment, I am pleased to recognize Thorndike Press* as one of the leading publishers in the large print field.

Founded in 1954 in San Francisco to prepare large print textbooks for partially seeing children, NAVH became the pioneer and standard setting agency in the preparation of large type.

Today, those publishers who meet our standards carry the prestigious "Seal of Approval" indicating high quality large print. We are delighted that Thorndike Press is one of the publishers whose titles meet these standards. We are also pleased to recognize the significant contribution Thorndike Press is making in this important and growing field.

Lorraine H. Marchi, L.H.D.
Founder/CEO
NAVH

* Thorndike Press encompasses the following imprints: Thorndike, Wheeler, Walker and Large Print Press.

CHAPTER
— ONE —

From the last will and testament of Love-Divine Brockett King, executed and read by Mr. John Anderson, attorney, one week after her funeral:

"I leave all of my property and holdings to the Tea-Olive Public Library, with my attorney arranging for the sale of my property and the distribution of the funds to the library. However, there is one exception to this gift: that little wooded area we've always simply called 'the woods' is to become the property of the Tea-Olive Bird Watching Society. The woods comprise approximately the thirteen acres, more or less, between Highway 64 and the edge of my yard, bounded on the north by Singing Creek and on the south by that present roadway to my house. I hope that from now on, the bird-watchers — all of them my friends — will call it the King's

Wood Bird Sanctuary (named for my late husband, the Reverend James King, may God rest his beautiful soul!), and that it be owned jointly by all present and future members of the Tea-Olive Bird Watching Society, of which I have been an active member since its inception all those many years ago. I ask that my executor arrange for surveying the area and assisting the bird-watchers in establishing a deed. Should the Tea-Olive Bird Watching Society ever cease to exist, the woods will become the property of the town of Tea-Olive, Georgia, with the provision that the city managers will maintain it as a bird sanctuary forever.

Also, if for any reason in the future the library ceases to exist (something I can hardly imagine), any remaining funds will revert to the town of Tea-Olive itself, to be used for the betterment of the community, according to the decision of the town council.

Note to the ladies of the Tea-Olive Bird Watching Society: Please protect this little sanctuary I have left to you all. You know my heart on this subject, and I trust that you will convey my wishes to all future members. I fear that the

8

cancerous-growth development of the cities around us will one of these days reach our own little town in these sweet hills below the Appalachian Mountains, and these acres must be protected. I cannot face my Maker (as I am sure to do soon) without having made everlasting provisions for the human friends and the feathered friends who have brought me so much joy, and this provision will assure that only appreciative, loving eyes will be cast upon the birds. Lastly, thank all of you for being my friends, thank you for the many hours of bird watching we have enjoyed together, the endless cups of tea sipped around one another's kitchen tables, and the fine singing in church on Sunday mornings.

One last thing I need to say: I've had everything any lady could ever ask for. I was born into a loving family, I married the great love of my life and had him by my side for almost fifty years, and I have been fortunate in having such good friends in the bird watching society, as well as in my community and my church. I have truly been blessed. So if anyone ever asks what my last words were to you, tell them I said this: 'Thank you all! I sure did have a good time.'"

CHAPTER
— TWO —

When he finished reading the will, the attorney glanced at the three women who were sitting in his office in quiet attentiveness, with their ankles crossed and their motionless, gloved hands resting in their laps. Somehow, their appearances comforted him in a primal manner, perhaps inspiring a memory of his own mother, and he smiled as he inhaled the clean aroma of soap and bath powder as it wafted around the room, circulated by the fan in the high ceiling of the office in the ancient courthouse.

He was surprised by the depth of his appreciation for these women — these *ladies,* in the greatest sense of the word, an honorary title bestowed upon gentle Southern women who did good works in the community, attended church and Bible study regularly, behaved appropriately at all times, and set good examples for the few younger women who lived in the small town of Tea-Olive, Georgia. He allowed himself the luxury of studying the women for long moments, noting the peaceful yet somewhat bruised gazes of their eyes and knowing that, as delighted as they must be about Love-Divine's gift to their bird watching society and to the town library, each of them was still mourning the passing of a good and dear friend.

Finally, he allowed himself to reach for a sealed letter that had been packaged with Love-Divine's will and handed it across his desk to Love-Divine's closest friend, Beulah-Land Everett (more simply called Beulah by most people), who handled it with a hesitation that came from accepting what would become the voice of her dear friend from beyond the grave. Beulah put the letter into her purse, while two other members of the bird watching society — Wildwood and Sweet — looked on silently. They appropriately concealed their happiness at gaining the woods for the bird watching society — and, as manager of the local branch library, Wildwood was also particularly surprised and happy about the gift to the library. But they said nothing, retained somber faces, and glanced from time to time at Beulah, deeply appreciative of Beulah's strong leadership abilities.

11

Beulah was certainly a strong-willed and physically well-rounded woman (some would have called her pleasingly plump, but not to her face), who prided herself on her general practicality and insistence on wearing sensible shoes. All of the members of the society were women who were at the center of activities in the small town of Tea-Olive, Georgia. But because Beulah was also the president of the bird watching society, she received special deference from the other members, particularly on the day when the society had received such a wonderful gift from Love-Divine. Too, they were all long-time volunteers in the local library's Homework Helper Program, a free service for academically at-risk youngsters, and members of the Service Saints at the Baptist Church, a Bible study group of ladies who balanced their study of Holy Writ with services to the needy in the town. The Service Saints took meals to shut-ins, provided transportation to the elderly for doctor appointments or grocery shopping, and held bake sales once a quarter, with the funds going to the church.

As the ladies sat in the attorney's office, they all seemed to glow with that special shine of women who *do good* for the community and who love the Lord with all their hearts. On that day, two members had been unable to attend the reading of Love-Divine's will: Memphis, who ran a small tearoom and was unable to close up her shop because of the early lunch customers her tearoom usually attracted, and Zion, who owned a small herd of Jersey cows and sold milk, cream, and butter out of a small creamery in her own home just outside of town. But truth be told, the other members hadn't really expected Zion to show up. She always had so much work to do, and whenever they did manage to convince her to attend some function or the other, she spent the entire time sighing and rolling her eyes and fidgeting in her chair, such was her impatience to "get back to the barn," as she explained it.

"When I'm there, I'm in the right place," Zion said. "And besides, the only reason I said I'd be in the bird watching society is because you all can't yak all the time! You *have* to be quiet!"

And none of them were offended by Zion's blunt directness. She had a terrible growl in her voice most of the time, but they all knew that deep down, she had a good heart.

All of the ladies, save for Memphis, had

been born right in Tea-Olive and therefore bore "hymnal names." Perhaps that would seem odd to strangers, but it had long been a tradition that girl babies were named after lyrics of hymns in the Baptist Hymnal and boy babies were named straight out of the Bible. So the men were John and Paul, Peter and David, Matthew and Aaron. And the ladies were named Grace (for the hymn "Amazing Grace"), Joy (for the hymn "I've Got the Joy, Joy, Joy, Joy, Down in My Heart!"), Beulah (for the hymn "Dwelling in Beulah Land"), Wildwood (for the hymn "The Church in the Wildwood"), Zion (for the hymn "We're Marching to Zion"), Love (for the hymn "Love Lifted Me"), Love-Divine (for the hymn "Love Divine, All Loves Excelling"), and Sweet (for the hymn "The Sweet By and By"). But the sad thing was that no one knew exactly how that tradition started, and if there had ever been anyone who knew, they were long committed to the red earth and eternal silence.

Memphis was the exception to the tradition of hymnal names. During the Korean War, her mother — one of the many Graces ("Amazing Grace") in town — was expecting a child, so she went to stay with her aunt in Tennessee while her husband was overseas. When the war was over and he came home, they returned to Tea-Olive with a baby girl named Memphis. As soon as people in town heard her strange name, they went through their hymnals, trying to find a hymn with the word *Memphis* in it. But to no avail. And her mother's whimsy at naming her after the city where she had been born followed her throughout her life in Tea-Olive and made her something of a novelty.

After the attorney had finished all the business and closed the folder on his desk, he gazed amicably at Beulah, Wildwood, and Sweet and cleared his throat. "I have a cousin in Augusta who's a surveyor," he offered. "If you like, I'll call him and set up a time so he can come out and take care of business for you ladies."

"Thank you," Beulah whispered.

"And now," the attorney said, standing up and bowing slightly to the three women, "I will start trying to liquidate the remainder of Miss Love-Divine's estate so that the funds may be transferred to the library, as she so stipulated."

"Do you have any idea of how much it will be?" Wildwood ventured, speaking the words gently and keeping her eyes cast down.

15

"Not really," the attorney confessed. "There's the farm, of course, and we will have to get it put onto the market. But being so far out in the country, I'm not sure that it will bring a sizable amount. There are also some investments. The Reverend King, as you know, was a frugal man."

"Well," Wildwood added, letting her eyes meet those of the attorney, "whatever it is, the library is certainly grateful to her."

"Put the land on the market?" Beulah asked, with alarm in her voice.

"Yes. Sell it. Liquidate the estate," the attorney said.

"But you wouldn't sell it to a developer, would you?" Beulah's suddenly louder voice seemed to vibrate in the small office.

The attorney smiled. "No, ma'am. Not to a developer," he said, and then, studying the pained expression on Beulah's face, he added, "It's such a small farm — not even a working farm at this point — that I'm sure no developer would want it."

"I've heard there was one — a developer, that is — snooping around about the old Maxson place, and it's not far from here." Beulah's voice sounded out her deep concern.

The attorney shook his head. "That's a

16

much larger tract of land, as I understand," he explained. "But growth is going to come to us, sooner or later," he said softly. "When the cities start overflowing, people start wanting homes farther out. And, too, development brings jobs you know."

"Oh, I know," Beulah said with misery in her voice. "But it brings other things, too. Things we don't want — heavy traffic, strip malls, and . . ." She stopped, lowering her voice to a whisper: "Nude dancing clubs — such as that."

"And new schools and new churches and perhaps even a new library," he said, smiling and nodding his head toward Wildwood.

"Come on, Beulah," Sweet said, taking Beulah's arm. "I'm sure John will be as interested in protecting our little community as we all are." Beulah cast a suspicious glance at the attorney. She knew that Sweet was an eternal optimist who always expected everyone else to be as honest and kind as *she* was.

Beulah was not so optimistic. She knew for a fact that sometimes a dark curtain can ripple in an invisible breeze and give us a glimpse of unlikely monsters.

When the women had exited the court-

17

house, they hesitated on the sidewalk. Wildwood glanced at her watch. "I have to get to the library, but we'll get together and figure all this out."

"It's nice she left so much to the library," Sweet commented.

"Oh, indeed it is!" Wildwood let a little bit of her elation show.

"Well, I'll let you all know when the surveyor is going to come out," Beulah said. "I'm sure we will want to follow him around, so we will know exactly what belongs to the society. Let's all just pray — pray hard — that no developer will buy it. Now, I have to get on home. I'll call you tomorrow." As the women prepared to take their leave, they went into a gentle flurry of air-kissing each other's cheeks and waving with fluttering fingers.

How shocked and repulsed those good, church-going, Bible reading ladies of the Tea-Olive Bird Watching Society would have been if they had known that in only a few short months, they would find themselves in the unthinkable position of plotting to commit a murder. But even when they found themselves caught up in such an unlikely and horrific plan, they never were able to use the word *murder*, because of the commandment, "Thou shalt not kill." So

18

that later, they called it by far more gentle names, names that belied the brutal truth of the matter. They couched that terrible resolve in more positive terms: *saving our friend, doing what has to be done, living up to our duty.*

Beulah saved her private letter from Love-Divine until she was in her own sweet sanctuary — sitting at her kitchen table with a tall glass of iced tea in front of her. She slit open the heavy linen envelope and withdrew the creamy pages, folded just right and with Love-Divine's copperplate handwriting going across the pages in perfectly straight lines.

"My dear Beulah-Land . . ."

the letter began, and already Beulah was smiling, for Love-Divine was ever formal and correct, and she always used Beulah's full hymnal name.

"You know now of my leaving those little woods to the bird watching society, and I trust that you are pleased with this arrangement. Of course, the majority of my estate goes to the library, and I know Wildwood will be grateful for

19

that. As you well know, the Homework Helper Program is dear to my heart!

As for this letter — I simply want to thank you, once again, for that long trip to the coast you took me on last month. You knew how very much I wanted to see the shore birds for the first and last time in my life, and I am ever grateful. It was a long drive you made, with your trunk all loaded with lawn chairs and a picnic lunch and blankets for spreading on the sand and with me piled up in your backseat, resting as well as possible and looking like a nine-months-pregnant lady! Isn't it strange how that happened? All my life, I wanted a child, and when I was young, I even used to pretend that I was expecting a child! You are the only person in the whole world who knows that little secret. Even my own husband didn't know, of course. But I loved my pretend-swollen stomach, loved that a pretend baby was growing in it. That life was in the making! I use to rub my hands all over it and even sing to it! That seems so strange, now that I'm older. And here at the end of my life, the swollen stomach still isn't life at all. It's death. I have a hard time remembering that, and maybe I shouldn't try to re-member it at all. Maybe it's a great comfort for me to know that death will come to me from the very place where life could have arisen, had it been God's will. Maybe you understand what I am saying, as you never had children either. And I think that wanting a baby so much is what got me interested in birds. They are so much like babies — small, fragile, fine-boned. But children grow up to be bigger, stronger people, while birds never do! They are always fragile, and we must never, ever hurt them. We must protect them, admire them, and appreciate them.

But I'm probably making you sad with these words, so let me go on to what I wanted to say the most: I will never forget that wonderful day we spent at the shore, watching all of the birds I had never seen with my own eyes: the lovely little spotted sandpipers, the royal terns, that juvenile white ibis, the marbled godwit, and finally, that wonderful snowy egret. And all those beautiful seagulls hovering over us, riding the ocean breeze like little kites and shrieking at us for tidbits of our sandwiches. I remember the smell of the

21

*ocean and the sand we got in our shoes,
and I remember licking my lips and
tasting salt on them. Bless your heart,
you made that all possible for me, and I
will never — ever — forget that day.
Thank you from the bottom of my heart,
dear, dear friend. Love, Love-Divine
Brockett King."*

Beulah refolded the letter carefully and
put it back into the envelope and leaned it
up against the sugar bowl, where she could
see her full hymnal name written in Love-
Divine's beautiful handwriting. And after
all, it was Love-Divine herself who got the
Tea-Olive Bird Watching Society established. Such a simple start it had been:
One early spring, a mourning dove had
made her nest in a low tree right outside of
Love-Divine's kitchen window, and after
every inevitable spring afternoon thunder-
shower, she would look out at the bird,
making sure it was OK. During the storms
themselves, Love-Divine watched the bird
being pelted with heavy, warm raindrops
and flattening herself on the nest as light-
ning flashed around her and the loud rolls
of thunder shook the very roots of the
nesting tree. And what struck Love-Divine
the most was that the bird never left the

22

nest, no matter what. She just flattened her small body against the forces of nature that are a part of the always-tumultuous Southern springtime, incubating the eggs and zealously guarding them, insuring the soft, distinct cooing of her offspring for the future. From that small miracle, Love-Divine developed a great love for all birds, and that was why she organized the bird watching society.

The women who formed the society had more in common than just an appreciation for birds of all varieties and the good works they accomplished in the community: Each and every one of them had experienced devastating loss or terrible betrayal in their lives, and to a member, they had learned to live with that. They shared yet one more common denominator: childlessness. Though they never spoke of that barrenness, each one of them retained a memory of sweet expectation, as they waited for long years for fruition from their own bodies. That shared memory was still among them, whether they were older and simply dreaming about what they had missed — Sweet, Beulah, and Zion — or whether they were relatively young and still hopeful — like Wildwood — or young but successfully distracting herself — that was Memphis.

Sweet was the only member of the Tea-Olive Bird Watching Society who had never been married. Both Beulah and Zion were widows, as had been Love-Divine. Wildwood was what folks in Tea-Olive called a "grass widow," a kind euphemism for a divorced woman and a term that was meant to salvage some of her dignity. Wildwood was the only divorcée in the whole town, and women who believed so strongly in traditional marriage sometimes gazed at her in an ever-so-slightly reproachful manner, but some of the women gazed at her in admiration — gazed openly upon a woman who had chosen to reject her own husband. No one ever knew exactly what had caused Wildwood to do something so unorthodox, because she never spoke of it herself, and of course, no one would have broached such a sensitive subject themselves. In fact, when they started using the term grass widow to describe Wildwood, none of them really knew where that expression came from. But Wildwood, ever the good librarian, sensed their curiosity, so she made sure to leave the library's large *The American Heritage Dictionary of the English Language* open to the page that explained the term, placing a small stick-it note to indicate the term itself. She knew full well that if only one person noticed that term and read its definition, word about the meaning of "grass widow" would spread through the town. And she was right.

Memphis had been married for several years to a young man from the flatlands of South Georgia before he was killed in a tragic automobile accident. At that point, she returned to Tea-Olive, and when she came back home, she never spoke of the tragedy, simply explaining in a good-natured tone that she much preferred living "above the gnat line," a terminology that separated their own North Georgia community from similar, but gnat-infested ones in South Georgia.

All of these good women felt a great need to nurture, which they satisfied by taking care of one another and by watching the many birds that nested around their town, fixating every spring on the various nestings and watching as the migratory birds flew away in the fall.

With Zion as the single exception, they were all active in the Homework Helper Program at Tea-Olive's small branch library, where they patiently helped small children who gripped their pencils too tightly, worried their bottom lips over arithmetic problems, and took an agonizingly long time in sounding out unfamiliar words. Through all of that, they were patient and loving, even when some of the children — those from homes in which personal hygiene was not encouraged — smelled like small, terrified animals that had been hiding in dank burrows far belowground.

CHAPTER
— THREE —

Early in the following week, several of the ladies went to those familiar woods, gazing around at the small copse of trees with new appreciation, and following the surveyor around as he measured, drove stakes into the ground, and made careful calculations in his notebook. Even though the women were all members of the bird watching society, anyone who was a more avid birder probably would have found their observation techniques quite amateurish, but they never professed to be completely occupied by the activity, as all of them had other demands upon their lives and their time. Still, their joy in spotting any kind of bird was always genuine in every way. They dutifully studied their bird identification books, but that was really the extent of their preparations for walking around and listening for any sound that would prompt them to raise their binoculars and murmur small sounds of appreciation.

On that particular day, Zion had asked that the surveying not take place until afternoon, saying that she had cows to milk and butter to churn that morning, and so it was after two in the afternoon when they gathered to watch the surveyor.

"If Zion had only told me she was behind in her chores, I could have gone in to help her yesterday," Beulah complained, whispering to Sweet. "I know I work for her only part-time, but I would have gone in to help her out, and she wouldn't even have had to pay me a penny for that."

"Well, you know how she is," commented Sweet, again whispering. "She doesn't like to ask for help. I'm still surprised she lets you help her out part-time."

"You all whispering something about me?" Zion suddenly demanded. "You have something to say, just say it right out."

"No, that's OK, Zion." Beulah tried to soothe her, and then she added what she hoped would be a distraction: "Did you ever see such glorious fall colors?" Her sweeping arm indicated the trees all around them. And indeed, autumn was in its fullest bloom, with the gentle foothills all around town and indeed Tea-Olive itself fairly undulating in riotous shades of red, orange, and yellow. Likewise, King's Wood (as they were obediently calling it, following Love-Divine's request) was also in its fullest autumnal glory. The sassafras and sweet gum leaves were a deep, vibrant red and hickory, and ginkgo leaves a bright, neon yellow. On the edge of the woods, close to the road stood a monstrous bitternut hickory tree that in winter revealed its bitter, crooked skeleton for all to see, loaded with winter-black crooked fingers that beckoned, like monster-hands. Other than the bitternut, the only tree that attracted attention was an Eastern white pine that towered almost a hundred feet in the air, far outreaching the other, more standard trees in the wood.

Only Beulah had been privy to Love-Divine's thoughts about the huge white pine: "Whenever I look through my kitchen window at the woods, I always think about a long ago time when a stray seed held in its tiny heart all the potential for that magnificent tree! And how did that miraculous seed manage to come so far south of the North Georgia mountains, which should have been the southernmost region in which it could survive? How did it arrive in these foothills and what were the odds of its landing in that rich soil at the edge of the woods, taking hold, and beginning its miraculous transformation? I believe with all my heart that God simply wanted that tree to grow right there."

Gathering under the great elm, the women from the bird watching society certainly had Love-Divine on their minds that day. Beulah had kept private the last letter Love-Divine had written to her, because no one else in the group knew about the trip they had made to the seashore. If the others had found out beforehand, they would surely have wanted to go along, and she had something entirely more calm and beautiful than having Love-Divine sitting in the middle of their *oohs* and *ahs* about the water birds. Instead, Beulah and Love-Divine had enjoyed a quiet, peaceful day filled with unspoken delight. That was the gift Beulah meant to give, and she had done so.

Now, because of Love-Divine's generosity, the club members followed the surveyor around gratefully. Beulah, Zion, and Sweet — who were called the senior members — had been joined by one of the slightly younger members: Wildwood. But Memphis, the other younger member, was unable to join them in the woods because her tearoom would still be serving a late tea/luncheon. Wildwood and Memphis were called junior members not because of their younger ages, but because they were relatively new to the whole business of bird watching.

Wildwood had been quite a handful for her mother when she was young — wearing strange-looking clothes and smoking cigarettes right out in public, something that caused her mother no end of distress. But when Wildwood matured, she became the sedate and unflappable librarian at the Tea-Olive branch library.

Memphis, who was not able to go to watch the surveying of their new land, and despite her un-hymnal name, was nonetheless a charming younger woman who, until she opened her tearoom, had worked in a local doctor's office. The most novice of all the birders, Memphis studied her guides regularly and was finally beginning to be able to identify several types of birds without her binoculars, but work in her tearoom always took precedence over bird watching.

While they were in the woods, Beulah glanced at Love-Divine's little house, sitting empty now and looking so lonely.

"I wonder what will happen to that house," Beulah said. "Surely, someone will buy it."

"But who?" asked Zion. "Not enough

31

land for big-time farming. And there's no other kind of work here, except the Dairy Queen or the kitty litter factory."

"That's true."

"Poor Love-Divine!" Zion said suddenly. "She had such an unfulfilling marriage!"

"What?" the others chorused.

"You better hush your mouth!" Beulah admonished. "How could you say such a hurtful thing?"

" 'Cause it's true!" Zion declared. "She told me so herself!"

"Why, surely you're just as wrong as you can be about that!" Wildwood cried.

"Listen," Zion lowered her voice to a conspiratorial whisper. "Long years ago, I stopped at that very house right there." She pointed to Love-Divine's old house. "I wanted to bring some butter beans from my garden to Love-Divine and the *good reverend.*" She snorted the last two words. "It was a Tuesday evening, and I was just going to leave the bushel basket on their back porch for them, assuming as I did that they were at the church league softball game. You do all remember how crazy he was about playing on that league, don't you?"

They all murmured in agreement, for it was widely known that, as a close second to his love for the church, the Reverend King loved playing softball. Played it, in fact, right up until his final illness prevented him from swinging a bat. And every single time he played, Love-Divine had been in the stands to cheer on the team.

Zion continued: "But when I went up to the porch, I saw Love-Divine sitting there all alone. When she saw me, she started to get up out of her chair and go inside. But then I guess she thought better of it, because she knew, of course, that I'd already seen her. So when she came to open the screen door for me, I could tell she'd been crying. She tried to cover it up, but I could tell, just the same. 'You OK?' I asked her, and you should have seen what happened then!"

"What?" They were all entranced by Zion's long-held secret.

"She started bawling! Wrapped herself around my neck and just sobbed. Said that the *good reverend*" — here, she snorted the words again — "seems he wasn't the perfect husband everybody thought he was. She'd never before opened her mouth to say a word against him, but she did that night. And I never heard her speak ill of him again."

"So if he wasn't a perfect husband, what

was he?" Wildwood persisted.

"He was just . . . a typical man," Zion spat.

"But in her will, she called him her *beloved husband,* and she even asked that this sanctuary be named after him!" Beulah argued. "And look at all the time she took such good care of him when he was in his last illness!"

"She kept her secret," Zion explained. "She kept her secret and if it wasn't for me, she would have taken it to her grave."

"What secret?" Wildwood demanded.

"Something that should remain a secret," Zion pronounced, speaking slowly and trying to resist the urge to tell. In the end, she couldn't keep her mouth shut: "Well, just so you all will know, he never did appreciate how hard it is to be a preacher's wife. Just didn't show any gratitude for all her hard work."

"I'll bet he's not the only preacher to be guilty of something like that," Beulah said. "It takes a brave woman to marry a preacher," she added. "I'm glad my sweet Paul worked in the flour mill all his life. It may not have been exciting, but it was good work, and he always had his Sundays off."

During this entire exchange, Sweet had

steadily backed up, with her hand over her heart, until at last, she was at a distance where she couldn't hear what was being said. To her mind, if Love-Divine had wanted the world to know of any disappointment in her marriage, she would have told it herself, and to hear the others speaking openly about what they would never have said in front of Love-Divine herself made Sweet incredibly sad, in a very strange way.

Beulah put an end to the uncomfortable gossip and tried to take the conversation to a kinder topic. "Listen, ladies, when we're through here, I'm going to treat you all to afternoon tea at Memphis's new tearoom. Have any of you seen it yet?"

With the welcome change in conversation, Sweet had rejoined the others, and she and Wildwood shook their heads, but Zion snorted. "I've been scared to look!" she pronounced.

"I hear she's done a good job with it," Beulah defended. "But let's go see for ourselves. So we can celebrate this wonderful sanctuary Love-Divine left to us."

CHAPTER
— FOUR —

Memphis lived in an enormous Victorian house that her parents had turned over to her when she returned home newly widowed, and her parents had retired to Florida. But when they moved away, she ambled around the large, empty house, unsure of what to do with herself. Her part-time work as the doctor's receptionist seemed suddenly unsatisfying, so she joined the Tea-Olive Bird Watching Society and started learning the many elements of good birding. She also signed on to help with the Homework Helper Program at the library, for which her friend Wildwood was ever grateful. Still, those activities failed to completely satisfy her. Almost in desperation, she planned a trip to England, something she had always wanted to do. Aside from the boys who went off to war so long ago, no one in Tea-Olive had ever been to England, and Wildwood was excited about Memphis's trip and saw the opportunity for a wonderful library program.

When Memphis returned home, they set up a date and time, and Wildwood set up the slide projector in the meeting room. Everyone looked forward to hearing about Memphis's trip and seeing her pictures. But to their surprise, the only slides Memphis brought back were of tearooms. No pictures of castles or moats, no Big Ben, no London Bridge — just one tearoom after another. People who were watching the slides were polite, of course, but everyone wondered what on earth could have so fascinated Memphis about the English tearooms. Later, they discovered that the fascination went much deeper than they ever realized, because Memphis set about creating an authentic tearoom right in the front parlor of her big house. For weeks, the sound of hammers and electric saws came from the house, then movers delivered eight or ten small tables and many fancy chairs. Luckily for Memphis, the property was already zoned for residential/commercial use, and the last thing she did was to have a carpenter at the furniture factory design and erect a tasteful sign: MEMPHIS'S ENGLISH TEAROOM. Smaller print below announced: SCONES, SPECIALTY JAMS, CLOTTED CREAM, THE FINEST IN ENGLISH

TEAS, ALL SERVED IN AN AUTHENTIC
ENGLISH ATMOSPHERE.

Finally, one day she tied a large bouquet
of balloons to the sign, and the tearoom
was in business. Among Memphis's first
customers were members of the Monday
afternoon Bible study group from the
Methodist Church. They tittered appreciatively at the lovely décor, and they fully
appreciated the paper-thin teacups and the
delicious scones. Wisely, Memphis had
added some Southern treats to the menu
as well: miniature pecan tarts, cheese straws,
and delicate, almond-flavored cookies, all
served in miniature muffin papers of soft,
pastel shades. For a reasonable price, each
table of four ladies was served a three-
tiered tray of assorted sweets and all the
specialty teas they wanted to drink. The
good report from the Methodist Bible
group spread throughout town quickly,
and they were followed by the Baptist
Women's Bible study, the Presbyterian
"Beautiful Day" Bible study, and eventually,
by the Veterans' Auxiliary group from
another nearby town. But because the
"meetings" of the Tea-Olive Bird Watching
Society were always conducted outdoors,
they had not had the chance to meet at
Memphis's new establishment. Now,

however, a celebration of Love-Divine's gift was a perfect excuse for them, and of course, Beulah was happy to have something to distract them from further discussing any particulars of Love-Divine's marriage.

"You all go on to the tearoom, if that's what you want to do," Zion announced. "As for me, I've got work to do, and I've already wasted enough time tromping around in the woods."

"Oh, please, Zion," Beulah protested. "Come on and go with us. You'll enjoy it."

"I'll enjoy making sure that little teenager I hired to help me this afternoon hasn't eaten all of the ice cream and cleaned out the till, to boot," Zion insisted. "You all just go on. I'm not really much of a tearoom person anyway," she laughed. "More of a camp-coffee person, I guess."

"Well, if you change your mind . . ." Beulah started.

"I won't," Zion said.

When the surveying had been completed, they all left the bird sanctuary to go home, get cleaned up, and meet at the tearoom later in the afternoon. All except Zion, of course. And when Zion went home and entered the spotless barn where her Jersey cows were all patiently waiting for the early evening milking, she felt her heart swell

39

with the sweet, undeniable comfort of being exactly where she was supposed to be.

"Hi, ladies," she spoke softly to the cows. "Now this is better than any old fancy tearoom, don't you think?"

Memphis welcomed Sweet, Beulah, and Wildwood into the tearoom, and they were pleasantly surprised at what she had done. The room, already large and with a high ceiling, was freshly wallpapered in a charming English violet print, with matching curtains at the windows. The heart-of-pine floors had been completely refinished, and ceiling fans twirled high above, sending a waxy, scented-candle coolness throughout the room. She seated them at a table covered with a cutwork starched cloth and handed them the small menus. Once they had selected the goodies that would grace their multilayered tray and the teas they would have, Memphis disappeared into the kitchen.

"Memphis has certainly done a beautiful job of this tearoom," Beulah said. "Look! She even has a window air-conditioner, for when the weather gets so hot."

"I wonder if she'll serve iced tea in the summer?" Wildwood mused idly.

"She certainly will!" Memphis chortled, backing through the swinging door and bearing a large tray containing their treats and tea things. "Iced teas like nobody around here ever had — flavored ones, you know, like blackberry iced tea and honeysuckle iced tea and lighter summer-fare sweets as well — chilled fruit balls and sherbet and thin, delicate cookies." She unloaded the tray and poured their tea into fragile cups.

"You've made it look wonderful, Memphis," Wildwood offered, while Sweet and Beulah murmured their agreement. "We ought to have the next library board meeting here. That would certainly cheer up the members, I think. And make for a happier meeting."

"You just let me know," Memphis agreed. "I'll fix up something extra special."

Beulah put an enormous blob of clotted cream on her plate and proceeded to dig into it.

"Aren't you going to put that on a slice of cake or something?" Memphis asked. "That's the way it's supposed to be eaten, I think."

"Plain is just fine with me," Beulah whispered, using her tongue to retrieve a blob of clotted cream from her lips.

41

While they sipped their tea and softly moaned in appreciation for the scones and clotted cream, a tall, solid man with a somewhat wild-looking mane of white hair came out of the bank, got into a black car, and backed out, turning and heading out of town. He was a stranger in Tea-Olive, something rarely seen.

CHAPTER
— FIVE —

Like Memphis, Sweet had inherited a large, old-fashioned house in town from a distant relative of her father's. This, of course, was in addition to the ancestral land she had inherited from her own great-grandfather, land she had grown up on and that she still owned. But unlike Memphis, who lived in the entire house except for the tearoom, Sweet had divided her house into three apartments, one of which she lived in herself. Even though the initial costs of having all those carpenters and plumbers come in to effect the changes were high, once that tab was paid off, the additional rents kept Sweet in an easy, fiscal solvency and also enabled her to leave untouched some of the investments her father's relative had made.

The smallest of the apartments was rented out to an elderly lady who desired no company except for that of her cat. The second was currently rented to the town doctor's licensed practical nurse, a pleasant young woman who accompanied him on his rounds of the county hospital and on his trips out to the rural areas to provide house calls. There, he tended the people who were so much like the original settlers — fiercely proud, self-reliant, and accustomed to a hardscrabble life of coaxing their food from the soil. For them, calling a doctor was reserved for the most dire of ailments — perhaps a baby turned around backward or a raging fever that defied all of their home remedies. For these people, the nurse held a special kindness, and once or twice she had even spoken to Sweet about them — their pride and abject poverty. Sweet always listened politely, remembering her father and his ancestors, who were probably very much like these rural folks the nurse liked so much.

Sweet allowed herself the largest and sunniest apartment, which had been made out of the former main living room and front bedroom. She'd had a comfortable bathroom installed in what had been a large closet in the old home, and she had decorated her home in all of her mother's sturdy Victorian furniture. She was happy and comfortable, and in the evenings, when she heard the elderly lady calling in her cat or the shower running in the nurse's apartment, she felt a strange sense of comfort in having other people nearby. It was a comfort she would not have been able to describe perfectly, just that it seemed to satisfy a tiny, strange longing deep in her heart, for fond memories of a family and a husband and a long marriage — although she reminded herself often that poor Memphis didn't have fond memories of a man who, basically, deserted her.

Sometimes, usually in the middle of a long, sleepless night, Sweet would create a make-believe marriage of many years to a kind, gentle man who still looked adoringly at her. At such times, she almost convinced herself that the memory was a real one, but it always melted away with the rising of the sun.

The next week, the same big, black car returned to Tea-Olive, following another car with a TOP OF THE HILL REALTY sign on its side, and both cars slowly made their way down the road toward Love-Divine's place. But on that same day, it so happened that Beulah and Sweet were in the King's Wood Sanctuary, looking for a woodpecker Zion had reported seeing there the day before.

"Look!" Sweet whispered, putting her

hand on Beulah's arm. Beulah lowered her binoculars and followed Sweet's pointing finger. The realtor's car and the black car turned in at Love-Divine's driveway. The realtor got out immediately, a petite woman wearing a hot-pink suit, and she approached the driver's side of the black car with a grin on her face.

"Isn't this absolutely *pastoral?*" In the quiet noontime, her voice carried easily to where Beulah and Sweet were standing. And they watched while the door opened on the black car and a tall, very distinguished-looking man unfolded himself, stood up, and shaded his eyes with his hand, seeming to look directly at the two bird-watchers. He had broad shoulders and a shock of unruly white hair. They both ducked down a bit, instinctively.

"He can't see us because of the trees," Beulah whispered. "And besides, we have a perfect right to be here. It's *our* sanctuary now."

"Yes," Sweet answered. "But us being here, with binoculars and all, might make it look like we're spying!"

"Spying?"

"Snooping," Sweet clarified.

Beulah grinned. "Well then, let's snoop!" And although they still remained crouched, they raised their binoculars to see more clearly what was transpiring in Love-Divine's own driveway.

"Who is that anyway?" Beulah asked. "He's not someone I've ever seen before."

"Goodness! He's a handsome man, isn't he?" Sweet answered. "I wonder where he's from?"

"Not from around here," Beulah confirmed. And as the realtor and the man entered the house, Beulah whispered, "You stay right here, Sweet. I'll be right back."

"Where are you going?" Sweet inquired.

"Just a little closer, to where I can see the tags on those cars. I know good and well they're not from around here."

"Well, go on and satisfy your curiosity then," Sweet said, and Beulah, still crouching, moved away deeper into the woods. After about a hundred yards, she once again approached the edge of the trees and trained her binoculars on the automobiles. The black car bore a New York State license plate, and while she couldn't see the other car's tag, she could easily read the sign on the side of the car: TOP OF THE HILL REALTY, AUGUSTA.

"Aha!" she whispered, feeling a strange little rush, as if she were truly a spy and had discovered something important.

Quickly, she made her way back to where Sweet was waiting for her.

"New York State!" Beulah whispered. "And the realtor's car is from Augusta."

"You reckon he's thinking about buying Love-Divine's house?" Sweet asked.

"That's what you get a realtor for," Beulah answered. "I just hope he isn't a developer!"

About this time, the tall man and the neon-pinked realtor came out of the back door and walked out to the small barn behind the house. Beulah and Sweet watched them closely, as they stood talking in the backyard for long minutes, with the realtor sweeping her arms out as if to explain to the man exactly how much property there was, and with him reaching up and smoothing his snowy hair against the breeze. They talked some more, and then nodded, shook hands, and both retreated to their cars. As they backed out of Love-Divine's driveway, Beulah commented, "She sure was smiling and nodding her head. I'll bet you anything he's going to make an offer."

"Well, no matter what the offer is, I'll bet the executor will accept it. Not too many chances of folks around here being interested in it," Sweet commented. "And if he really is going to live in the house himself, it might be fun to have a real, live Yankee right here in Tea-Olive!"

"Why, I don't think that would be fun at all, especially for him," Beulah argued. "He wouldn't understand a thing about how folks around here do things."

"Maybe not," Sweet responded. "But I'll bet we could teach him."

That comment drew a sharp glance from Beulah, but she said nothing except, "Let's get back to seeing if we can spot that woodpecker. If Love-Divine's house has been sold, we'll hear about it soon enough."

"Maybe I'll call Wanda this afternoon and do a little snooping of my own," offered Sweet.

"Wanda?"

"Don't you remember her? She used to go to the Presbyterian Church. Worked over at the army base and moved to Augusta to be closer to her job."

"What about her?"

"Well, the lady who owns the house Wanda rents is a realtor, and she's from Augusta too. So maybe Wanda can find out what's going on," Sweet explained.

"If the place is sold, it will be in the newspaper anyway," said Beulah. "But it might be more fun to find out *that* way."

"By snooping, you mean?" Sweet teased.

"Exactly! Now where on earth is that woodpecker?"

As it turned out, Wanda's landlady did some calling around, and when Wanda called Sweet back, she relayed the facts in a delighted tone.

"Listen, Sweet, this man really is a big somebody!"

"What do you mean?" Sweet asked.

"Are you ready for this?" Wanda did love telling a big story.

"I'm ready, Wanda — spill it!" Sweet laughed.

"He's a *judge!*" Wanda practically shrieked. "A real, honest-to-goodness judge!"

"A judge of what?" Sweet asked.

"A judge of the court, Sweet. A real judge of a real district court in New York!!"

"Well then, what's he doing in Tea-Olive?"

"Well . . . ," Wanda couldn't help drawing out the explanation. "It seems he's getting ready to retire, and he wants to become a gentleman farmer. So that's why he's looking for a small farm. I've heard that he also looked at one in South Carolina, so maybe he won't make an offer on the place near Tea-Olive."

"I guess we'll just have to wait and see," Sweet replied, trying to hide her disappointment.

"Sweet? Are you okay?" Wanda's solicitous voice drew a sigh from Sweet.

"Well, Wanda, just between thee and me, he's a gorgeous man! Do you know if he's married?"

"Widowed, I hear," Wanda said. "And Sweet, I'm surprised at you! Aren't you a little long in the tooth to be messing around with puppy love?" Sweet thought for a long moment before she realized that she truthfully had no answer to that question. "Like you said, we'll have to just wait and see," Wanda said. "And in the meantime, you work on your girlish figure and get yourself a new hairstyle."

"What's wrong with the hairstyle I have now?" Sweet demanded.

"It's dated, honey," Wanda warned. "Now you do like I said, and I'll cross my fingers for you that things work out with you and the judge!"

"Well. Just don't say anything, Wanda," Sweet begged.

"Your secret is safe with me," Wanda assured her. "Besides, I don't keep up much with anyone else from Tea-Olive anymore. You're the only one who seems to remember me."

"I remember you, Wanda," Sweet said. "I remember how we were both in the grocery store one day, and none of us really knew you very well — because we all went to the Baptist Church and you went to the Presbyterian. And besides, you worked and had to drive so far, so you didn't have time to be in the bird-watching club or Homework Helpers or anything like that."

"Yes," Wanda answered. "I lived in Tea-Olive only long enough to settle my great-aunt's estate — just a few months. But I remember one day when we were both in line at the grocery store, and for some reason, I told you about my kitty, Verdi, and how I was going to have her put to sleep."

"Verdi," Sweet repeated. "I had forgotten about that."

"Well, Verdi was elderly and very sick, and you, Sweet, you offered to go with me to the vet to have the deed done. I will remember that forever!" Wanda's voice was filled with genuine gratitude. "You did go with me, and I will always thank you for that."

"Well, I could tell you were in a great deal of pain, and you needed someone to comfort you," Sweet said.

"I certainly did need that," Wanda confessed. "Thank you!"

"You're welcome," Sweet said. "And thanks for the information about the judge."

After Sweet replaced the receiver, she absentmindedly reached up and touched her hair — felt the stiffness of hair spray and wondered if it was, perhaps, time for a new hairstyle. Something younger and softer.

CHAPTER
— SIX —

As close as the members of the Tea-Olive
Bird Watching Society were to one another,
Wildwood and Memphis both respected
and admired the easy familiarity among
Beulah, Sweet, and Zion and knew that it
was the end product of an unusual three-
some friendship that went all the way back
to their days in the first grade at Tea-Olive
Elementary School — at a time when neither
Wildwood nor Memphis had even been
born.

Beulah and Sweet had grown up far
outside of the town on adjoining farms,
and those two little girls first met when
Sweet's mother had taken ill and Beulah's
mother took Beulah by the hand and they
walked the half mile or so to Sweet's house,
carrying a basket full of fresh biscuits and a
Mason jar full of honey. Beulah and Sweet
were then only four years old, and they had
both been extremely timid with each other
at their first meeting.

"Run outside and play with Sweet," Beulah's mother had instructed, all the while Beulah was staring at the pretty little girl with white-blonde hair and enormous, cornflower blue eyes.

"That's right, you girls go ahead and play outside and let us visit a spell," Sweet's mother instructed, at which point Sweet reached around Beulah's mother, took Beulah's hand, and matter-of-factly drew her out of the bedroom and out onto the wide front porch.

"Wanta see my playhouse?" Sweet asked, and Beulah nodded solemnly. Still holding Beulah's hand, Sweet led her across the side yard and down a dirt trail that ended in a broken-down scuppernong arbor. Ducking down, Sweet led Beulah into what appeared to be a perfectly arranged area where the arbor still stood, an area complete with bits of ribbon that decorated the dead vines and bits of broken pottery that were arranged into the soil in a mosaic of outcast shards of old plates and cup handles.

"This is my very own house," Sweet announced, and Beulah smiled at her. Sweet went on, "This is a place for thinking nice thoughts and being happy, but if you want, I can show you something that will make" — Sweet's voice dropped low into a conspiratorial whisper — "all the hair stand up on the back of your neck!"

"What?" Beulah's curiosity was instantly engaged.

"Blood, that's what!" Sweet said.

"Whose *blood?*" Beulah asked.

Sweet's face grew serious, her thin, blonde eyebrows drawing together. "A Yankee soldier's blood! Com'on," Sweet commanded.

They left the beribboned bower and approached a large barn. Sweet led Beulah around the side of the barn to a smaller, unpainted building that was built to stand on jagged piles of slate rock.

"There!" Sweet whispered, pointing to a dark stain on some of the rocks.

Beulah held her breath. It certainly did look like a bloodstain, but she also knew that Yankee soldiers hadn't been on the land in many years. As young as they were, both Beulah and Sweet were familiar with the terrible war that had taken place between the North and the South; some of those skirmishes actually taking place on the ground upon which they were standing.

"My great-great-granddaddy hit a Yankee soldier in the head with a log of stovewood, and that's where his blood

56

spilled onto the ground!"

"It is?" Beulah was both repelled and fascinated by the stain and by the story that had grown up about it.

"And when the other Yankees started to hang my great-great-grandfather," Sweet went on, "he *laughed!*"

Beulah tried to imagine what kind of man would actually laugh while he was facing death, but she didn't know how to formulate the question. And right at that moment, both of the girls heard Beulah's mother calling to her.

"I gotta go," Beulah announced.

"Come back and play again," Sweet invited.

"It's too far for me to come alone," Beulah explained. "But are you going to Tea-Olive Elementary in September?"

"I sure am!" Sweet chirped.

"Then we can ride the school bus together," Beulah said.

"That will be fun!"

Indeed, Beulah and Sweet sat together on the bus that first day of school, giggling nervously and wondering what school would be like, and because the school was small, they did wind up in the same classroom, accomplishing the same activity on that first morning: *color the man's hat brown; color his shoes black; color his shirt blue.*

At recess, Beulah and Sweet walked around together, silently studying everything they could about the "Town girls," and whispering back and forth to each other about them, how easily they mingled with the other town girls and how they were timid around children who rode the bus in from the rural areas. Just as the bell rang, sending them all back inside the school building, Beulah noticed a dark-haired girl who had remained standing apart, leaning against the playground fence and actually glowering at everyone. Beulah had never seen anyone be able to make such a terrible-looking face. Everything about it screamed, "Leave me alone!"

But Beulah being herself, that face only prompted her to approach the girl. Sweet followed along but remained somewhat back, wondering what this exchange might provoke in such a ferocious-looking child.

"Hi," Beulah said. "I'm Beulah and this is Sweet. What's your name?"

For a moment, the dark eyes seemed to shoot sparks, but then, incredibly, the corners of her mouth turned up a little.

"I'm Zion," the girl said. "And I don't live in town."

"We don't either," Beulah explained. "But I didn't see you on the bus this morning."

"I'm on the other side of town," Zion explained. "I live on a farm."

"So do we," Beulah said, and seeing that the exchange wasn't so frightening after all, Sweet came closer.

"How come you look so mad?" Beulah asked, in childlike bluntness.

"Why, I guess I just look the way I look!" Zion retorted. "I'm not really mad *all the time*. I just like looking that way."

"Why?" Beulah pressed, causing Sweet to take one step backward.

"I don't know," Zion confessed. "I'm just me, I guess!"

Something in the tone of Zion's voice tickled Beulah and she started laughing. Sweet eventually joined in, and at the last, even sour-faced Zion had to laugh as well.

And from that very small exchange on the playground the first day of first grade, Beulah, Sweet, and Zion bonded in a friendship that would last for most of their lives.

At recess on the last day of school that first year, the three of them sat under a tree beside the school building, making daisy chains out of clover blossoms, serious-faced and deeply wounded by the fact that they would not see one another during the long summer. But then Sweet came up with an idea: "Let's all go to Vacation Bible School together!" Sweet said, her voice surging with delight. Zion and Beulah gazed at her without comprehension. "Listen," Sweet went on, "if we go to Vacation Bible School together, Beulah, you and I can walk into town from home, and so can Zion."

"That's a long walk," Beulah said. "I don't know that Mama would let me do that."

"Well, she would if you tell her we're just going to the church, I'll bet!"

"Zion, do you think your mama would let you walk into town alone?"

"I guess so," Zion offered. "She'd be real happy to see me wanting to go to Vacation Bible School."

So before they boarded the different buses that would take them into the rural areas outside of town, they exchanged phone numbers and their clover daisy chains, as a pledge of their friendship and their plans for getting to see one another during the long summer.

And indeed, all of the parents consented, and so the three girls resumed their friendship the first week of August at the First Baptist Church in town, where the Vacation

Bible School was run by the minister's lovely young bride, Miss Love-Divine. She was sweet and pretty and gentle with the children, and they all glowed under her supervision and her smile. Beulah, Sweet, and Zion made small collages that depicted Bible stories, sang "Jesus Loves Me" about a thousand times, and smacked their lips over the tart pink lemonade and coconut-flavored cookies.

Beulah had been right about it being a long walk from the farms into town, but the morning part of the walk was entirely enjoyable, with the soft mist of summer mornings hanging in the pastures; but in the hot afternoons, the walk was much harder, with the August sun beating down on them and dry dust rising up under their feet. Still, the sweetness of being all together once again was, they all agreed, worth the long afternoon walk home.

That strong friendship among the three lasted all the way through grammar school and into junior high, and at that point, with awkward embarrassment, they began to develop the bodies of young women. Zion stayed as thin as a rail, but height-wise, she shot up until she was just under six feet tall, an event that seemed to take place almost overnight. For a week or so, she walked around with her shoulders hunched, but Sweet and Beulah vowed not to scold her for that.

"She'll stand back up straight soon," Beulah assured Sweet. "Zion isn't one to go around feeling sorry for herself." And Beulah had been right; Zion soon started standing straight and tall, and she attracted the attention of the coach right away. As he watched her, he envisioned wonderful, winning basketball games, for surely Zion was the tallest young woman he had ever encountered. When he approached her about trying out for the basketball team, she hesitated.

"The practices are after school, right?" she asked.

"Yes," the coach confirmed, squinting up into her face.

"I have to help on the farm in the afternoons," Zion explained, and there was a pride in her voice that revealed she liked taking care of her father's small herd of Jersey cows.

"Well, let me know if you change your mind," the disappointed coach said.

Now Sweet and Beulah began to develop the soft curves of young women, Sweet especially having a charming figure. But

Beulah, in those tender years, began what would be a lifelong fight to keep her weight down. She avoided candy and soft drinks, but when her mother would place a large platter of hot cornbread on the table, Beulah reached for the freshly-churned butter and applied it with a heavy hand. Sweets, she could avoid with no trouble, but bread . . . any kind of bread . . . slathered with butter was her constant downfall.

When the three friends reached high school, the boys were instantly attracted to Sweet, with her demure charm, and most of the time between classes, tall, lanky Zion and short, plump Beulah stood around, watching the gaggle of boys trying to get Sweet's attention. And indeed, Sweet could have had any number of dates, but her mother forbade any such activity, and as always, Sweet did as her mother demanded, and without complaint.

After high school, the friends were compelled to part, with each going on her own path. Beulah went off to a secretarial school in Augusta; Sweet's mother insisted that she attend a Baptist women's college in Virginia, where she majored in early childhood education; and Zion — not surprising anyone who knew of her zeal in tending her father's dairy herd — won a 4-H scholarship to go to the

University of Georgia to major in animal husbandry and dairy science.

Beulah finished secretarial school first, and she came home to a good job in the local doctor's office. She bought a good used car that enabled her to work at school, but still to remain at home with her aging parents. Sweet stayed on at college, learning everything she would need to qualify her as a teacher at the same Tea-Olive Elementary School where she and Beulah and Zion had first met. Zion completed one year in her study of dairy science, and at the end of that year, her father called her home to stay. Zion's mother had been ill, and she was needed at home to tend to the mother and to help out on the farm. Zion never indicated that she resented that interruption of her education; instead, she simply started putting into practice all that she had learned, and the farm's animals thrived under her meticulous care.

The three friends got together as often as possible, and they never lost their interest in one another and their basic friendship. When first Sweet's parents passed away and then Beulah's, both of them left the rural area and moved into town. The old farmhouses eventually fell apart, but the land remained. Sometimes, on Sunday afternoons, Beulah and Sweet would take a picnic lunch out to the old homesteads and eat their sandwiches sitting on the old concrete steps of the smokehouse where the stain still remained on the rocks.

When Zion's parents died, she remained in the family home, alone, totally occupied by taking care of her cows and running a small creamery — where Beulah was her best part-time helper.

Because of these deep and long-lived friendships, Zion, Beulah, and Sweet were completely comfortable and easy around one another, and whenever they happened to speak of that shared past in the presence of Wildwood and Memphis, the younger women enjoyed their stories immensely.

Perhaps the only manner in which the difference in the generations showed was in the older women's adamant dislike of "progress." Once, when gently trying to defend the benefits of progress and development, Wildwood and Memphis murmured most respectfully about the issue, hoping that their gentle good manners would offset any tendency of Beulah and Zion to rant and rave. But it hadn't worked. Rant and rave, Beulah and Zion certainly did, while Sweet, in typical fashion stood back and smiled gently, looking at the floor.

CHAPTER
— SEVEN —

During the weeks following the judge's appearance in Tea-Olive, speculation among the people ran rampant about the judge and his visit to Love-Divine's old place. Sweet, especially, found herself in an extremely strange mood — almost reminiscent of what had been a long-ago, petulant feeling of wanting something new and exciting to see and think and talk about. The summer when Sweet and Beulah turned fifteen years old, Sweet had gone through a phase — that's what her mother had called it — where she yearned for anything that could take her mind, if not her body, out of the dead, hot rural landscape. Her sighs grew heavy and her lovely eyes held the hint of a mysterious pain that she could not name.

"You're just going through a phase almost all girls go through," her mother explained after she had watched Sweet prowl around the hot living room and emit deep sighs every few minutes. "It's not a small thing when a girl is turning into a woman, young lady. So don't you think you're the only one who has ever felt that kind of restlessness."

Sweet wanted to ask if her mother had gone through the same terrible and wonderful feelings, but she was feeling too petulant to ask. She simply heaved another sigh and went out to sit in the swing on the front porch, to rock it back and forth slowly, listening to the squeak of the chains and believing that if she didn't get to go somewhere and do something — anything — she would simply die on the spot. So she got out of the swing and went walking, barefoot, down the long clay road that would bring her to Beulah's house.

Beulah had been sitting in the front porch swing herself, shelling butter beans and humming to herself. When she saw Sweet coming down the road, she put the beans aside and went to meet her. Without a word, she took Sweet's hand and led her to the front steps that, at that time of day, were mercifully shaded by some tall evergreens. By the time they sat down, Sweet was in tears.

"What's wrong, Sweet," the young Beulah had softly inquired. "Tell me about it. You know you can talk to me about anything!"

Sweet wiped her hot, wet cheeks with the back of her hand.

"I don't know how to say it," she confessed with misery in her voice. "Maybe it's this: Sometimes I get so tired of this hot, dead, dry place, I just want to die!"

Beulah thought for a moment and then she said, "You remember that movie we got to go see last summer? The one about all those young folks at the beach?"

"I remember," Sweet said. "But what does that have to do with anything?"

"Well, after we saw that movie, I wanted more than anything in this whole world to be a pretty, rich girl and get to go to the beach and hang out with those handsome boys and have them think I was pretty," Beulah confessed softly. "I wanted that so bad, I thought I'd just die!"

"You never said anything to me about that," Sweet complained.

"I didn't say anything to anybody," Beulah said. "I just carried all that hurt and longing around inside of me, until one day, Mama noticed that something wasn't right about me, and she sat me down for a long talk. She said that every young girl goes through something like that, but you just have to wait it out and then you'll be fine again."

"Something like what?" Sweet asked.

"Wanting something and not knowing

what it is," Beulah answered. "Or sometimes it's just not wanting what you have
and thinking you're going to die!"

Sweet took a long, ragged breath. "Yes,"
she had said simply. "Oh yes!"

And of course, Beulah's mother had been
right. Sweet simply waited and waited until,
one fine morning, that terrible longing was
gone!

But now, it was back in full force all those
long years later; it was exactly the same
feeling, but she knew not to say a single
word about it. Mature women shouldn't
have emotions like teenaged girls! What
she could allow herself, so privately, was
a complete fascination and a strong
speculation that the judge would buy Miss
Love-Divine's place.

Sure enough, as if Sweet herself had
secretly willed it to happen, yet another
excited phone call from Wanda revealed
that the judge had signed the final contract
and would be moving to Tea-Olive within
a matter of weeks.

Of course, Sweet couldn't keep the
information about the house to herself, so
she told Beulah, who told Zion, who told
Wildwood, who told Memphis and then,
because of Memphis's tearoom, word went

out all over town like wildfire.

When the editor of the *Tea-Olive Gazette* heard the news, he jumped on the story right away. He had only two days to develop the new lead story, and he spent the better part of one day chasing down a phone number in New York for the judge so that he could corroborate the facts. When, at last, he had a number, he dialed it.

"Good morning, sir!" he chirruped when the judge answered.

"Yes?" The voice was extremely careful . . . even frosty.

"This is Tom — I'm editor of the *Gazette*, our little weekly newspaper here in Tea-Olive, and I want to print an article about your becoming a new resident."

A long silence from the other end and then a hearty guffaw. "Well, if you think this is something people will be interested in reading about, sure!" the judge responded lustily.

"Oh, I'm sure everyone will be interested in learning something about a real judge."

"Yes? Well, what can I tell you?"

"Would you please tell me why you became interested in this little town?"

"It's pretty personal," the judge mused. "But you can just say that I spent every summer of my childhood in a small town much like Tea-Olive, with my stepgrandfather."

"*Step*grandfather?" the editor asked, not being sure that he heard correctly.

"That's right," the judge confirmed. "Oh, he was a wonderful man. Taught me how to catch fish, clean them, and fry them up over an open fire."

"That sure sounds wonderful," the editor agreed. "Can you tell me his name?"

"Yes. He was Zechariah Carver. Died many years ago."

"I'm sorry," the editor said. "Now, when do you think you will be moving in at the old Love-Divine place?"

"The what?" The judge was clearly confused.

"The old Love-Divine place," the editor repeated. "That's what folks around here call it."

"Interesting," the judge commented. "I'm going to have some extensive remodeling done, so it will probably be a month to six weeks before I can occupy the house."

"Well, we're certainly happy to have you come and live here," the editor purred. "I'm sure you will be a credit to this community."

"Hope so," the judge responded. "Certainly hope so. I always try to support the community in which I live."

The story appeared in the next edition. Headline: RETIRED NEW YORK JUDGE TO BECOME RESIDENT OF TEA-OLIVE. And the brief article followed:

The town of Tea-Olive is about to grow, with the confirmed acquisition of the property of the late Love-Divine Brockett King by a retired New York State judge, the Honorable Hyson Breed. We all welcome him most heartily and trust that he will become a valued and active member of this community. The judge has told your reporter that he was attracted to Tea-Olive because of happy childhood memories of summers spent with his stepgrandfather in a similar town. The judge plans extensive renovations to the house and the outbuildings, prior to moving in. We all sincerely welcome you, Judge Breed.

Everyone in town read the article with growing excitement, especially Sweet, who, quietly and without saying anything, drove all the way into Augusta and came back with a new and flattering hairstyle. Of course, everyone in town noticed the attractive new style, but few said anything directly to Sweet about it. Still, Beulah and Zion did glance at each other somewhat uneasily.

And then, for everyone except Sweet, things pretty much returned to normal in the small town, with Beulah spending every morning helping Zion with the milking of the small herd of Jersey cows and the afternoons either helping in the Homework Helper Program at the library or meeting with her Bible study group. Further, she hosted a meeting of the United Daughters of the Confederacy at her home, an activity that prompted a thorough housecleaning and two days spent baking tempting cookies and finger cakes, and preparing a wonderful fruit punch.

Zion, as usual, was occupied with taking care of the cows, straining and putting up milk for placing in the large cooler in the shop portion of her home, churning home-made ice cream, and as always, scrubbing the milking parlor and all of the equipment until it was spotlessly clean. Wildwood spent more time working at the library than usual, since one of her assistants was on maternity leave, and Sweet spent most afternoons in the sanctuary, not really looking for birds, but training her binoculars on Love-Divine's empty little house and daydreaming shamelessly about the judge — handsome man! — actually moving in. Everyone noticed Sweet's slightly dreamy mood, but of course, no one said anything about it to her. Zion openly snorted when she realized that Sweet seemed to be "in love," but Sweet didn't even notice that loud snort.

Sweet went to the sanctuary almost every day, and finally, her vigilance was rewarded. The judge's big black car pulled into the driveway, followed by several trucks, some loaded down with new lumber, some with new bathroom fixtures, and one with nothing but new wiring products. Sweet watched breathlessly as the judge got out of his car and started shouting orders to the men in the trucks. He was wearing a spotless white shirt with the sleeves turned up and his shock of unruly white hair caused several ancient butterflies to flutter around in Sweet's unaccustomed stomach.

Over the next couple of weeks, anyone who went to the sanctuary heard only the sounds of nail-pounding, electric saws, and grunting men. Of course, they saw few birds, because the noise had temporarily frightened them away. Sweet, of course, went to the sanctuary most often, always hoping to get a glimpse of the judge through her binoculars. Beulah came every few days, just out of curiosity, and Zion came not at all.

"Don't know why everybody is so interested in him!" she commented to Beulah. "Why, they don't know a blessed thing about him!"

During the time of renovation and work on the outbuildings, the judge stayed at a motel fifteen miles away, near the interstate highway. It was also reported that the first morning he had breakfast at the café beside the motel, he had stared, open-mouthed at the generous order of grits on his breakfast plate.

"Grits?" he chortled. "I'd forgotten about grits!"

The waitress was surprised by his reaction. The café catered to interstate travelers, so sometimes customers came in who didn't realize that if you ordered two scrambled eggs, for example, you would, of course, get the eggs, but you would also get grits — always, and without ever having to specifically order them. The café owner refused to change that old tradition, and on occasion, a plate would come back to the kitchen untouched, with the waitress's request for a new plate and no grits. But never before had the waitress seen anyone totally surprised and delighted by an order of grits. When he glanced up at the waitress, she thought that she could see tears in his eyes.

Immediately, he dug his spoon into the puddle of melted butter right in the center of the grits and lifted a snowy spoonful toward his mouth. But he paused to inhale the mild aroma of well-cooked grits and melted butter before he took the first spoonful. His eyes closed and his mouth lifted into a blissful smile.

"Grits!" he said again. "I don't know how I could have forgotten all about them!"

And how did folks in Tea-Olive come to learn about the judge's reaction to grits? Because someone had a cousin who was a good friend of the waitress's mother, and the story of the judge and the grits arrived in Tea-Olive in a matter of minutes after it happened. Anything and everything about the judge was of great interest to everyone.

The judge showed up at the house every morning and stayed until the workmen left at dusk. When work was finally finished in the house, the workmen refurbished the small barn and started in on what seemed like miles of fencing. A paddock at the barn, fencing all around what would obviously be turned into a pasture, a separate shed for farm implements, and even pasture fencing around the small peach and apple orchard. Finally, the fence was put up between the King's Wood Bird Sanctuary and the driveway. The only section not fenced was the pecan orchard, which contained thirty or forty bearing trees.

When all was done according to the judge's instruction, a large moving van arrived, and the judge stood by the doorway, directing the men as they took boxes, china barrels, and oversized, dark furniture into the various rooms.

Then the day came when the judge moved out of the motel and into his new home. At first, everyone politely left him alone, knowing that he needed time to settle in. And he was seldom seen in town. In fact, the one and only time he went to town was to visit the courthouse, where he did a whole afternoon's research on Love-Divine's old property. And he showed an intense interest in the copy of her will that was a matter of public record. He read the papers that showed how the executor had disbursed funds from the estate. The clerk later related that the judge had asked only one question: "Where is the library?" And of course, she had given him that information.

When a reasonable interval of time had passed, the people in Tea-Olive took a more active role in welcoming the judge to his new community, and he seemed to be a relatively personable, if somewhat private, gentleman. He was immediately invited to attend the Baptist, Presbyterian, and Methodist churches, and the Reverend and Mrs. Brown from the Methodist Church actually made a call on him out at Love-Divine's old place. Mrs. Brown (a native of Tea-Olive, her hymnal name was Victory-in-Jesus, but almost everyone in town called her simply Vicky), later informed almost everyone in town about what she saw there.

"Well, my husband was interested in the improvements to the barn and the brand-new tractor, and the judge certainly seemed to enjoy showing off all his new possessions and sharing his plans for that 'gentleman's farm.' Of course, I was most interested in seeing what he'd done to the house, and goodness me! He certainly made some big improvements. Especially the kitchen — all new appliances and countertops, and a big rack that holds copper cookware! I'd say he's going to be looking for a wife to go in that kitchen!"

When those words made their way around town, Zion pronounced, "If he so much as winks at *me*, I'll treat him like any other rat that gets into my barn!" To which Beulah nodded and added, "I wouldn't want another man, not after all my good years with my sweet Paul." And Sweet blushed mightily and said, "I imagine he'd like a younger wife. Someone like Wildwood or Memphis." But Beulah harrumphed and said, "Well, there's not much good pickings around this town, that's for sure." At the last, Sweet added, "But he certainly cuts a dashing figure." Beulah and Zion stared at her. "What I mean," Sweet amended, flustered, "is that he's a very nice looking man."

"Well, Wildwood and Memphis better watch out, just in case," Beulah added, frowning.

CHAPTER
— EIGHT —

Wildwood and Memphis were among the very few younger women in Tea-Olive, because it was common knowledge that when young women left the town, whether to work or go off to school, very few of them ever came back. Wildwood and Memphis were the two exceptions to this migration away from the small town. And no one really blamed young people who left because the chances of finding good work were few and far between, so they had to choose between the kitty litter factory, the Dairy Queen, and a few small stores. For those with an education, there were the schools, but with the population diminishing, the classes were ever smaller and the open teaching positions rare.

In the past, life had been simple for those who wanted to remain in the area. Young men grew up and worked on the family farms, which most of them had been doing since they were children.

Young women waited for one of these young men to ask them to be their wives, and then they joined the small army of farm wives who raised chickens, canned the summer produce for the winter, nursed young animals and kept them close to the heat of the stove, made quilts out of outworn clothing, and prepared huge midday meals for the hardworking men. Those opportunities were few now, since so many of the family farms were standing empty.

After high school graduation, Memphis went off to a culinary institute in Augusta, because she had always enjoyed food preparation and thought it would make a good career for her. After she finished at the institute, nothing would satisfy her except going to live in Atlanta, even though her mother tried to warn her about the rapid-fire pace of living there. In Atlanta, Memphis became a team member in a catering business, and she learned that part of her job was to drift silently among the guests in the mansions of wealthy Atlantans, passing trays of finger foods and cocktails. Even though she requested being allowed to prepare some of the dishes, the proprietor of the catering firm dissuaded her from that.

"You just don't realize how demanding

some of our most important clients can be," she explained. "Everything has to be perfect!"

"But how will I ever learn, if all I do is act as a server?" Memphis had retorted.

"Your time will come," the proprietor assured her.

But it didn't. Not in two long years. And Memphis began having some negative thoughts, such as: "If I'd wanted to be a waitress, I could have done that closer to home!" And too, Memphis was a dutiful daughter, an only child, and the thought of her parents aging without her presence burdened her heart.

Two corresponding events eventually drove Memphis to leave Atlanta. First of all, her apartment rent went up considerably and without notice, and her meager salary was already stretched to the limit. The second event occurred at a catered party in one of the great north Atlanta mansions. The hostess took exception to the filling in the cocktail puffs, stormed into the kitchen where the catering staff were working at top speed, and threw three trays of the puffs onto the kitchen floor.

"Get out!" the hostess raged. "Get out! And don't think for a single minute that I'm paying for such slop as you've served to my guests!"

Within an hour after the pastry puff incident, Memphis was already driving on the interstate, with all her possessions thrown into her car. In town, people were talking about her impending return, and a rumor went around that she had left a great deal more than just a job. Gossip had it that she had married, and that her new husband had already left her. Memphis herself never spoke of such. And on the day she turned into the broad driveway of her parents' Victorian home in Tea-Olive, she felt that she had truly come home for the very first time.

Wildwood's venture into the world outside of Tea-Olive was equally devastating but more serious in nature. After finishing one year at the community college, she, too, ventured to Atlanta.

"What is it about these children, that they just have to go live in Atlanta?" people in town asked among themselves. But they already knew the answer: young people wanted excitement and adventure, and that was in short supply around Tea-Olive.

Wildwood got a job in a public library in Atlanta, where she spent the first year reshelving books and "reading the shelves," which meant going down each row, making sure that the books were in good condition and shelved properly. She didn't mind that work at all, because Wildwood's own brand of excitement and adventure came in the six-foot one-inch frame of Arthur, who was a loyal library patron. He checked out copious amounts of crime and adventure books, and every day that he came to the library, he made sure to find Wildwood in the stacks and pass some general pleasantries with her. His slow, rural Alabama speech pleased her, and finally, when he asked if she would like to have coffee with him after she got off from work, she accepted.

They started meeting at the coffee shop just down the street from the library several evenings a week, and the chemistry between them swept both of them along in a flood of hand-touching and eye-searching, and finally to dinners in each other's homes. At first, Wildwood had been a little embarrassed to have him come into her drab little apartment, but when he did come in, he filled that small place to the very hilt with his bigness and goodness.

Finally, Wildwood asked Arthur to come to Tea-Olive with her one weekend, to meet her parents. He accepted the invitation on the spot, and her parents both liked him immensely. Wildwood's mother secretly began planning a wedding that would take place in the First Baptist Church, but even when she hinted about her plans to Wildwood, Wildwood herself remained unresponsive. So it was not a complete surprise when Wildwood phoned them about two weeks later and announced that she and Arthur had been married by a justice of the peace in Atlanta. What was a surprise, however, was that only two months later, Wildwood moved back home, without Arthur. Wildwood was somewhat silent and withdrawn, and she had been home for around two weeks when she told her parents that she and Arthur were divorcing. She gave no reason, and her parents accepted her right to privacy.

"Listen, honey," her mother crooned. "You live in a world far different from the one I was in at your age. In my generation, we had no choice but to try and hitch ourselves to a good man. I certainly did, but I was just lucky. You young women have many more opportunities, and you *can* make choices."

"I know, Mama," Wildwood whispered, and then she added, "thank you."

Wildwood seemed perfectly contented to be back in the quiet town of Tea-Olive, and she contented herself with writing in her private journal and remaining polite but somewhat cool to her friends. In this way, she brought home the fact that she was not going to discuss her private life with anyone. In only a few short months, the old manager of the Tea-Olive Public Library had to retire because of health reasons, and Wildwood got the job.

Likewise, Memphis's luck changed for the better. She was hired to manage the lunchroom in the high school, and she did such a great job that in less than a year, she was the major chef. The youngsters were delighted with the meals she prepared, and at last, she was doing the work for which she had trained so hard.

So Wildwood and Memphis were the only two young women who left Tea-Olive but who came home again. And stayed.

CHAPTER
— NINE —

From the very beginning, people in town treated the judge with great deference, and the town merchants certainly benefitted from the judge's seemingly endless resources. At the hardware store, the judge ordered all of the farm implements he would need, a huge order that brought a foolish grin to the owner's face. After the order was complete, the owner and the judge engaged in all-important small talk, with the judge querying the owner about nearby ponds for good fishing.

"He's sure a fine fellow," the owner later confided to his wife. "Seems to be so down-to-earth and friendly."

At the bank, the judge established all of his accounts, and in a private meeting with the bank president, he revealed his strong penchant for total and complete privacy, as far as his finances went. The president assured him that he himself would handle any and all transactions, therefore bypassing any young teller who might be tempted to discuss the judge's business. The president grinned widely after announcing such a rare and personal service, and the judge shook his hand, touched him on the shoulder, and thanked him most sincerely.

"Could you ever ask to meet a finer man?" the president wondered later.

So in addition to the people liking his just-a-regular-fellow attitude, they held him in great reverence — for after all, he *was* a retired judge!

So very soon — too soon, some said — the judge was invited into the most important organizations and positions in the town: the library board, the Kiwanis Club, even the town council, but he gave his regrets for each invitation, explaining that work on the farm was his top agenda right now. But he also said that later, when he had more time, he would gladly reconsider, especially showing an interest in serving on the town council. When pressed about his plans for the farm, he freely detailed the cattle he would like to raise, the modern chicken coop he had constructed, and the small cannery he had built behind the barn, for putting up the fruits of what he anticipated to be a large "kitchen garden." In other words, it seemed to folks in the town that the judge was simply preparing a farm that would provide him with everything he needed, and he certainly didn't seem interested in selling any of the products. "Oh, maybe some specialty fruits to local shops," he admitted. Other than that, he was pretty quiet about the farm, and he joined in the traditional procedure of coming into town on Saturday afternoons, to have his hair trimmed at the local barber shop, to talk and visit and compare the size of fish caught in the creek or the status of the current rainfall.

For nearly a month, people held their breaths, waiting to see which church the judge would attend. All of the ladies in town, even the happily married ones, took to dressing up even more for church than they usually did. They all waited and watched, but finally, they had to confess that the judge wasn't coming to any church in town.

"Perhaps he drives over to Augusta?" someone surmised.

"I don't think so," was the response. "I think he just plain out isn't a church-goer at all."

Such a thing was almost unthinkable in Tea-Olive, but the people quickly forgave him for that failing because of his genial good manners and jolly demeanor. They even forgave him when he hired a farmworker from out of town.

"Why didn't you hire someone local?" the hardware store owner asked him.

"Because I am an extremely private man, and a local would spread gossip about me from day one," he answered, smiling and shrugging his shoulders. To the people in town, their lives were always an open book anyway, and their words and actions were immediately known to everyone, but they accepted the fact that, to the judge, privacy and decorum seemed to be the standard he set. So some of them clucked their tongues, but they accepted that the judge was "a fine man, but a little different."

The members of the Tea-Olive Bird Watching Society waited a polite extra length of time before calling on the judge, to welcome him to the community. But while they waited, they all did more "bird watching" than usual, and always in the King's Wood Sanctuary, and so they kept a close eye on what was going on at the farm. Among them, they would never have said that they were spying, but secretly, each of them knew that's exactly what they were doing. Sweet, especially, trained her binoculars more frequently on the farmhouse, hoping to catch a glimpse of the tall, stately judge.

"Everyone simply calls him the judge," she complained. "Why doesn't someone call him by his given name?"

"Because Hyson Breed simply isn't very easy to say," Beulah offered. "It's just so much easier to call him the judge."

While they all waited for a polite length of time to pass, they watched not only the judge's farm, but they also spotted several pileated woodpeckers, whose medium-pitched laugh was interspersed with the rapid-fire *rat-a-tat* of its beak against the hard trunk of a tree. At dusk another day, they heard the soft, downy *whoo-whoo* of a great horned owl (they thought!), though they never could spot him. And they were all thrilled when the cry of a red-tailed hawk shattered the softer sounds in the woods. They finally spotted him, although he flew away before most of them could get their binoculars trained on him.

"I saw him!" Beulah yelped, suddenly aware that she was hearing the sounds that she and Sweet had heard so many times when they were children growing up in the higher hills north of Tea-Olive. "Listen, Sweet! Did you hear the hawk?"

But Sweet wasn't listening. She had her

binoculars trained right on Love-Divine's old house, and the only thing on her mind was the judge. So Beulah was left alone with the memories of her ancestors as well as Sweet's.

As the story went, Sweet's ancestors — through her father's side of the family — were the first settlers in the Tea-Olive region. Tough-minded Scots-Irish immigrants looking to start a new life in what was then the English colony of Georgia, they were all headed farther south, but among the seven wagons, two broke down at exactly the same time, in a spot between the rolling hills of North Georgia just below the Appalachian Mountains. Josiah O'Rourke, unofficial but revered patriarch of the band of seven families on the trek for a good place to settle, declared that since two of the wagons had broken down at exactly the same time, it must have been a sign from the Heavenly Father that they were to settle right there.

So they set about parceling out the land for growing fields and pastures and built log cabins out of trees they felled themselves. Their first winter was a mild one, so that instead of struggling to survive, they all lived happily off of the harvest of squirrels, rabbits, wild turkeys, and doves that the men brought home from long days of hunting. But one day, when the men were hunting, they all noticed a strange, very sweet aroma in the woods.

"Am I smelling a *flower?*" one of them asked.

"Can't be!" another exclaimed. "Not in the middle of December."

But it was certainly a flower, as they soon discovered by following the scent to a large bush with dark leaves and miniscule, white flowers. So that day, when the men came home with their hunting pouches loaded with quail and rabbits, they each brought a small branch of that wonderful shrub with them, to give to their wives.

On one long expedition to a local trading post, the men learned that the shrub was called a tea-olive, and from then on, whenever they went hunting, they always brought home some of the branches. Later, the settlement of those seven families came to be called Tea-Olive, Georgia.

When spring came for those first settlers, the oxen that had pulled the wagons were hitched to plows, and the men worked hard, breaking up the land, while the women and children followed behind them in the rich furrows, dropping in seed corn. Other women and children worked "kitchen gardens," which yielded tomatoes and butter beans, radishes, and pole beans. And in this way the settlers grew close to the land.

During the American Revolution, the men fought hard for the new country, and when independence had been won, they rejoiced at simply being back home on their own land — this time in their own free country. Later, in the Civil War, the men fought for independence again, for an independent Confederate nation. But that time, they lost, and when the few survivors came home, it was to abject poverty and shame. Still, they survived, and for all those generations that followed, Tea-Olive was always the place they called home. And they were nearly all as tough and as strong as those Scots-Irish ancestors.

Some people said that Sweet's particular brand of gentility, much more highly refined than almost every other lady in town, was the result of her mother's influence. For her mother had not grown up in the hardscrabble world of wrenching a living from the soil, but from her good fortune of being the pampered only daughter of a wealthy Virginia family. Gentle good manners and refined behavior were demanded unerringly from Sweet, from the time she was merely a toddler. But it was from her father that Sweet inherited her love and reverence for the land.

"Never give up the land," Sweet's own father had whispered to her on his deathbed. "Never! Do you hear me?"

"Yes, Papa," Sweet had answered, and she meant it.

So that lovely afternoon all those years later, as the ladies roamed around King's Wood Bird Sanctuary, Beulah was really in a place of long ago and with people who had been gone for many generations. Still, she and Sweet carried some of those strong traits within themselves. Beulah could only hope that Sweet carried enough of the traits to keep her from making a fool of herself over a man none of them knew very well.

CHAPTER
— TEN —

After many such afternoons spent in the sanctuary, the ladies felt that a reasonable length of time had passed for letting the judge get settled in, and they worked together to bake a high, white, coconut cake. At last, they went to call upon the judge, as social custom dictated, and Sweet had butterflies in her stomach for days, but she had the decorum and good sense not to mention that to any of the others.

So on a Saturday afternoon, the ladies of the Tea-Olive Bird Watching Society descended upon Love-Divine's old house, came up onto the porch, and knocked softly at the door.

"Who is it?" came a booming, deeply masculine voice from inside, but they could hear no footsteps approaching the door. So they glanced uneasily at one another and knocked yet again. "I SAID WHO IS IT???" came the enormous roar that made every one of them flinch a bit.

All except for Sweet, who privately thought that the voice carried deep and thrilling tones of wonderful masculinity and authority.

"It's the Tea-Olive Bird Watching Society, judge, and we've come to welcome you to the community!" yelled Beulah. And at last, they heard footsteps coming toward the door. Heavy footsteps that set the porch floor to vibrating. The judge opened the door to come face-to-face with a group of ladies wearing Sunday-best dresses and with ultrapolite smiles on their faces, smiles that soon turned to glances of disbelief, for the judge was wearing a brilliant red silk robe over khaki pants and a blazingly white T-shirt. They all gasped a little, never before having seen a man in a silk robe, much less a bloodred one. Beulah recovered herself first, and she thrust the cake toward him.

"Welcome to the community," she sputtered, as he reached out to take the cake into his huge hands. Sweet, especially, noticed the bulging veins in the back of his hands and imagined those same hands swinging a gavel to silence an entire courtroom full of people.

"Judge, please allow me to introduce the members of the Tea-Olive Bird Watching Society." Beulah pressed forward, starting to introduce the members using their full hymnal names, not realizing how strange those names were going to sound to him. "This is Zion. She is named for the hymn, 'Marching to Zion' and she runs a small creamery on the edge of town. I'm sure she would welcome you as a new customer." Zion turned a deep red and studied her shoes. "And this is Wildwood. She is named for 'The Church in the Wildwood.' She works in the local public library and will be happy to issue a library card to you." Wildwood smiled and nodded her head. "This is Memphis, the only one of us not given a hymnal name, but that's OK," Beulah added. Memphis nodded her head and smiled at the judge. "And this is Sweet." Beulah indicated the slender, nervous Sweet, who was sporting a new hairstyle, as Wanda had recommended. "She is named after the hymn, 'Sweet By and By.' "

"How do you do," Sweet responded, and she was the first among them to extend her small hand toward the big man. Now the judge, who had become more and more incredulous as Beulah introduced the hymn-named women, looked deep into Sweet's eyes and smiled. Sweet blushed prettily and slowly withdrew her hand from his strong grip. Beulah finished up the introductions: "I am Beulah, named after the hymn, 'Beulah Land,' and I am the president of our little bird watching society."

After the introductions were finished, they all experienced a small moment of awkwardness. Then he addressed Wildwood: "You work at the library?"

"Yes, I do," Wildwood confirmed, blushing and hating herself for it.

"You came into an inheritance from the previous owner of this property, didn't you?" he inquired.

"Why yes," Wildwood said. "We are deeply appreciative to Love-Divine for making the library the beneficiary of her estate."

At that, the conversation stopped abruptly, with the judge wondering if he would have to invite them into his home. He clearly didn't want to do that. Talking and joking with the men in town was one thing, but a bevy of women in his living room would be quite another. At the same time, the women were all wondering if he would invite them in, and if he did, would it be proper for them to enter a house where a man was wearing a red silk robe, even if it was worn over his clothes?

As usual, Beulah took over the awkward situation. "Well, we have to go now, but we hope you enjoy the cake. And once again, welcome to the neighborhood."

"Bye now!" they all chorused together, and they went back toward Beulah's car, being careful not to titter among themselves while he was watching from the doorway. As they drove away, one small hand fluttered briefly through the open window of the car, and the judge stood for a long time with the perfect coconut cake in his large hands. Finally, he looked down at it.

"Sweet," he said.

CHAPTER
— ELEVEN —

To Wildwood's delight — and eventual dismay — the judge came into the library only about a week later and filled out an application for a card. Wildwood issued one immediately, not waiting the customary few days she normally required. She even typed the card herself and handed it over with a flourish. As he took the card, he looked around the library's main room with a frown.

"How about a tour?" he asked Wildwood.

"Of course," she answered, and proceeded to show him the children's area with its brightly colored carpeting and numerous floor pillows, then the small reference area and the heritage collection.

"What's a heritage collection?" the judge asked, thumbing the corner of an ancient book.

"It's where we keep books and files relevant to the town's history," Wildwood explained. "As well as genealogy information that goes back to colonial times."

At that moment, the Homework Helper children burst into the library, their high-spirited noisiness disturbing the velvet silence. The judge looked at the children and drew his nostrils tighter as their warm, animal aromas reached him.

"Good heavens!" he exclaimed. "What are those noisy children doing in here?"

Wildwood had to resist her urge to tell the judge to lower his voice so that the children would not hear his disparaging remarks. "These are the Homework Helper children who come after school twice a week for extra assistance," she explained, trying to keep her voice mannerly and well-modulated.

"And who helps them?" he asked. "You?"

"Yes, I help when I have time," Wildwood said. "And we have some wonderful volunteers as well."

Then Wildwood made a valiant attempt to change the course of the conversation away from the children: "I heard that you were invited to join the library board of trustees," she ventured. "We hope that you will consider such a move in the near future."

The judge seemed a little surprised when she changed the subject, and he gazed at her steadily before he said, "Well, yes. I'll certainly consider it. I always want to do my part in the community."

Later, Wildwood told her mother, "He seems a little rough around the edges, but I still think it would be a great honor for our little library to have him on the board."

Only a few days later, Wildwood's wish was granted. The judge became a board member. When he arrived at the library for the first board meeting, he was wearing an immaculate, finely tailored suit and a dazzling white shirt with a tie. Wildwood showed him into the conference room that was used for the meetings.

"Please make yourself comfortable," Wildwood said, indicating a chair at the large, oval table. "The other board members will be here soon."

Introductions were in order that evening, because while everyone in town knew the judge, he knew few of them. Wildwood handled the introductions carefully, noting that the other board members, who wore casual attire — the women were wearing freshly ironed housedresses and the men were wearing clean shirts with the sleeves rolled up — seemed quietly surprised at the judge's immaculate suit and silk tie. And perhaps his magisterial bearing and expensive attire set the stage for something strange: all of the other members, even people who had been on the board for many, many years seemed to defer to him almost immediately, became quite timid in his presence, and whenever he said anything, everyone listened with rapt attention.

But Wildwood was completely surprised when his first question was about the after-school Homework Helper Program.

"How many children does that program serve?" he asked Wildwood. She looked through the folder in front of her and said, "Well, right now, we're serving about eleven children."

"That's not many," the judge responded. "Is it worth the expense?"

No one said a word for long minutes. They knew, as did everyone in town, that the program served low-income children who, without the extra help, would fail over and over again and eventually probably drop out of school altogether.

"We think it's an important program," Wildwood finally said, softly. "It serves children who haven't had many advantages." In vain, she looked around at the other board members, seeking some support. None of them met her gaze.

"But it serves so few children," the judge insisted.

"It's a voluntary program," Wildwood explained. "We try hard to connect with the children who need this help, but many times, their parents or caregivers have never had any advantages themselves, and so they fail to understand how valuable the program really is." As she spoke the last words, she changed her tone and looked pointedly at the judge, clearly indicating that he, himself, didn't understand. But her tone was lost on him.

"It's still expensive, both in the cost of materials and in library staff time," the judge said. "I think we should attract more children or else close it down."

At that point, not only Wildwood, but all of the other board members realized that the judge truly didn't understand about the children the program served. Because after so many long years of racial segregation, Tea-Olive was only one of the thousands — perhaps hundreds of thousands — of small towns throughout the South that were trying to provide some kind of service to help children overcome all the years of deprivation their parents and grandparents had suffered and which still affected the children of today. But what would the judge know of that? Someone who had lived his whole life in upstate New York would never be able to understand.

Wildwood looked around at the other board members, but they still said nothing. What mystic transformation had taken place in that room? The judge! He simply walked in and without a shot being fired, he smiled and nodded his head and acted the perfect gentleman, while he simply took over *everything*. Without any argument, he became the guiding force in the whole board. Wildwood could hardly believe what had happened.

"It's an important program!" she sputtered, unwilling to lie down like a frightened lamb and allow this smiling stranger to destroy the program so many underprivileged children depended upon!

"It's important to *you*," the judge almost whispered. "It's only important to *you*." The other board members shuffled their papers and looked at their hands.

"The program must survive," she said, close to tears of frustration.

"Then I suggest, madam, that you find a way to fund it," the judge said, and again, no one rose to Wildwood's defense.

The meeting had been adjourned for only a few minutes when Wildwood called Beulah and told her about what had happened.

"He's a library board member?" Beulah questioned. "Already? Why, nobody even really knows him yet!"

"But he's a retired *judge,* Beulah." Wildwood was again close to tears.

"That doesn't mean he's necessarily a good man," Beulah mused. "Doesn't tell us one single thing about him really, except that he got elected to a district court in New York."

"Well, he seems to be polite and courteous, but he's on the board now, and I really believe that he means to shut down the Homework Helper Program!"

Beulah was incredulous. "Why on earth would he do that?"

"He said it's too expensive, what with the materials and the drain on library staff time." Even as Wildwood spoke those words, she still could not comprehend them. "He said I should seek other funding, if the program is to survive."

Beulah thought long and hard. "Well, we could get one of the volunteers to manage the program," she mused. "Is Thankful Broderick still volunteering?"

"Yes, she is," Wildwood answered, feeling better by knowing that Beulah was sharing her determination that the program survive.

"Well, she's a retired teacher, so she's

fully experienced, and I'll bet she would manage the program for you, if you asked her."

"I never thought of that," Wildwood admitted. "I'll certainly ask her."

"As for money for materials," Beulah continued, "we could have a bake sale and raise a little money. I don't think the materials cost that much, do they?"

"Not really, but our budget is already so tight, so maybe that's why the judge thinks we should shut it down. And another thing I've been thinking about is this: sometimes, when somebody gets to be the new person on a board or a commission, they feel that they have to do *something*, and if they can't think of one thing, then they will think of another!"

"And there's yet something else we can add to the list of things that need thinking about," Beulah said.

"What?" Wildwood couldn't imagine what Beulah was talking about, but she valued the fine mind that resided beyond Beulah's spectacles.

"Are we all just going to roll over and play dead?" Beulah asked. "Let one board member change the program without a fight?"

"I can't fight by myself," Wildwood

admitted. "I've already told you how everyone else on the board seems to be cowering before the judge!"

"Well, maybe that's what we need to change," Beulah murmured.

"But how?"

"You just let me think on it a little bit," Beulah said. "There is a solution, I just don't know what it is, right now."

"Yes," Wildwood said. "Thank you, and let me know what you think the solution can be."

Very early the next morning, Beulah drove to Zion's creamery. And Beulah's work there was worth much more than the small salary Zion was able to pay, because Beulah loved driving out of the town and into the openness of the countryside, especially so early in the morning. Going to Zion's was like stepping back into another time — a time before freeways and satellite dishes — before everyone was in such a hurry. A time before everyone was so afraid of "development." Strangely, Beulah recalled a letter Love-Divine had written to the editor of the local newspaper, and which he had published in its entirety several years ago, when they all first started becoming worried about suburban sprawl and how it would affect the quality of life in places like Tea-Olive. She had liked the editorial so much that she had fairly committed it to memory:

Dear Editor,

I am writing this letter on behalf of those of us who fear "development." Yesterday, I drove over to Agriville to see an old school friend with whom I had lost touch. I was simply amazed at what is happening to that once beautiful little town. It's closer to the interstate highway than Tea-Olive, but I fear that, eventually, the same things will happen here. The residents of Agriville are able to hear the roar of fast-moving traffic faintly in the dead quietness of rural nights. Super shopping centers have risen like mysterious, giant mushrooms in the places where, only a few months ago, honey-colored Jersey milk cows grazed in knee-deep, dew-glistened grass, their brown eyes glowing like strange flowers between the flicking, dark-tipped ears.

"Development" scrapes the land clean, then paves it over, marking it into parking spaces and loading

zones, huge, flat, acres-large monstrosities of parking lots, where the broiling summer sun softens the pavement and people returning from the air-conditioned environs of the store itself find their cars floating in waves of uprising heat and with the door handles too hot to touch with the bare hand. Changing — always changing, with a kitty litter factory springing up on what used to be a proud, old homestead, and local "meat and three" country cafés being joined by Tex-Mex stands and strange small restaurants, where folks who still wore freshly ironed coveralls to town on Saturday could dine on Chinese noodles floating in a delicate chicken broth.

But in other ways, very little has changed about Agriville. The churches — Baptist, Methodist, Presbyterian, African-Methodist Episcopal, and Holiness — keep a tight hold on the old traditions of long Sunday morning services, a shorter Sunday evening service, Wednesday night prayer meeting, and of course, choir practice and the annual Homecoming: All-Day-Singing-and-Dinner-on-the-Ground.

But it seems to me that "development" causes some terrible changes, and we should all try to keep our simple way of life in this beautifully simple little town.

That letter had so deeply impressed Beulah that she cut it out and put it into the back of her Bible. Now, driving to Zion's house, out in the countryside, she hoped more than ever that so-called progress would not come and spoil their town.

Beulah pulled her car around in back of Zion's house. The lights were already on in the milking parlor, and while Beulah tied on her heavy-duty apron, she could see Zion with her bucket of soapy water washing the udders of the twelve little sweet-faced Jersey cows.

"Put on your boots," Zion ordered, and Beulah obediently slipped off her shoes and worked her toes into the spotlessly clean rubber boots. Zion was a complete stickler for cleanliness, whether it was the barn in which her cows stayed the night or the rooms in which the cows were milked and all of her dairy products were made.

"Makes me so mad!" Zion was complaining.

"What does?" Beulah asked, as she

began rinsing the udders and drying them with a soft towel.

"Got rats in my barn again," Zion muttered. "Gotta get them exterminated right away."

Beulah made no comment; she just continued rinsing and drying. She always thought that the turgid udders were fascinating, what with the bulging veins and the weight of all that milk. As she rinsed and dried each one, Zion came behind her to attach the long arms of the milking machines. Soon, the machines filled the milking shed with a steady thrum, thrum, and the shed itself filled with the comforting aroma of warm milk.

"Wildwood called me yesterday evening," Beulah said. "Guess they've put the judge on the library board, and Wildwood's scared he wants to cut out the Homework Helper Program."

"The library board? Already?" Zion was parroting Beulah's exact words of yesterday. "Why, nobody even knows him! Not really." Zion's voice held contempt, but that didn't surprise Beulah, because ever since she had become a widow, she didn't "truck" with men at all. In fact, she once even bragged that she had never met a man other than her late husband whom she liked in the least little bit. "He's sure moving in fast," Zion added. "And I think it's probably a lot faster than we know."

"What do you mean?"

"I had a phone call last night, too."

"Wildwood called you?"

"Not Wildwood. Memphis."

"What about?" Beulah finished drying the last udder and stood up.

"About seeing that blessed judge" — here, Zion let a small humph enter her voice — "and Sweet!"

"What? Where?" Beulah's mind was racing.

"Seems they were having tea together yesterday afternoon and leaning forward toward each other, whispering and laughing. They stayed at the tearoom an uncommonly long time, and Memphis said she even caught them playing patty-fingers!"

"What?"

"Touching each other's hands and acting silly. That's why I say he's moving a lot faster than we know."

Beulah couldn't imagine what was going on in Sweet's mind! Why, the man was a perfect stranger! But then she remembered Sweet's comment about the judge being a handsome man, and goose bumps came up on her arms. It surprised her that Sweet would even consider going out for tea with him! Beulah thought for a long moment before she spoke. "You free later this afternoon?" Beulah asked, and Zion eyed her suspiciously.

"Why?"

"Because I think we need to do some bird watching. Something about the judge just doesn't strike me right. And because he's a retired judge, folks are too trusting of him. I'd like to go hunt for that woodpecker again and take a good look-see at what's going on out at Love-Divine's old house."

So later that afternoon, Beulah and Zion stood well back in the trees at the bird sanctuary, with their binoculars trained on the judge's "gentleman's farm." All of the fencing had been painted white, and the new tractor gleamed in its shed. The pasture was now dotted with Jersey cows, and chickens scratched and clucked in their pens.

"Well," Zion commented, "he may be a retired judge, but he isn't very smart, I would say."

"Why?" Beulah asked, perplexed.

"Not smart enough to have a roll-bar on that new tractor," Zion said, training her binoculars on the tractor again. "Go to driving on a hill and a tractor can turn over on you real fast."

"That's right," Beulah agreed.

"My papa," Zion added, "why he wouldn't have driven a tractor without a roll-bar for anything in this world." She trained her binoculars on the small herd of cows.

"Wonder if he's going to sell milk from those cows?" Zion mused. "Not room enough in this little town for more than one creamery, and he's a rich, retired man and me just a poor woman trying to pay my electricity bill!"

Beulah knew that Zion was getting herself worked up and that if she didn't distract her, Zion would go into one of her full-blown diatribes against giant superstores and interstate highways and how they were sure to impact the town — change it forever. Of course, Beulah agreed with Zion about that, but she never seemed to get quite as riled up as Zion about it.

"Easy, Zion," Beulah crooned. "I expect running a creamery is a lot more work than he's willing to do." But just then, Beulah and Zion spotted the judge's hired man walking across to the barn with buckets in each hand.

"Doesn't have to do it himself," Zion growled. "Got a hired man to do it all for him!" Beulah was trying to think of how to settle Zion down when — right before their very eyes — Sweet's little blue sedan pulled into the driveway. Both of the women took in sudden, shocked breaths, but they didn't lower their binoculars.

Sweet, her new hairstyle set off by a soft blue dress, got out of the car and draped a matching scarf around her neck before she approached the judge's front door. After Sweet had knocked, she looked directly toward the sanctuary, and as usual, Beulah and Zion ducked down instinctively. But when the door opened and Sweet, smiling broadly, had entered the judge's house, they stood up straight again.

"You know what I keep thinking about?" Beulah asked.

"Heaven only knows," Zion answered.

"I keep thinking about what Vicky said after she and the good reverend made their call on the judge."

"What did she say?" Zion asked.

"That the judge was going to be looking for a new wife to go in that new kitchen he's got."

"It's all too fast," Zion said. "We need to talk to Sweet. Doesn't look right for a single woman to go visiting a single man without anyone else in the house."

"The hired man is around," Beulah said, trying to make herself feel better about what they had seen.

"He's not inside the house," Zion said simply.

"I'll go talk with her this evening after prayer meeting," Beulah said. "Looks to me like she's simply lost her mind!"

"Well, let's get out of here," Zion suggested. "This is all making me too uncomfortable!"

True to her word, Beulah approached Sweet after prayer meeting was over, taking her elbow, guiding her down the steps, leading Sweet to her car, and getting into the passenger seat of Sweet's car, without so much as an invitation.

"What on earth?" Sweet breathed.

"Sweet, somebody's got to talk some sense into you before you get into water that's way over your head." Beulah allowed her full concern to come out in her tone. Sweet immediately looked out of the window of the driver's side, as if to dismiss anything Beulah might say.

"You know exactly what I'm talking about, don't you?" Beulah nudged.

"Maybe I do and maybe I don't." Sweet pouted.

Just like a naughty child! Beulah was thinking. *And what on earth can make a grown woman — old enough to be a grandmother, if she'd ever had any children of her own! — go so hard against her own upbringing?*

"I'm worried about you." Beulah tried the gentler track. "Is there anything you want to tell me?"

"I don't know what you mean." Sweet didn't try to keep the annoyance out of her voice.

"Zion and I were at the sanctuary today, and we saw you drive up and go into the judge's house." There! It was said right out loud.

Sweet's face was incredulous. "Were you all spying on me?" she demanded.

"No, we were not spying on *you*," Beulah said, and she didn't add: we were spying on the judge. "We were looking for a woodpecker, and we couldn't help but notice when you went out to the judge's house. What were you doing there, Sweet?"

"That's really not any of your business," Sweet said, but in a gentle tone that conveyed her unwillingness to be rude.

"Well, it can't be for any good, Sweet," Beulah argued. "I don't have to tell you about life in a small town! People are going to talk, and it's going to hurt you."

"I've been hurt before and survived," Sweet said. "And besides, I believe that his intentions toward me are purely honorable."

"You don't know anything about him," Beulah reminded her.

"I'm *learning* about him," Sweet defended herself.

"Just don't be blind, Sweet," Beulah cautioned. "And don't go to his house anymore and make yourself the object of gossip. Go out to dinner with him. Maybe even go to a movie, though that's a pretty long drive. But just you be careful!"

When Beulah got out of Sweet's car, she felt that she had failed in her mission to warn Sweet — to warn her about what, she wasn't sure. But about *something.*

Over the next few weeks, Sweet and the judge were the hot items of gossip in town. They drove down to Athens to take in dinner and movies, and they sat together on Sweet's front porch, rocking and talking. They even spent a weekend together at Lake Lanier, something that really set tongues to wagging furiously.

"I can't believe her behavior!" someone said.

"She's living in sin!" pronounced another. "Better for them to get married than for Sweet to burn in hellfire!"

And Sweet herself presented the same proper demeanor as she had always shown, but in the supermarket, she could hear whispers while she selected a cantaloupe melon and in the beauty parlor other women refrained from speaking until Sweet was having her hair blown dry and couldn't hear them for the noise. And when the attendant turned off the dryer, the other women fell silent. Sweet noticed these things, but for the first time in her life, she didn't care what anyone said. She was finally — finally! — going to have the husband she had always dreamed of having, and that was all that mattered to her.

The judge accomplished other things during his ardent courtship of Sweet. He quietly bought partial ownership in a small construction firm in Athens, and someone said it was the same company that had refurbished the house for him and put in all the fencing. He also began fostering extremely positive relationships with the town "fathers," the good country men who composed most of the town council. He placed another big order for farming implements and an upright freezer at the local hardware store. In fact, the order was so large that the proprietor — who was also a town councilman, smiled for days on end. Next, the judge made a large donation to the Tea-Olive Men's Service Club, whose president was also on the council. At the local florist's, he placed an ongoing order for red, white, and blue carnations to be placed on the graves of veterans in the Tea-Olive cemetery every Veterans Day and the Fourth of July. The florist was delighted to receive such good business, and she spoke highly of the judge to her husband, who was on the council as well. The judge bought a side of beef from a local beef producer (to go into the new freezer), and yes, that producer also just happened to be on the council. At last, he went to a local jewelry shop and purchased the largest diamond ring he could find. At that, the jeweler could not resist whispering in the barber shop that he thought the judge was getting ready to pop the big question to someone.

During all of this activity, the judge changed the way he dressed, wearing freshly ironed shirts open at the neck and actually smiling and laughing with the people of the town.

"Why, he's like a changed man!" some of them exclaimed. "Maybe that's what being in love can do for you!" And no one was surprised at all when the judge was invited to join the town council. After all, he was such a personable man, and he certainly did help the town's economy.

These things, he accomplished by day, but at night, he continued his wooing of the already-smitten Sweet. Zion and Beulah had tried numerous times to talk to Sweet about what was happening, but she was completely impervious to all their concerns. They all went bird watching several times, including Wildwood, who had a rare day off from the library, and Sweet openly and without any embarrassment kept her binoculars trained right on the judge's house instead of on the birds.

"What are you looking for?" Beulah asked her, finally.

"I just want to be able to see him," Sweet answered, turning her soft blue eyes on Beulah. And Beulah had seen that expression before, but always on the faces of young people who have been bitten by the lovebug — who were hopelessly, madly, in love; she had never seen that expression on the face of a mature woman. It made such a strange combination, that mixture of sweet madness and the soft lines around Sweet's eyes.

"He's going to ask me to marry him," Sweet said in such a soft voice that Beulah and Zion could hardly hear what she was saying. They stared at her with open mouths, and Sweet blushed a deep pink. "I'm sure of it!" she added, with a note of triumph in her voice.

"No!" Zion shouted. "You make him wait! You don't even know him!"

"I know that I'm in love with him," Sweet said. "Oh, I'm in love for the very first time in my life!" Sweet crooned, even turning in a small circle.

At that moment, the judge came out of the back door, and without another word, Sweet walked out of the woods and down the hill to him.

"I don't think there's anything we can do to stop her," Beulah lamented, watching as the judge and Sweet embraced.

"Well, she's certainly not a child. She's a grown woman with a sound mind, and legally, she has the right to do anything she wants to do."

"But it's going to be a disaster," Wildwood said.

"I suspect you're right," Zion agreed. "And when it turns into that disaster, we'll have to be here for Sweet. Help pick her up and dust her off and hope she learns, once and for all, not to be so trusting!"

"So . . . do we just go along with her on this?"

"Nothing else we can do!" Zion fumed. "We're too old to pout!"

"And I have to be especially careful here," Wildwood reminded Beulah and Zion. "Say what you will, he's a member of the library board and now on the town council, and I need my job!"

"So you've decided to cave in to him, too?" Beulah asked.

"I don't know what else to do," Wildwood said. "The rest of the board members have already caved in, and I can't fight him without them. And the town council makes all of the important decisions about the library — usually with the recommendation of the board, of course."

"All we can do now," Beulah said, "is pray for Sweet and go ahead and plan a bridal shower for her." Zion shuddered, but she said nothing more.

CHAPTER
— TWELVE —

Sure enough, the judge presented Sweet with that huge diamond ring and even got down on one knee to propose to her, and that right in Memphis's tea room! The other customers murmured "Aah!" and for Sweet, that moment almost stopped her heart from beating. All of the emotions that she thought everyone but her had experienced — the heart-stopping delight, the delicious clouding over of any imperfections, the joy of being the center of someone's affection — now belonged to her, at last! She accepted his proposal on the spot, and an announcement of their engagement was printed up in the next issue of the *Tea-Olive Gazette*.

And contrary to what Beulah, Zion, and Wildwood would have thought, the judge had, indeed, begun being intimate with Sweet in a particular way: by telling her in detail about his largely unhappy childhood, when every single year his family sent him off to boarding school, and even when he came home for holidays, they were cold and distant to him. But he also told her of his only childhood joys — those of spending every summer with his stepgrandfather in a little town not far from Tea-Olive.

"The summers were wonderful," he confessed to Sweet. "It never dawned upon me that my family in New York were simply trying to get rid of me during the summers, just the way they sent me off to boarding school every fall, because I was never happier than when my stepgrandfather taught me how to fish, how to plow . . . and with a mule, no less!" And how those hot, wonderful, lazy summer days in the South composed the only times of happiness in his life, which was why, when it was time for him to retire from the bench, he started searching for property that reminded him of those times.

"And now I have *you* as well," he murmured to Sweet. "I have you to make me happy!"

Contrary to the way Beulah, Zion, and Wildwood were worrying about the rapid courtship and impending wedding, the other ladies in Sweet's Bible study class thought her impending marriage was wonderful and exciting.

"Why, he just swept her right off her feet!" they said and "How romantic!" they exclaimed. So they planned a shower for her and had a special meeting to decide upon a wedding gift.

"This won't be as easy as buying gifts for a young, first-time bride," they decided. "She already has all the household things she needs."

"What about giving them a wedding trip?" another suggested. "It wouldn't have to be terribly expensive — perhaps a three-day stay at a nice hotel at Lake Lanier?"

"They have already been up to Lake Lanier," scoffed another, bringing blushes and downcast eyes to all of the others.

"That's all in the past," someone said. "I'm sure she has prayed for forgiveness for that blatant indiscretion by now. So I think a gift of a few days for them to go away is just a fine idea. And too, such a nice gift will show the judge that we aren't a bunch of hayseeds!!"

So the good ladies from Sweet's Bible study class arranged for a gala wedding shower at Memphis's tearoom, and they made sure that Memphis knew there was to be no skimping on the food or the teas. They ordered a big cake from Memphis's own kitchen, and the day before the shower, they descended upon the tearoom armed with huge bouquets of fresh flowers, spools of white satin ribbon, and crystal candleholders. When they left, the tearoom, already beautiful in its own right, had been transformed into a magical setting for love and happiness.

Beulah and Wildwood attended the shower, of course, because they were in the same Bible study class with Sweet, but Beulah also said that the Tea-Olive Bird Watching Society should properly throw their own small shower as well.

"Why do we have to celebrate something we're all so worried about?" Zion asked sensibly.

"Because it's the proper thing to do," Beulah argued. "And besides, we have to let Sweet know that we support her, even if things do turn out badly — as I suspect they will!"

"Let's just hope we'll be wrong about that," Wildwood added.

So they, too, worked with Memphis and arranged a small but tasteful tea for Sweet. Zion even agreed to attend, marking the first time she had ever been in the tearoom. And she surprised everyone by swapping her typical coveralls for a dress for the shower, and she even wore fingernail polish. To Beulah, it seemed incredible to see that type of decoration on Zion's strong, square hands and strangely, it made Beulah's eyes fill up.

The society gave Sweet a framed Audubon print and their heartiest congratulations, as was the proper thing to do. But secretly, they glanced at one another, and without saying anything aloud, Beulah silently prayed, "Please, Lord, be with Sweet!"

"So now, tell about plans for the wedding," Wildwood asked, trying to keep her voice light and pleasant. Sweet blushed and stirred her tea.

"Well, we're not going to have a church wedding," Sweet said, and the others looked up sharply.

"Not a church wedding?" Beulah stammered. "I didn't know there was any other way to have a wedding."

"We're just going to a justice of the peace," Sweet explained. "That's the way the judge wants it to be."

"Why are you still just calling him the judge?" Zion asked, and they all noticed the edge in her voice. "Doesn't he have an honest-to-goodness name?"

"Hyson," Sweet whispered. "But that seems so personal!"

"It had better be personal," Zion growled. "For Heaven's sake, Sweet, you're going to *marry* him!"

"I know," Sweet answered, and Wildwood knew for a fact that she saw in Sweet's expression the very same expression she had seen in the library board members' faces when the judge joined. Complete agreement and acceptance. So Wildwood was thinking: *What is it about that man that makes everyone — including me! — just roll over like some subservient old dog, begging to have his stomach rubbed, hoping against hope that man won't kick him to death? And what is it about* us, *that we would assume he's so much better than all of us? Just because he's from New York? Just because he's a retired judge? What do we really think of ourselves? Maybe we've finally come to believe that we are Southerners like those usually portrayed in movies and on television: inbred, uneducated, and bigoted. How could we have come to believe that horrible lie?*

Whatever the answer was, she wasn't sure she wanted to know it.

While Wildwood was wondering, Beulah was thinking fast and hard. Somehow, she had to find a way to make Sweet wait before marrying the judge.

"Sweet, we all really want to give you a nice wedding," she started out, drawing startled glances from Wildwood and Zion.

Beulah went on desperately: "You know . . . in the church, with flowers and your friends all around you. Music and magic and romance!" she added at the last, and the softness in Sweet's eyes told her that she'd made an impression.

"Well, I don't know," Sweet murmured. "I'm not sure the judge would go along with that."

"It's not just *his* wedding, Sweet," Beulah argued. "It's *yours* too, and I think he will do whatever you like."

Sweet was smiling and nodding her head. "All right, I'll ask him," Sweet said at last.

"Ask?" Zion fairly exploded. *"Ask?"* she repeated.

Sweet was as startled as Beulah and Wildwood at Zion's outburst. She stammered around and then finally said, "Well, I'll talk it over with him." She lifted her chin and cocked her head in Zion's direction, to let Zion know that she had overstepped her bounds and had better let things go, at least for now.

"Ladies! Ladies!" Memphis singsonged the words in an effort to lighten the atmosphere at what had been a delightful little wedding shower. "Let me pour you some more tea — it's blackberry and simply delicious!"

Wildwood sat back, studying the women around her and going back over the small, unpleasant incident. *What is it about us,* she wondered silently. *What is it about us . . . about Southern women . . . that we always have to doctor everything up with good manners, obsessing about not hurting anyone's feelings, with not telling the truth as we see it because that would be unmannerly! What a dangerous tradition!*

Beulah and Zion began planning a small wedding, even while they were washing and drying udders and attaching the milking nozzles.

"*You* plan it," Zion growled. "I don't want anything to do with it."

"Listen, Zion, the only reason I championed the idea of a real wedding was to make Sweet wait a little longer. If we can get them to agree to a 'real' wedding, we'll have to have a few weeks to plan it. Maybe . . . just maybe . . . Sweet can get to know him better in those few weeks."

"No, that won't happen," Zion pronounced. "Sweet is out of her mind, in love, and she won't allow herself to see anything bad about him."

"And we don't know anything really bad about him, either," Beulah protested. "But I think she ought to get to know him better before she takes her vows."

"That would be nice," Zion said dryly, as she began straining milk through the cheesecloth.

A couple of days later, Sweet called Beulah.

"It's no go, Beulah. The judge won't hear of a church wedding."

"But why?"

"He said that he doesn't like fancy-dandy things," Sweet explained. "So we're going to do this the way he wants."

At that point, Beulah knew that nothing was going to slow down Sweet's headlong plunge into matrimony. "Well, if there's anything I can do for you, let me know," Beulah offered, trying to keep the bitter disappointment out of her voice.

The only thing that Sweet would let Beulah do was to accompany her to pick out her wedding dress; she specifically didn't invite Zion because she knew that Zion was very impatient with things like shopping or getting your hair done, or "primping," as Zion called it.

"Foolishness!" Zion would have trumpeted. "Pure, feminine foolishness!"

Wildwood and Memphis both had to work, and so that left Beulah and Sweet, which was exactly the way Sweet wanted it to be. In the store, Sweet tried on several dresses, finally settling on a pale blue with a matching jacket. Beulah watched as Sweet turned this way and that in front of the mirror, her face radiant and eyes glowing. And Beulah remembered herself all those years ago, doing the same turning and with the same radiant hopefulness filling her heart as she prepared for her wedding to her sweet Paul.

So Beulah's heart was hopeful but heavy as she watched her dear friend, Sweet, who was getting ready to alter her life completely.

"Do you think the judge will like my dress?" Sweet asked, almost in a childlike way.

"I think so," Beulah assured her, though of course, Beulah had no idea of what the judge's taste was like. Still, he seemed to be agreeable and courteous, so Beulah was sure that he would compliment Sweet on her dress, whether he really liked it or not. At the same time, the deep feeling of foreboding arose in her so strongly that she couldn't stop herself from saying to Sweet: "Are you sure you wouldn't be better off to wait a little while? Get to know him better?"

"Oh no," Sweet's voice was unconcerned and even singsong.

So in only a week, the ladies of the Tea-Olive Bird Watching Society stood along the judge's driveway, holding bunches of colorful balloons and tossing handfuls of rice as the big, black car headed down the driveway toward the justice of the peace and then the three-day honeymoon at Lake Lanier.

That same afternoon, Beulah was scheduled to work with nine-year-old Tobia Johnston through the Homework Helper Program at the library, and because Beulah had arrived early, she had the chance to chat with Wildwood for a few minutes. Beulah pushed the book cart for Wildwood, who was trying to get most of the books reshelved before school let out and the children arrived in the library.

"Have you had a chance to talk with Thankful Broderick about perhaps running the Homework Helper Program for you?"

"I've got it on my list to do today," Wildwood said. Then she shelved one more book, stood up, and squared her shoulders. "Maybe I hate to make that call because it will mean the judge has made us change the way we do things here."

"Change is always hard," Beulah commented.

"Yes," Wildwood agreed. "Especially change that isn't for the better!"

At that moment, they heard a small flurry of noise at the front of the library, and a large group of children came in, carrying their backpacks and chattering together excitedly. One small boy, Tobia Johnston, spotted Beulah, and he grinned and waved at her. She waved back.

"Time for work," Beulah said.

Along with the children, three more volunteers arrived, with Miss Dabney among them. Miss Dabney had been the head librarian at a small branch for African-American children, back during the days of segregation, and she commanded great respect from everyone in the community because of the way she conducted herself and her small patrons during the era when they all had to get accustomed to integration. She was a woman of great dignity, and when her eyes met Beulah's, she nodded her head, smiled, and took her place at one of the small tables, with her Homework Helper charges on either side of her. Likewise, the other volunteers settled in, and Beulah guided Tobia to their own table. She cast a quick glance at Thankful, who was beginning to work with her own assigned student and noticed some tired-looking lines around her eyes.

For a little over an hour, Beulah sat beside Tobia, overseeing his homework, and she became almost fixated on his small hand — the way his dark fingers clutched the pencil. She also noticed the badly frayed cuffs and collar of his shirt, and when their time was up, she spoke to Tobia carefully.

"Tobia, do you think your mama would mind if I made you a present of a new shirt?"

His dark eyes widened. "Yes, ma'am," he spoke gravely. "She sure would mind! My mama says we don't take charity." He was silent for a moment, and then he added earnestly, "She's proud, my mama is! She works hard." With a faint glow of bravado, he nodded his head and smiled.

"Well, maybe we can do this another

way." Beulah was really only thinking out loud. "Let's say we have a game going on between us."

"Game?"

"Yes. And this is the game: If you bring your spelling grade up for the next marking period, I'll bring you a new shirt as a prize! Your mama doesn't mind if you win a prize, does she?"

"Oh, no, ma'am!" he brightened and momentarily placed his hand on Beulah's. "Well, I gotta go now," he said. "Gotta help my mama get the little ones fed some supper and into bed before she goes to work."

"Does a grown-up stay with you all while she's at work?" Beulah was surprised when she heard her thought spoken out loud.

"I'm the grown-up!" Tobia bragged. Beulah resisted the strong urge to pull him into her arms. Instead, she reached into her purse, took out a piece of scrap paper, wrote her phone number on it, and handed it to him.

"Well, if ever you need help with anything, day or night, you call me," she said.

"Yes'm!" And then he was gone. Beulah stayed sitting in the small chair at the table in the children's section of the library, thinking about Tobia and the other children who took part in the program. If only the judge could *see* them, get to know something about the hard lives most of them lived, then surely he would see the value of the program and not even think of trying to shut it down!

"Well," she finally said to the empty table, "if Thankful won't take over the program and run it for Wildwood, I guess I'll just have to do it myself!"

After church on Sunday, Beulah, Wildwood, and Memphis drove out to see Zion, and even though Zion didn't go to church, she still believed in keeping the Sabbath.

"As much as I can," she once explained. "Cows don't know it's Sunday, so they have milk just like any other day. I can't let them stand around heavy and uncomfortable just because it's Sunday." But in the afternoon, Zion would take an atypical rest, by sitting idly in a rocking chair on her front porch, drinking lemonade or sweet tea. When Beulah, Wildwood, and Memphis drove up, Zion got right up and went into the kitchen, so that by the time they came up the front steps and sat down themselves, she had something cold to drink waiting for them.

At first, they rocked and sipped silently, and then Beulah said to Wildwood, "Look, I've been thinking about it, and if Thankful won't take over the Homework Helper Program, I'll do it myself."

"Why, thank you, Beulah." Wildwood's voice was warm with gratitude but rough with the acknowledgment that she, herself, would no longer be running the program. "It's not terribly time-consuming," Wildwood continued. "Just keeping track of the volunteers and being there for them if they run into any problems. That and keeping the lines of communication open between the volunteers and the teachers."

"I can donate some supplies," Zion added, and the others glanced at her in a surprised way. "Well, I can!" Zion added forcefully. "I don't have much, but I can help a little bit."

"Thank you, Zion," Wildwood sputtered. "I'm sorry if I acted surprised."

"Well, *I* am certainly surprised," Beulah added.

"I know, I know," Zion muttered almost under her breath. "You all think just because I act tough as nails all the time, I don't have any heart!"

"Oh, I know you have heart," Beulah

protested. "When I see how tender you are with your cows, I know you have a big heart. I just didn't know it extended to *people*. And by the way, did you get rid of those rats out of your barn?"

"Sure did," Zion bragged. "Poisoned every last one of them!"

Her clear delight made Wildwood wonder just exactly how tender Zion really was.

"Dirty vermin!" Zion added.

"And speaking of vermin," Beulah said. *"The judge"* — she emphasized the grandeur of the title — "will be bringing Sweet back to Love-Divine's old house day after tomorrow. I sure hope they enjoyed themselves up at Lake Lanier, but I'll be so glad to see Sweet again."

"I don't know why you seem to dislike him," Memphis spoke up. "He seems to be a nice man, and I think you're probably just prejudiced because he's not a Southerner."

Before Beulah could speak, Wildwood interrupted. "Well *I* married a Southerner, and believe me, it didn't make a bit of difference when we started having trouble."

"You've never told us anything about that," Memphis complained. "We're all such good friends, I think you should be able to share it with us and let us comfort you."

"I don't need comforting," Wildwood said roughly, drawing startled glances from the others. "I'll never need comforting again in my whole life!" Her adamant tone signaled to the others that the subject was closed.

Once again, it was Beulah who tried to smooth things over.

"Maybe we ought to take a casserole over there tomorrow, so Sweet won't have to worry about fixing a meal the minute they get back."

"That's a fine idea," Wildwood said. "I can make my chicken, sausage, and mushroom casserole and take it over tomorrow afternoon."

"But how will you get in?" Beulah asked.

"I'm sure that handyman-person the judge has hired will be around to put it in the refrigerator for you all," Zion said. "We certainly wouldn't go into the house without them being home. That wouldn't be right."

"I'll make some yeast rolls," Beulah said, "and bring them over to you in the afternoon."

"And I'll contribute some fresh, good country butter," Zion added. "That will make a nice supper for Sweet and the judge."

"Well, I'm really not doing it for *him*," Beulah confessed. "But if I want to do it for Sweet, I suppose it will have to be for him as well."

"I'll donate a cake from the bakery," Memphis offered. "Chocolate?"

"Chocolate!" the others chorused in unison.

With their feelings all aired out and with the problem of the Homework Helper Program resolved, they all sat together in companionable silence, enjoying the relative peace of a Sunday afternoon.

The next morning, Beulah dialed the phone number for the judge's farm. As she had hoped, it was answered on about the seventh ring by the handyman.

"This is the judge's residence," he said, and Beulah could hear how uncomfortable the words were in his mouth. Clearly he had been instructed on how to answer the judge's phone.

"Oh . . ." Beulah hesitated. "Listen, you don't know me, but I'm a good friend of Miss Sweet. I know that she and *the judge* . . . will be coming home tomorrow, and we wanted to bring by a casserole for their supper. And please, what is your name?"

"Jim," he answered.

"Well . . . Jim," Beulah continued, "if it's convenient, we'll come by around four thirty today and give you the casserole."

"Yes, ma'am," Jim answered. "I'll be glad to put it in the judge's refrigerator for you. And I'm sure they will appreciate your trouble."

When Beulah hung up the phone, she tried to picture in her mind exactly what Jim looked like. Probably just a good, country man who needs that job and who has to swallow plenty of crow to keep it. She couldn't stop herself from shaking her head.

At exactly four thirty, Beulah pulled up into the old, familiar driveway of what had been Love-Divine's house and took the casserole, the yeast rolls, Zion's good country butter, and Memphis's chocolate cake out of the car. A lean, tall man approached her, pushing his cowboy-style hat onto the back of his head.

"Jim?"

"Yes, ma'am," he answered, reaching up and removing the hat completely.

Beulah laughed softly. "I'm sorry I can't shake hands," she explained, balancing the

145

casserole in one hand and the tray holding the rolls, butter, and cake in the other. He smiled and reached out for the casserole. "I'm Beulah," she said, and he nodded his head and smiled. Why, he had beautiful, laughing blue eyes and straight teeth. Perhaps not at all the kind of man she pictured as hired help on a farm. For a brief moment, she thought about her own internal tirade about stereotyped Southerners. Could she be guilty of the same thing? Why had she assumed that a farmhand would be dirty and unmannerly? Then she noticed his ramrod posture. Perhaps he was a military veteran who was down on his luck.

"I'll put these into the judge's refrigerator right away," he promised. "And thank you for going to this trouble." But Beulah hardly heard him because her eyes had wandered over to the equipment shed, where Sweet's familiar car was parked. And what concerned Beulah was that the right rear tire was flat.

"Why, what happened to Sweet's car?" Beulah asked.

"Don't know," Jim answered. "Just that when I came out this morning, it was flat."

"Well, I hope you will please have it fixed before they get back."

"Can't do that, ma'am," he answered uneasily.

"But why?" Once again, Beulah could hear reluctance in his voice.

"Judge called me this morning, to check on things, and I told him about that flat tire and how I would get it fixed right away." He paused and seemed to squirm in discomfort.

"And?"

"Ma'am, he told me to leave it alone."

"He told you *not* to fix it? Why?"

"I don't know, ma'am. It's just what he said."

Gazing at Sweet's disabled car, Beulah once again felt that same strong foreboding. Why on earth would the judge not have his handyman fix the tire? Beulah knew how important Sweet's car was to her. For Sweet, that car of hers was a symbol of her independence, her ability to take care of herself.

"Well, thank you, Jim," Beulah said warmly, but as she went back to get into her own car, she glanced at Sweet's car yet again.

"I wonder what that's all about?" she whispered to herself. "Could it be that the judge wants to take care of her car himself?"

And the answer to that question bruised her heart.

"No."

CHAPTER
— THIRTEEN —

The next morning, while Zion and Beulah were taking care of the morning milking, Zion noticed Beulah's unusually quiet mood.

"You got something on your mind?" Zion asked, in her usual gruff way.

"I don't know." Beulah was clearly distracted.

Once they got all of the milking machines attached to the bulging udders, and the parlor was throbbing with the sounds of the machines and the sweet aroma of warm milk, Zion wiped her hands on her apron and stuck her face right into Beulah's.

"Might as well spit it out," Zion growled. "You know you can't keep things to yourself."

"Sweet's car . . ." Beulah started.

"What about it?"

"It's got a flat tire."

"And?"

"That handyman, Jim, said the judge told him not to fix it."

"Well, maybe he wants to do it himself," Zion surmised. "Him being so newly married and all."

"I don't think so," Beulah said. "There's just something about it that bothers me."

"There's lots about the judge that bothers lots of people, I think. Even though everybody keeps talking about how nice he is," Zion added.

"They'll be back today. I hate for her to see that flat tire."

"What's made you so protective of Sweet all of a sudden?" Zion was always one to get to the bottom of things.

"It's not all of a sudden," Beulah protested. Then she added, "It's just since the judge came."

Zion snorted. "Everything got all heaved up every which way once he got here," Zion agreed.

"There's something wrong," Beulah murmured. "There's something wrong, and I don't know what it is."

"We'll have to wait and see," Zion pronounced. "But I know you aren't very good at waiting."

Beulah wanted nothing more than to call

Sweet on the phone, but she thought that would be rude. Even if they had already gotten back, folks always gave newlyweds a little privacy, and this should be no different. But she kept staring at the phone and resisting the urge to reach out for it. Finally, she did reach for the phone, but it was the number of the Tea-Olive Library that she started to dial before she remembered that Wildwood was at a regional meeting and wouldn't be back until later in the week.

Finally, Beulah couldn't stand it any longer, so she took her binoculars and headed for the bird sanctuary.

With resolution, Beulah walked through the woods until she came to the edge that overlooked Sweet's new home. Staying in a slightly hidden location, she sat down on the ground and trained her binoculars on the house. Sweet's car still sat under the shed, and the tire was still flat. That made Beulah's heart lurch. She had half a mind to go down there and change the tire herself! Because maybe the judge told Jim not to change it, but he certainly didn't tell her. But there was a problem with that plan: she simply didn't know how to change a tire. That's something Zion would have known how to do. She should have thought of that during the morning.

As Beulah watched through the binoculars, Jim came out of the barn and started across the yard to his own little caretaker's cottage. His walk was easy and unconcerned, so perhaps he was pretending the farm was his place, and not just somebody else's property. He certainly looked the part. She watched him until he went into the cottage.

How easy it was for her to envision herself and Love-Divine sitting on that porch together, with Beulah a young bride and Love-Divine as a minister's wife who had taken the young Beulah under her wing. Love-Divine had taught her about cooking for a husband and running a household and provided a motherly companionship that Beulah had treasured forever.

"It goes by too fast!" Beulah said aloud. "Everything changes and it's all gone." That thought depressed her beyond measure, so she got up, brushed off her slacks, and went back to her car.

But the next day, she was back at the sanctuary, and this time, the judge's black car was in the driveway. She ducked around until she could see Sweet's car, and yes, the tire was still flat. So much for thinking that he wanted to change her tire himself! And then some sort of a strange sound caught her attention. A bird? But not a bird she'd ever heard before. She trekked along in the woods, following the sound, and then she realized that it was coming from the house itself. She hoisted her binoculars and trained them onto the back porch. And what she saw almost made her gasp. On the back porch was a birdcage, and that's where the sound was coming from. A canary, perhaps? But the kind of bird didn't really matter. What mattered was that Sweet would never — ever! — want to see a bird living in a cage.

That was completely unlike Sweet!

The bitter feeling that crept into Beulah's chest was almost unbearable. How did Sweet come by that bird? It had to have been a gift from the judge, and if that were the case, he understood far less about Sweet than she had previously thought. And if he tried to give her such a gift, why didn't Sweet tell him straight out that birds kept in cages saddened her? Perhaps she didn't want to hurt his feelings? Well, Sweet had better steel herself to be more direct with him; he didn't seem to be someone who would take a polite hint at all.

Beulah's head was reeling. She wanted to march right down there and talk to Sweet, but she knew that would be too terrible a breach of good manners. So she simply satisfied herself that Sweet was back and that after a reasonable length of time, she could find out from Sweet herself exactly why there was a caged bird on her back porch.

Beulah told Zion about the caged bird, but Zion didn't seem to think there was much to make of it.

"Lots of folks like to keep canaries," she reasoned.

"But not Sweet!" Beulah protested. But Zion merely shrugged her shoulders.

Toward the end of the week, Beulah finally got in touch with Wildwood.

"I'll meet you at Memphis's tearoom after you get off from work," Beulah suggested. "I've got some things to tell you about."

"And I've got some things of my own to tell you," Wildwood answered. "See you there around five thirty?"

"That sounds fine."

Beulah felt vastly relieved that Wildwood was back from her regional meeting. Unlike Zion, who was so stoic about almost everything, Wildwood empathized with anything that bothered a soul. And Beulah's soul was certainly bothered.

"Just some iced tea this time, Memphis," Beulah ordered. "Make that two iced teas, please. Wildwood will be here in a few minutes."

"You talk to Sweet since the honeymoon?" Memphis asked.

"Oh no," Beulah shook her head. "It's too soon."

"I guess so," Memphis agreed, "but that honeymoon stuff is usually for young folks, isn't it?"

"I think that good manners apply to any age." Beulah smiled.

When Wildwood arrived at the tearoom, she looked tired, and she had something behind her eyes that caused Beulah some concern.

"Wildwood, honey! You look tired to death!"

"It was a long drive," she said. "And long, long meetings and not very good news, I'm afraid." She sipped her iced tea gratefully.

"Well, we've already figured out how to manage the Homework Helper Program without it costing the library any money or staff time," Beulah reasoned. "Whatever comes along next, we can manage that as well."

"I'm not so sure," Wildwood said, heaving a sigh.

"Tell me," Beulah directed.

"It's budget cuts again." Wildwood stopped trying to keep the misery out of her voice.

"We'll figure something out," Beulah crooned. "We've got a good Friends of the Library group. We'll all pitch in to help."

"It's more than that," Wildwood whispered. "Beulah, they're talking about shutting down some branches."

"What?" Beulah was incredulous. "Not Tea-Olive, surely!"

"Surely," Wildwood said. "Their reasoning is that the Woodall branch can serve our patrons just as well, and it's only sixteen miles away."

Beulah sat in stunned silence. It was true that the more affluent families in town could easily take their children to the Woodall branch, but what about the children who did not come from affluent families, especially the ones in the Homework Helper Program? Suddenly, Tobia's earnest face appeared in her mind. *Tobia!*

"Some . . . children . . . wouldn't have a

way to go that far," Beulah said simply. "They're the ones who will lose out if we lose our branch!"

"I know," Wildwood replied patiently, willing to wait while Beulah digested the terrible possibility of those children, once again, being left behind.

"But what about the funds Love-Divine left to the library?" Beulah asked.

"Yes, we could use that money," Wildwood said. "But that would hold us only a year or so, and then that money would be gone and we'd be right back where we are now. We need to put those funds into an endowment and raise more funds to join it, then eventually, the income from that invested money could sustain the library for years."

"Well, that sounds encouraging," Beulah admitted.

"But it isn't going to help us right now," Wildwood explained.

"Then we'll find another way!" Beulah fumed. "We won't give up! That's all there is to it!"

"I don't know how we can stop what's happening," Wildwood confessed. "If the town council agrees that the library should close, we won't be able to stop it."

"Yes we can!" Beulah fairly shouted.

"We'll get the Friends of the Library . . . no, we'll get every living soul in town to rise up in protest!"

Wildwood waited for a few moments, and then she breathed, "Even the judge?"

"Well, yes — even the judge!" Beulah's mind was racing.

"Do you understand, Beulah, that he has the power and . . . the charisma . . . to stop such a movement among the people? And that he is on the town council himself as well?"

"I do," Beulah announced in a solemn voice. "This will take some thinking."

Memphis came to refill their glasses, and she could tell that they were discussing something important and private, so she brought new ice cubes, filled their glasses quickly, and then discreetly disappeared back into the kitchen.

"How did the judge get into the middle of things he doesn't know anything about?" Wildwood wondered aloud.

But at that question, a proverbial lightbulb clicked on right over Beulah's head. "Love-Divine's will!" Beulah almost shouted. Then she lowered her voice, squinted her eyes, and leaned toward the center of the table, whispering, "Listen, put it all together, Wildwood. He's bought

157

into a construction company in Athens, he's gotten himself on the town council, and . . ." Here, Beulah hesitated and closed her eyes. "And if the library closes, Love-Divine's money reverts to the city."

Wildwood studied Beulah's anguished face while all of those facts settled themselves into her mind. "You mean that he would use the money to build . . . something? And have his own company do the building?"

Beulah nodded slowly. "Yes, that's precisely what I think. But again, we have to be careful."

Wildwood heaved a deep sigh and drew a hand across her forehead. "Oh, let's not think about it right now," Wildwood pleaded. "Now, what was it you wanted to tell me about?" Wildwood asked.

"It can wait," Beulah said. "It will have to wait!"

CHAPTER
— FOURTEEN —

Beulah's mind was a tangle of thoughts when she left the tea shop. She had a big campaign to develop and run, and the first step would be to ask Wildwood to call an emergency meeting of the Friends of the Library. Wildwood herself would know who were the important people to name for a town-wide letter-writing campaign to the town council. But then, they still had to deal with the judge, and there was only one way to do that — through Sweet.

The least Beulah could do was wait one more day before calling Sweet, and even then, it would certainly be a breach of good manners to bother someone so newly married. But this was too important to put off. She would get Sweet to plead their case to the judge. Surely a newlywed husband just returning from his honeymoon would listen to his new bride and do everything he could to make her happy. Sweet would matter more to him than any amount of money he may be able to wrest away from the town and pay to his own company! Sweet was the ace in Beulah's hand!

The next afternoon, Beulah dialed the number for Love-Divine's old house and held her breath while it rang. After it rang about seven or eight times, she was ready to hang up when Jim answered: "This is the judge's residence."

"Jim?"

"Yes, ma'am," he answered.

"This is Beulah. Miss Sweet's friend? We met when I brought a casserole out there the other day."

"Yes, ma'am. I remember."

"May I please speak to Miss Sweet?"

"Uh. Ma'am, the judge and the missus left this morning for New York to visit some of his family."

"They did?" Beulah's hopes faded. "Do you know when they're coming back?"

"No, ma'am, I sure don't. But if you will give me your phone number, I'll let you know as soon as the judge calls and tells me they're coming back."

Beulah gave him her phone number and hung up. It was hard for her to believe that Sweet was going all the way to New York State, and Beulah didn't know a thing about the trip.

"I guess I'll have to get used to that," Beulah told herself. "Now that she's married, there will probably be plenty of things going on in her life that I don't know about." Once that sad thought had passed through her mind, Beulah realized that they had gained a brief reprieve from worrying about the judge. With him gone, they could move ahead with their call-in, write-in, petition-signing campaign: Save Our Library! She would call Wildwood right away with that news. And as soon as Sweet and the judge returned from New York, Beulah would ask her to convince the judge for them.

By late afternoon, Beulah had already designed the petition forms, called all of the volunteers of the Homework Helper Program with the news, and rough-drawn a poster for the cause. Wildwood had called an emergency meeting of the Friends of the Library and, taking advantage of the judge's absence, had also requested an emergency meeting of the library board of trustees. With Beulah and Wildwood fanning the flames of passion, Beulah was reasonably sure of a community outcry that would reach the hearts of the town councilmen, whose hands held the fate of their little branch.

But after all of that activity, Beulah was left strangely electrified, and she was unwilling or unable to content herself at home. It was unusual, but not unheard of, for Beulah to show up at Zion's creamery for the late afternoon milking, so she went to Zion's, followed around behind her friend, rinsing and drying udders. Zion, of course, noticed the worry lines in Beulah's forehead, but as was her custom, she patiently waited, knowing that Beulah could never carry anything alone for very long. But this time, Beulah was strangely silent and for such a long time that Zion finally asked, "What you got on your plate, Beulah-Land?"

That reference to her hymnal name drew a smile from Beulah and unleashed a torrent of words — about her worry for Sweet, the threat to the library, and Sweet's unannounced trip with the judge to New York.

"Bring me around one of those petition sheets," Zion said. "And I'll get all my girls here to sign it." She swept her arm across the milking parlor and the sweet-faced Jersey cows.

"The cows?" Beulah was confused.

"Yep. They all have people-names anyway.

Nobody would ever know the difference."

"Well, *I* would," Beulah confessed, blushing a little.

"I know they'd sign it," Zion went on. "Cause they always agree with me!" With those words, she stuck the milking machine nozzle onto a tender teat a little harder than usual, making the cow twitch.

"Zion! You're just terrible!" Beulah laughed. Zion smiled up at her with only a slightly malevolent look on her face. "Whatever we have to do, we'll do it," Zion pronounced.

CHAPTER
— FIFTEEN —

Three long days passed, during which time the library board of trustees, minus the judge, met and agreed to support the drive to Save Our Library and the Friends of the Library unanimously voted to launch a campaign that would require taking the petition sheets by hand up and down every street in town. They also decided to put petition sheets in the teachers' lounges in the schools, and one zealous Friend even offered to take petitions into the county hospital so that sick folks could also sign it. The letter-writing campaign was to be set up by Hope Zeiner, who was a retired schoolteacher herself and could help people word the letters so that no two were exactly alike. The volunteers from the Homework Helper Program also said that they would assist their students in writing letters as well, telling the "powers that be" about what the branch library meant to them. Beulah and Wildwood were much pleased that such a sense of optimism and enthusiasm existed. But they both knew they had to work as fast as possible, get the fires going good and hot before the judge returned. After that, it would be up to Sweet to persuade him to vote against closing the library.

On the morning of the fifth day, Beulah's phone rang.

"Miss Beulah?" It was Jim. "I had a phone call from the judge just a few minutes ago, and he and Miss Sweet will be back this coming Monday."

"Oh, thanks so much for letting me know," Beulah said. "I really appreciate it."

As soon as she hung up, she dialed Wildwood at the library. "They're coming back on Monday," Beulah reported. "Now, I think you ought to take down that Save Our Library banner over the front door, just for Monday. I'd hate for the judge to see that before I've had a chance to talk to Sweet. I really think she's our only hope for winning him over."

And on the much-anticipated Monday morning, Beulah finished helping Zion with the morning milking, and then the two of them headed straight for the sanctuary with binoculars in hand. No matter what time they got home, Beulah had to see Sweet right away.

"What I can't figure out is why anybody would ask him to join the library board without really getting to know him first," Zion snorted. "That was just purely stupid! That, and putting him on the town council. And everybody who helped put him there deserves to be kicked by a mule!"

At a little past three o'clock, the black car came up the driveway to Love-Divine's old house. Jim ambled across the yard and took luggage out of the trunk while the judge got out and went straight into the house, walking rapidly.

Beulah adjusted her binoculars. She could see Sweet still sitting in the passenger seat. Jim finally noticed that she wasn't getting out of the car, and he put down the suitcases in the driveway and opened the passenger's door. When Beulah saw Sweet, she could hardly believe her eyes! Even from that distance, a large, angry bruise spread itself right across Sweet's left eye!

"What on earth!" Beulah breathed, causing Zion to use her own binoculars to see what Beulah was muttering about.

"Good Lord!" Zion spat. "What happened to her?"

"I don't know, but I'm going to find out."
As Beulah stepped out of the sanctuary, she
saw Jim take Sweet's arm and guide her toward the steps.

"Sweet!" Beulah yelled as she ran across
the yard. "Sweet! Wait a minute!"

Sweet's hand automatically came up to
try to cover the bruise. Jim stepped back,
staring at his shoes.

"Honey! What happened?" Beulah
begged. "How on earth did you get that
awful bruise?"

"I . . ." Sweet was almost too embarrassed
to even speak. "I had a fall."

Beulah narrowed her eyes at Sweet. "You
had a fall? A fall is what did that to your
face?"

"A fall," Sweet repeated. Jim discreetly
retrieved the suitcases and carried them up
onto the porch, giving Sweet and Beulah
some privacy. Zion came walking across
the yard at a more leisurely pace, following
Beulah's wild dash. Beulah looked at Zion
and shook her head the least little bit,
trying to indicate that Zion not question
Sweet about the bruise, but Zion was Zion
and not prone to taking discreet little hints
about anything.

"Did somebody belt you one?" Zion
asked in a loud voice. "Looks like you've

been in a prizefight!"

"I fell." Sweet again tried to cover the bruise.

"You sure that stinking man you married didn't do that to you?"

"Oh yes," Sweet whispered. "I'm sure."

At that very moment, the judge came out onto the front porch. The minute Beulah saw Sweet glance at him, she was positive that Zion had hit the nail right on the head. Yes, that stinking man had done this to Sweet!

"Come into the house, Sweet," he commanded, ignoring both Beulah and Zion.

"I'm coming," was all Sweet said, leaving Beulah and Zion standing speechless in the yard.

When they walked back across the yard and went into the sanctuary, they said not a single word, both of them too shocked to speak. By the time they reached their cars where they were parked on the side of the highway, Zion had developed two brilliant red splotches on her cheeks, whereas Beulah had gone quite pale.

"What do we do?" Beulah whispered, feeling too fragile to even hear her own question.

"I know what *I'd* do." Zion's chin was shaking with anger. "I'd make sure he never

did anything like that again to *anybody!*"
Then she spat onto the ground, something
Beulah had never seen any lady do before
in her life.

"Vermin!"

CHAPTER
— SIXTEEN —

Beulah was so shaken by what she had seen and heard that she didn't even show up to help Zion with the milking the next morning. Wildwood tried to phone her to find out if she'd had a chance to speak to Sweet, but Beulah didn't even answer the phone. She just stayed in bed until almost noon, with the blanket pulled up over her head and tears silently leaking out of her closed eyes. But even though her body was inert, her mind was racing: *What a joke! What a terrible, terrible joke! We thought poor Sweet would be able to talk the judge into helping save the library. Why, she can't even save herself. But what to do? He's got too much power. I'll bet even the police wouldn't arrest a retired judge, for Heaven's sake! Dear Lord, please help me to find a way to help Sweet. Poor, dear Sweet.*

At that very instant, Beulah's mind stopped racing, and she knew exactly who to talk to about this heartbreaking mess!

She got out of bed, washed her face, drank a cup of coffee, and called Zion.

"I'm going to go see Reverend McKenzie," Beulah announced. "I've got to talk to somebody about this. It's just killing me! We have to do something. We just have to!"

"Yes," Zion agreed. "We have to do something! Stinking man!"

"I'm going right now, Zion. I'll talk to you later and tell you what he had to say."

Beulah dialed Reverend McKenzie's number at the church, and he answered the phone himself.

"Well, how are you, Beulah?"

"Not so good, I'm afraid," Beulah answered. "I need to talk with you, if you have time this afternoon."

"Of course! Say, I heard that Memphis has added a line of fine specialty sandwiches at the tearoom. Would you like to join me for lunch?"

"I don't think so," Beulah said. "I really need to speak with you privately."

"Certainly." Beulah could hear him rustling some papers. "How about two thirty, here at the church?"

"That will be fine. And thank you."

"We'll see you then."

★ ★ ★

After Beulah hung up the phone, she sat quietly thinking about how to give utterance to her suspicions about Sweet's predicament. And what on earth did she think a minister would be able to do about it? Perhaps go out and talk with the judge — let him know that Sweet's friends were concerned about her? And would that be enough to stop the judge? Would it? And what if she were wrong? What if Sweet really had fallen?

The Reverend McKenzie's office was decorated much in the way of a comfortable living room, thanks to Vicky's good taste. Beulah sank into a comfortable chair, and the reverend seated himself across from her, leaning forward and with his elbows resting on his knees.

"Now what can I do to help you?" he asked solicitously.

"It's about Sweet," Beulah began cautiously. "You know about the marriage, of course."

"Oh, yes — certainly do wish they had let me do the honors . . . in *church*." His tone was a little petulant.

"I'm not all that sure it would have been an honor," Beulah whispered.

"Why do you say that?"

Beulah took a deep breath. "Because I think he's already hit her." How strange those brutal words sounded in such a beautiful office and with such a good, kind man sitting across from her!

"*Hit* her? Are you sure?"

"Well, something sure happened to put such an awful bruise on her face," Beulah said.

"Did you ask her about it?"

"I did, and so did Zion, and she said she had a fall."

"Could that be possible?"

"I suppose so, but the way the judge got out of the car and went inside, leaving Sweet just sitting there? Jim had to help her out of the car."

"Jim?"

"He's the man the judge hired to help out at the farm."

"And what did Sweet say, other than that she'd had a fall?" he gently inquired.

"It wasn't so much what she said as the way she was acting."

"She was embarrassed?"

"Mortified," Beulah said, and felt peppery tears coming up behind her eyes. "And when the judge came back out onto the porch — while Zion and I were standing

173

with Sweet — he ordered her into the house, just like she was a dog or something!"

"That doesn't sound good," the reverend agreed. He got up, fetched a box of tissues that he held out to Beulah, and then poured a glass of water for her from a carafe on his desk. She took the tissues and the water gratefully, and he sat down again, studying her carefully.

"What can I do?" he asked sincerely.

"I'm not sure," Beulah answered. "I thought that maybe if you made a call on them, the judge would understand that Sweet has folks who are looking out for her. And maybe he wouldn't treat her that way again, if indeed, he did in the first place."

"Yes, she certainly has folks looking out for her — like you and Zion and Memphis and Wildwood — and she has her church family as well."

"I'd be willing to bet you anything that you won't see her at church again."

"Why do you say that?"

"She's too ashamed." Beulah realized that she had spoken the absolute truth. Sweet would die of embarrassment if her Bible class folks saw her in such a condition. Or if everybody in town found out about what the judge was doing and made it the subject of gossip. "I hope you will please be very discreet about this," Beulah added. "It could be embarrassing for Sweet. It could also be a very dangerous situation."

The reverend leaned back, with his hands tented under his chin, as if he were praying. But his steady gaze never left Beulah's face.

"Do you know if the judge has any history of this sort of thing?"

"No. I don't know. Just the way nobody here really knows much of anything about him — except that he can sure turn on the charm. When he wants to," Beulah added.

"Too fast," the reverend said.

"I beg your pardon?"

"Too fast," he repeated. "Folks around here just sized him up too fast."

"I think you're right about that. So what do we do?"

"How about this? I'll make a call on them and say that I heard about her fall and came by to see if there is anything we at the church can do to help while Sweet recovers. That way, the judge will know that folks are concerned about her, if he's guilty of hurting her."

"Yes, that's a good idea. I am just so worried about her!"

"Why don't you give her a call this afternoon, but don't say anything about my coming out to see them tomorrow or the next day," he cautioned. "And for the time being, let's just go along with the story about the fall. Until we know something different, at least."

As soon as Beulah got home, she called Zion and told her about the plan.

"I don't know why you have to pussyfoot around like this," Zion said. "Why don't we just go over there and confront him?"

"Because of Sweet," Beulah explained. "We've got to do this carefully and discreetly because of Sweet."

"He can hurt a lot more than just her feelings," Zion pronounced. "You know that, don't you?"

"I know it," Beulah said. "But I wish I didn't!"

"You hear anything more from Wildwood about the Save Our Library project?"

"No," Beulah confessed. "This new problem just seemed to eclipse everything else. We've got a lot more to worry about than whether the judge can throw a bucket of cold water into the works."

"You sure got that right," Zion agreed.

★ ★ ★

After Beulah made herself a glass of iced tea, she turned around and dialed Sweet's number. To her relief, Sweet herself answered.

"Hi, Sweet." Beulah tried to make her voice light and unconcerned.

"Oh, Beulah!" Sweet exclaimed. "I'm so sorry you and Zion had to see me looking so bad yesterday!"

"That's why I called," Beulah said, and when she heard Sweet's intake of breath, she quickly added, "to see how you're doing after taking such a hard fall."

"Oh, I'm better," Sweet answered. "I've had an ice pack on my face almost all day, and the swelling is going down."

"And Jim told me you and the judge had a nice, long trip to New York."

"Yes, it was a nice trip." Sweet's disinclination to add any details confirmed Beulah's expectations.

"Well, I won't keep you," Beulah said. "I just wanted to check on you and see that you were okay. Maybe we can go to lunch at the tearoom one day. I've heard that Memphis has added a specialty sandwich menu."

"I don't know," Sweet murmured. "There's a lot of work to be done around here."

"I know," Beulah said. "You just stay in touch."

"I will," Sweet answered. "Oh, and Beulah? Thanks for calling."

Beulah hung up the phone feeling positively deceitful. How could she pretend to go along with Sweet's story? And all in the name of not embarrassing or upsetting Sweet? *Always be mannerly, even if some total jerk is using your good friend's face for a punching bag!*

When Beulah arrived at the library for Homework Helper time with Tobia, she noticed that the Save Our Library banner had been put back up over the front door. Inside, a large conference table held stacks of petition forms and suggested support letters. Another pile explained the phone-in procedure, and a box held hundreds of SAVE OUR LIBRARY lapel buttons.

"So how is it going?" Beulah tried to sound light and confident when she spoke with Wildwood.

"So far, so good," Wildwood answered. "I tried to call you yesterday, but I guess you weren't home. Have you gotten to talk with Sweet about the judge?"

"No, I haven't. Something else came

up," Beulah said. "Listen, I need you to help me with a reference question, Wildwood."

"Sure." Wildwood had that same rapt expression she always wore whenever someone needed information. "What is it?"

"I need for you to be discreet here," Beulah warned.

"Beulah, you know that everything anyone tells me here in this library is absolutely confidential!"

"I know that," Beulah said. Then she glanced around, lowered her voice, and whispered into Wildwood's ear: "I need to learn more about the judge."

"Sure," Wildwood whispered back, and Beulah noticed that Wildwood didn't seem to be surprised at the request. Just then, as always on Homework Helper days, the front doors burst open and the children in the program streamed into the building. Tobia threw up his hand in greeting to Beulah, and the minute she saw his hopeful face, all of her cares and worries seemed to roll away.

CHAPTER
— SEVENTEEN —

"You'd better come to my office for this," Wildwood said over the phone the next morning.

"I'll be right over," Beulah answered. But before she left her house, she dialed Sweet's number. This time, the judge answered, and Beulah's heart went right into her throat. How could she possibly be polite to this possible monster?

"May I speak with Sweet, please," she said carefully.

"Uh, she can't come to the phone right now," the judge said, and immediately Beulah envisioned Sweet's bruised face. Had he hit her again? And perhaps again?

"I really need to talk with her," Beulah persisted.

"Well, I don't know what to tell you." The judge's voice took on an edge. "She simply can't come to the phone right now."

"Is she OK?" The question escaped from

Beulah before she could realize the words themselves.

"Of course, she's OK," the judge growled.

"She hasn't fallen down again, has she?"

The sharp click and the dead line told Beulah that she had carried things a little too far with the judge. Well, she *would* speak with Sweet that very same day, one way or another. But first, she needed to go see Wildwood and find out more about the judge.

When they were privately settled in the office, Wildwood took a folder out of her drawer and opened it.

"Well, he is definitely a retired judge," Wildwood confirmed. "And in his career, he made some pretty unpopular judgments."

"Then I guess there are a lot of people who would like to pay him back about that," Beulah mused.

"But there's more here," Wildwood said. "About his late wives."

"Wives? Late wives? He was married before? More than once?"

"Twice. And twice he's been left a widower." Wildwood hesitated. "Both were 'accidental deaths.' "

Beulah felt her heart thud against her

ribs. "Accidental deaths?"

"One was an automobile accident," Wildwood continued.

"And the other?"

"A home accident. The second wife fell in the bathroom and hit her head on the edge of the tub."

Beulah and Wildwood stared at each other for long moments before Beulah asked, "Were there investigations into these . . . accidents?"

"Yes, and both were ruled completely accidental."

Wildwood closed the folder. "Now I need for you to answer a question for me: Are you worried about Sweet?"

"Yes," Beulah breathed, and then like a pressurized hose, all of the words came pouring out of her. She told Wildwood everything, including the judge's refusal to let her speak to Sweet that very morning. Wildwood listened intently, showing emotion only when Beulah described the terrible bruise on Sweet's face.

When Beulah stopped talking, the two women sat in silence for long moments.

"What can we do?" Wildwood finally asked. "We don't have any proof that the judge is being rough with Sweet."

"I know we don't, but we have to do

something!" Beulah cried. "I'm going to talk with her or see her *this very day!*"

That afternoon, Beulah parked along the highway, walked resolutely through the sanctuary, went up to the front door of Love-Divine's old house, and knocked sharply on it. The harsh sound of her own angry knuckles startled her, so that when the door opened and she was face-to-face with the judge, she stumbled with her first few words to him.

"I need to talk with Sweet," she managed to mumble. "It's quite important." The judge looked down at her with a bemused expression on his face.

"She can't have any company right now," he said, and he started to close the door. But Beulah pushed back against him.

"I said that I need to talk with Sweet. If she doesn't want any company, let her come to the door and say that for herself."

The bemused expression faded, and in its place came a mask with glowering eyes and down-turned mouth.

"Good Lord, woman!" he exclaimed. "Is there no end to your meddling?"

And with that, he pushed the door shut, and she didn't have the strength to keep it open. The lock clicked into place, leaving

Beulah standing on the porch, trembling with anger. She went back across the yard toward the sanctuary, feeling that his eyes were boring into her back with every step.

Once she regained the anonymity of the woods, she sat down on the ground behind some heavy bushes and waited, watching the house through her binoculars. She watched as Jim headed to the barn, and then he came back across the yard and knocked on the back door. Beulah couldn't see who opened the door, but a short while later the judge came out of the front door, and he and Jim walked away toward the barn. That was exactly what Beulah was waiting for.

She ran, halfway ducked down, across the short distance between the sanctuary and the back door of the house. She didn't bother to knock, but simply let herself in, and she didn't call Sweet's name or anything else that would attract attention. On tiptoe, she went down the long central hallway and into the living room. Sweet was sitting in a chair, with her Bible open across her knees. When she saw Beulah, she took a quick breath and then reached up to cover the lingering bruise on her cheek.

"Beulah!" Sweet said. "What are you doing here?"

"I tried to speak with you by phone this morning, and the judge said you couldn't come to the phone. So I stopped by about thirty minutes ago, and he said that you couldn't have any company."

"I didn't know you called," Sweet confessed simply. "And I didn't know you came to the door."

"What's going on?" Beulah asked, casting an eye through the living room window and toward the barn. When Sweet didn't answer, Beulah looked back at her and saw that her face had collapsed into a pained expression that Beulah had never seen before.

"Something's wrong," Sweet managed to whisper. "I *didn't* have a fall."

"I thought as much! Go get some clothes together," Beulah ordered. "You're leaving here with me right now."

"No!" Sweet was adamant. "It was the trip to New York that got him all upset. He'll be OK, now that we're home."

"What happened in New York?"

"Well, his family is just real cold toward him, and I really don't know what he was expecting, but they acted like our coming to visit was just a big bother. Such cold people! It was really quite uncomfortable. I've never been an unwanted guest before."

"Did any of his people say why they were acting that way?" Beulah pressed.

Sweet hesitated, took a deep breath, and slowly let it out, studying her hands the whole time. "Well, there's an old aunt — formidable-looking woman — and she got me aside and said for me to be careful. I didn't know what she meant, and when I asked her, she said, 'We don't know for sure, but we suspect he's done some dirty deals before, and anyone who's his wife should be extra careful.' Well, I still didn't know what she meant, but she just shook her head and glared at me and said something about having to protect the family name."

"And you think it's the way the family acted that got him all upset?" Beulah asked.

"I don't know. When we started driving home, he was quiet, so I didn't press him for conversation. But when we stopped for the night, I asked him about it, and . . ." Sweet stopped talking and put her hand to the bruise on her face.

Beulah said not a word, but her mouth dropped open.

Sweet continued, "Then, the next day, while we were driving, he started talking about his stepgrandfather and how his only happy times in his childhood were at his farm in Georgia. So I figured that once we got home, he would be fine. Then he found out about that Save Our Library drive, and he was just furious. Said the library board waited until he was out of town, on purpose, and voted to support it."

"But what does that have to do with *you?*"

"Nothing, really. Just that when he gets mad or upset about one thing, he gets mad and upset about everything!"

For long moments, Beulah sat in silence, desperately wondering if she should tell Sweet about the judge's two wives — *deceased* wives. But as she studied Sweet's face, she decided against telling her. It would be too much and too soon.

"I'm going to have a talk with him," Beulah declared. "I won't stand by and know that he may hit you again!"

"No, Beulah! Please just leave things alone. He will get better, I'm sure."

"But he won't even let any of your friends talk to you or come to see you!" Beulah cried.

"That will get better, too," Sweet assured her. "Just let us get settled in, and I'm sure things will return to normal."

Beulah could tell that it was hopeless to try to persuade Sweet. Whatever hold the judge could get over people so fast had obviously taken in Sweet as well.

"I'll be back!" Beulah promised.

"No!" Sweet begged. "Just let me work this out myself. But be sure to warn Wildwood about the judge being so mad. He said it's downright dumb to have that library in Tea-Olive! Says it costs too much money to have it."

Beulah's heart screamed at her to tell Sweet what she thought was the real impetus behind the judge wanting the library to close. She heard the words in her own mind, though she did not speak them to Sweet: *Remember Love-Divine's will! If the library closes, the judge can get his hands on her money through the town council!* But Beulah's lips remained closed. Sweet had more on her plate now than she could say a blessing over!

"I'll tell Wildwood," Beulah promised. "And I *will* be back: We'll figure out something! We'll figure it out!" With that, Beulah hastened back down the hall, dashed across the backyard, and regained the safety of the sanctuary.

Once she reached her car, Beulah knew exactly where she was going. By the time Beulah arrived at Zion's barn, she was seething with a rage she had never known before. A rage that actually tasted bitter in her mouth, so that she dared not even open her mouth for the terrible words that may fall right out of it.

"I wish you could see your face," Zion laughed, trying to tease Beulah.

But then, Zion stopped laughing and looked at Beulah with a questioning expression. "Are you OK?" she asked.

"No, I . . ." Beulah began. But then she stopped. Beulah and Zion stood in silence for long minutes, staring into each other's eyes as if they had never met before. "I mean . . . I'm not sure," Beulah amended. Then she added in a whisper, "Sweet confessed to me that the judge did . . . hit her."

Zion drew in her breath sharply and then her eyebrows came together in concentration. "We have to be careful here," Zion warned. "If we do anything to make his temper blow up, we have to make sure that Sweet is out of harm's way when that happens."

"Yes," Beulah agreed. "I need to find out what the Reverend McKenzie thinks about the situation. He should have gone out there by now."

Beulah considered stopping by the church in person on her way home, but then she opted to call the good reverend on the phone because he might be able to see in her eyes the pain and rage she was trying so hard to control. Because Zion had been right: they had to be careful.

The reverend answered on the second ring.

"Yes, Beulah, I did go call on Sweet and the judge. Or rather, I called on the judge. Sweet was taking a nap."

"You didn't see her yourself? You didn't go in the house?" Beulah felt her heart drop right down into her shoes.

"Well, no," he explained. "I certainly didn't want to interrupt her nap."

Beulah said nothing, and the reverend continued: "The judge is a charming man, Beulah. I'm almost certain you are wrong in thinking he's being cruel to Sweet in any way. Why, he talked about her in the kindest manner possible, especially about how he thinks she had the perfect name for her gentle personality. He showed me all around the farm too, and I've never seen anyone more solicitous about his animals."

"Animals," Beulah repeated, senselessly.

"Listen, Beulah," the reverend went on, as if his sacred ears had picked up a hint of danger in her voice. " 'Vengeance is mine, saith the Lord.' "

"Maybe that's true," Beulah admitted, keeping a close watch over her tongue as she felt her ire rising ever nearer the surface. "But Reverend . . ."

"Yes, Beulah?"

"When that happens, I want a front-row seat."

"Why, Beulah, I've never heard you speak like this," the good reverend gently admonished her.

"I'm sorry, but it's the way I feel," Beulah whispered. "And I've found out that the judge had two wives before Sweet."

"What?"

"And they both died accidentally," Beulah added.

"What?"

"You heard me," Beulah said simply. After a long silence, she heard his voice, with a darkened tone in it. "You need to tell the sheriff about this, Beulah. And I'll pray for you all," the reverend said. "I'll pray very hard."

"Pray for Sweet," Beulah said. "Please pray for Sweet."

"I will do that as well," he assured her.

Beulah didn't fully realize that her next step in trying to help Sweet was already in

191

her mind. She simply found herself heading into town and going into the sheriff's office.

As in most small towns, she knew Matthew Anderson well, knew him especially well because the sheriff and his wife attended the same church as Beulah. When she came into his office, he stood up.

"Well, hello, Miss Beulah," he said genially. "I'm surprised to see you." He smiled and indicated a chair. When she was seated across the desk from him, she felt the full weight of responsibility that she would bear when the words came out of her mouth.

"What can I do for you, Miss Beulah?" he asked earnestly.

Beulah took a deep breath and began releasing the words. "I think that the judge is abusing Sweet," she said simply.

Matthew turned his head a little, looking sideways at her, and that small action indicated his skepticism. "And upon what do you base this belief?" he asked, picking up a pencil and moving a legal pad in front of him.

"She told me as much," Beulah answered. "And she's got a terrible bruise on her face."

"Did you ask her about it?"

"I certainly did," Beulah said. "At first,

she told me she'd had a fall. But then this afternoon, she confessed that the judge had struck her."

"And what do you believe?"

"I believe he hit her."

"Why would he do something like that?" Matthew asked her, and Beulah realized right away that there was no answer to that question. All her life she had been fortunate in being around good, kind people who respected and cared about each other. She had no comprehension of what it would take to make one person actually strike another person, much less what would make a big man hit a tiny little creature like Sweet. He must outweigh her by at least a hundred pounds! Her eyes filled up. "I have no idea," Beulah confessed. "Sweet just told me that when he gets angry about one thing, it spreads to everything else."

"Well, I expect a lot of people are like that," Matthew responded, as he jotted down some notes on the legal pad. "Perhaps she should consider charging him with assault?"

"Sweet?" Beulah cried. "Why, I can't imagine Sweet being willing to do something like *that!*" She hesitated for a long moment while the sheriff studied her carefully. Finally, Beulah looked down at her lap and added, "Besides, I think she's really in love with him. But there's another problem," she added. "The judge's first two wives both died accidental deaths, and I'm just wondering if they really were accidents."

The sheriff frowned. "So what do you want me to do?" he pressed gently. "If those deaths were officially ruled as accidental, I have no right to suggest otherwise."

"At least you can go talk with the judge," Beulah answered. "Let him know that some of us are suspicious about his behavior and that we are watching out for Sweet." Beulah was amazed at how easily the words came out.

Matthew shook his head a little. "I'll go out and see him today," he said, and then noticing the agony on Beulah's face, he glanced at his watch. "I'll go out there in about an hour. And I'll talk with Sweet as well. Let her know what her rights are, given that something like you are suggesting really happened — to Sweet, that is," he added, letting Beulah know that he wasn't about to bring up anything about the late wives.

"Will you please let me know what you find out?" Beulah asked.

"I'll call you this afternoon," he promised.

As Beulah left the sheriff's office, she

glanced up at the red, white, and blue, star-studded banner that was fluttering on the pole in front of the post office.

"Thank you," she said to it.

CHAPTER
— EIGHTEEN —

Since it would probably be several hours before Beulah could expect a phone call from Matthew Anderson, she couldn't bear to return home, to sit there watching the clock and waiting for the phone to ring, so she decided to drive up to Sweet's great-granddaddy's old place and take a good, bracing walk about that beloved property.

Somehow, she felt that walking around where Sweet's ancestors had walked would soothe and calm her jangled nerves. Would make her feel that not only Sweet's ancestors but all the saints of Heaven would be watching out for her. Ancestors, saints, the reverend, and now the sheriff. That felt good!

Long before the town of Tea-Olive developed, the area was occupied by farms spaced far enough apart to allow for plenty of land to grow crops. When Beulah turned off of the paved road and onto the unpaved Old Church Road, she knew that she was driving past fields that had once belonged to her own ancestors. One portion of a broken-down barn still remained on the land, and every summer, it was covered by kudzu so that it appeared to be some kind of a half-risen, hulking animal trying to free itself from the tenacious vines.

Four miles down the dirt road, Beulah pulled off to the side and got out of her car. How many times had she and Sweet come out to this old property to pick blackberries? She couldn't estimate, but it was many, many times. In the middle of the property near where a house had once stood, an enormous oak tree spread out its branches. It stood unbowed by winter winds or torrid summer heat. When Beulah and Sweet would come out to pick berries, they always packed a light lunch, and they would sit under the sweet shade that big tree provided and enjoy their sandwiches and the sun-warmed berries. Beulah could almost see Sweet's face — the wide-apart, innocent blue eyes and the berry-stained smile. Sweet! —

Beulah walked on with a deliberate stride, trying to work off her anger over Sweet's present predicament. And as she walked, she was thinking about Sweet's ancestors and her own — hard-working but gentle people who worked together, not against one another. People who took care of one another in sickness and who worked together at harvest time. Some of them people who had never seen a paved road and had never ridden in an automobile. They led what modern people would probably think of as terribly boring lives, yet the bottom line to them was *survival*.

That's what Sweet was facing now, but survival in an entirely different way.

Beulah walked for about an hour, cresting gentle hills and descending into shallow ravines. At the last, she topped a rise, and she could see the far-off gentle bulges of the Appalachian Mountains, a sight that always exhilarated her. But what exhilarated her even more that day was that a red-tailed hawk flew across the sky, emitting its high-pitched cry. It was such a magnificent bird that the mere sight of it brought tears to Beulah's eyes. Yes, magnificent . . . and free! She breathed deeply, gazing at the pristine world around her, and then she turned and started back toward her car and toward a town where good people had been fooled by the outward appearance and phony actions of a truly evil man. And to her friend, Sweet, who was *not* free, even as that poor little canary in its cage was not free! She shuddered.

True to his word, Matthew called Beulah late in the afternoon.

"Miss Beulah? This is Sheriff Anderson," he spoke softly.

"And?" Beulah was clearly anxious to hear what he had to say.

"Well, I've just spent almost an hour with the judge and Miss Sweet, and they are both as surprised as can be that anyone would think there was any trouble out at their place."

"What did they say?" Beulah inquired.

"They both said that Miss Sweet had an unfortunate fall," he said.

"Did you question Sweet right there in the judge's presence?" Beulah asked.

"Well, yes ma'am, I sure did," he admitted.

"Then I'm not surprised that she wouldn't tell the truth. If you didn't believe her, you'd leave — and she would be left alone with *him!*"

"Tell the truth, they both seemed so surprised and then a little upset that anyone had come to see me," he confessed. "The judge kept asking me who had talked to me, but I didn't tell him."

"Thank you for that," Beulah said.

"Listen, Miss Beulah, I think you're wrong about the judge. He's a fine, up-standing man, in my opinion, and I don't think he would ever lay a hand on a lady."

Beulah suddenly felt a debilitating weariness. "I see," she murmured. "Well, thank you anyway."

"Yes ma'am. You let me know if I can do anything else for you."

Just as soon as Beulah hung up the phone, it rang again. It was the judge.

"Are you the one who sent a minister and now a sheriff out to my house?" he demanded, his voice heavy with anger. "Are you?"

"Yes." Beulah's voice trembled, and that made her angry. "We're all worried about Sweet. She's our friend!"

"Sweet is my *wife!*" he bellowed into the phone. "Now I am telling you this once and for all. Stay away! Leave us alone! If you send anybody else out here to spy on us, you'll regret it."

"That sounds like a threat," Beulah said, her voice growing stronger.

"Take it any way you want to," he growled. "Just mind your own business

200

and leave us alone." And Beulah thought she could hear Sweet crying, just as the judge slammed down the receiver.

Beulah stood, trembling, for only a moment before she hopped into her car and drove out to see Zion.

Beulah was sitting at Zion's kitchen table with an untouched glass of iced tea before her. She had just finished telling Zion all about the tragic events of the day at Sweet's, with Zion frowning and shaking her head. And then she told Zion about the minister and then the sheriff both being fooled by the judge. Finally, she talked about the murderous sound of the judge's voice when he told her to leave him and Sweet alone.

"We've got to do something," Zion growled.

"But what?" Beulah wailed in frustration. "We've tried the church, and we've tried the law. What or who do we turn to next?"

Zion growled deep down in her throat, as if she were straining to drag something heavy from one place to another, deep inside of herself. Finally, she coughed and said, "If we could only get Sweet away from him long enough to talk some sense into her head!" Then Zion's eyebrows shot up almost to her hairline. "We'll kidnap her! Make her see what's going on! Then take her to the sheriff ourselves so she can talk without *him* being around. If he wasn't near her, I'll bet she would agree to letting someone help her. Maybe even to taking out an assault charge."

Beulah mused for several moments over Zion's suggestion. "I don't know about that," Beulah whispered. "Suppose she's really in love with him?"

"She could be," Zion said with disgust. "And she could also be afraid of him."

"We have to find out," Beulah agreed. "We have to know."

"So let's think about this a little bit," Zion suggested. "Figure out how to get Sweet away from him long enough for her to come to her senses and tell the sheriff the truth."

Deep into the night, Zion sat at her kitchen table alone, thinking hard about how she and Beulah could get Sweet away from the judge. In town, Beulah tossed and turned in a half-sleep, dreaming terrifying half-dreams about hog-tying Sweet and putting a gag in her mouth, loading her into the back of Zion's big truck, and speeding off down the highway into the darkness. But speeding off to *where?*

CHAPTER
— NINETEEN —

When Beulah arrived at Zion's the next morning, she went about washing and drying udders, as always, but she also glanced at Zion from time to time, trying to see if Zion had come up with a plan for getting Sweet away from the judge. But Zion's face remained blank and placid, her mind seemingly occupied with straining the milk and making sure that the cooler was at the right temperature. When they were done and the cows had been released to the sweet green pasture, Beulah broached the subject: "Have you thought of any way we can get Sweet to ourselves, even for a little while?"

"Yes, I have," Zion announced, with a jut of her chin. "We're going out there to get Sweet and take her to tea at Memphis's café, and we'll tell the judge that's where we're taking her and what time we'll have her back home. Then we'll just barge along with helping Sweet get ready, and the judge won't be able to do a thing about it. Short of shoving us to the floor, that is!" Zion laughed, but Beulah had gone pale at the thought of actually trying to get Sweet out of the house while the judge was there. "Besides," Zion added. "With that hired man around, the judge wouldn't dare raise his hand against either one of us, and if he does, then *we* will file charges of assault!"

"And *where* are we taking Sweet, to talk with her? If we tell the judge we're going to Memphis's tea shop, he'll just follow us, and even if he doesn't sit with us, he'll be intimidating Sweet, by his mere presence."

"Oh, we won't go to Memphis's at all," Zion laughed. "We'll bring her here — to my barn."

"To your barn?" Beulah could hardly believe her ears.

"Sure. No one would ever think to search my barn."

"We're going to *hide* Sweet?" Beulah asked, alarmed.

"Just long enough to talk some sense into her," Zion argued.

"And how long will that take?" Beulah asked.

"Don't know," Zion said. "As long as it takes, I guess."

Beulah had gone pale as a sheet of blank

paper. "Oh, Zion, maybe this isn't such a good idea after all," she wailed.

"But what's the alternative?" Zion asked. "Just leave her out there with *him* and maybe he will do worse than just hit her, in time?"

Beulah remembered the report that Wildwood had found about the judge's second wife and of how she died from a fall in the bathroom.

"I wish we had some proof," Beulah muttered.

"Oh, we've got proof," Zion said. "Sweet is the proof — her own face is the proof — if we can only get her to come clean to the sheriff."

Beulah and Zion were well-dressed and outwardly calm when they knocked on the door to Love-Divine's old house that afternoon. The judge answered the door, took one look at Beulah and Zion and slapped his forehead in exasperation.

"Look, am I going to have to take out a restraining order to keep you people out of our lives?" he roared, red-faced and sputtering.

"Perhaps," Zion answered coolly. "But that would probably look real funny to folks around here. We're friends of Sweet's from childhood, and we want to see her."

"Well, you can't!" the judge yelled, and a thick vein began bulging ominously in his left temple.

"Yes, we *can,*" Zion said, and she neatly stepped right around the judge and went into the living room, with Beulah close at her heels.

"Who the hell do you think you are?" the judge roared, his caustic voice drawing Sweet out of the back of the house. She stood rooted in the living room doorway, wiping her hands on her apron and with her mouth hanging open.

"Sweet, go take off your apron," Zion ordered. "We're taking you out for tea."

Sweet's glance went straight to the judge, and she stammered, "I don't think . . ."

"Then don't think!" Zion ordered. "Just come with us." Zion grabbed Sweet's arm, and then she turned to where the judge's huge bulk filled the space in front of the door. "Excuse us, please," Zion said politely. "I am taking Sweet out for a cup of tea, and I urge you not to raise your hand against any of us. There are at least two of us here who *will* press an assault charge if you put your hand on any of us."

The judge took a step to the side, his face incredulous that anyone — especially a woman — would speak so disrespectfully to him.

With Sweet still stuttering and glancing at the judge, Zion swept her along onto the porch and down the steps. Beulah remained frozen where she was standing, and the judge stared at her.

"Come on, Beulah!" Zion bellowed, sending Beulah scurrying around the judge and out into the yard, following Zion and Sweet to Zion's truck. They crowded into the passenger compartment and Zion spun the truck out of the yard with a roar of engine and gravel-spinning tires.

"What on *earth!*" Sweet managed to say. "What on earth are you thinking?"

"We're thinking that we need to talk with you," Beulah said. "And without the judge around."

"He'll just follow us to the tearoom," Sweet protested, with tears coming up in her eyes.

"That's why we're not going there," Zion answered, turning the truck onto the highway and stepping down on the gas pedal hard.

"What?" Sweet now seemed completely alarmed. "Where are we going?" she fairly shrieked.

"Somewhere else," Zion said. With that,

Sweet began to weep. "Oh, my God! Are you kidnapping me?" she screamed.

"We're performing an intervention!" Zion roared back at her. Beulah looked at Zion sharply. She had never heard of an intervention, but she didn't want to ask Zion what it meant, not in front of an upset Sweet.

Sweet continued to weep quietly the rest of the way to Zion's farm. When Zion turned in, she didn't stop her truck where she usually parked, but she drove on down and stopped behind the barn. From the other side of the pasture fence, the cows eyed them with pacific curiosity and then began quietly lining up to go into the milking parlor.

"Let's go into the barn," Zion said. "And then I've got to tend to the milking."

Beulah led Sweet into the barn, where they sat down together on a bale of hay. Zion remained standing. Beulah reached over and took Sweet's hand. "Listen, Sweet," Beulah began. "This isn't going to work."

"What isn't? Your kidnapping me?" Sweet shot back, glancing at Zion. "I *know* this won't work, and you all have just made everything worse for me!"

"Worse? How?" Beulah asked.

"He's going to be furious, you know," Sweet continued. "And he's going to take it out on me, even though I didn't have a thing to do with this . . . hateful scheme . . . you all dreamed up!" Sweet was becoming more and more agitated.

"It's the only way we could talk with you," Zion said defensively. "*He* won't let us get anywhere near you!"

"And that's going to get better now?" Sweet demanded.

"We're afraid for you," Beulah said.

"You're afraid for nothing," Sweet answered. "Listen, Beulah, I'm a married woman, at last, and I'm willing to put up with his little bit of temper."

"Little bit?" Beulah yelped.

"It's going to get worse," Zion warned. "You've got to stand up to him if you want this marriage to have a chance. If you let him get away with hitting you, it's going to get worse."

Zion's sincerity seemed to penetrate Sweet's protestations.

"What do you think I should do?" Sweet asked sincerely.

"Tell the sheriff what happened," Beulah said. "Get it onto a record somewhere, and maybe . . . maybe . . . that will make him not hit you anymore."

"Tell the sheriff?" Sweet repeated.

"YES!" came a booming male voice that caused all of the women to flinch.

The formidable figure of the judge was in the doorway of the barn, with the sheriff beside him.

"Yes!" the judge said again. "Tell the sheriff here how Beulah and Zion . . . your *good friends* . . . forced their way into my house and took you away against your will!"

"How about that, Zion and Beulah," the sheriff said. "Are you ladies guilty of kidnapping?"

"I think what you were going to tell the sheriff, Sweet, is that Beulah and Zion here have refused to let us newlyweds alone for a single minute. Isn't that what you were going to say?" the judge demanded.

Sweet blushed and looked down at the floor.

"Come with me," the judge ordered, and Sweet obeyed immediately. "I imagine you have something to say to these . . . ladies," the judge added. "I'll let you know later whether I want to press charges or take out a restraining order." So saying, the judge took Sweet's arm and led her out of the barn. The sheriff remained, tapping his foot and frowning.

"This is serious business," he said at last. "You all can't keep bothering the judge and Sweet like this. If he takes out a restraining order against you all, I'll have no choice but to arrest you if you bother them again."

"We're afraid for Sweet," Beulah murmured.

"Sweet herself will have to tell me if she thinks she's in danger," the sheriff said. "I can't do anything about what you ladies *think* is going on. Now you all go on home, please."

"I *am* at home, thank you," Zion snorted. "And I need Beulah here to help me with the milking."

"OK," the sheriff said. "Just you two find yourselves a hobby or something and leave the judge and Sweet alone. Do you hear me?"

"We hear you," Beulah murmured.

Beulah and Zion said not a word to each other during the milking, but when they were done, Zion said, "We should have thought it all out better."

"Thought it out?" Beulah asked, uncertain of what Zion was saying.

"The intervention," Zion said. "We should have planned it better."

211

"Well, we tried," Beulah lamented.

"*Next time* we'll do better," Zion pronounced.

"*Next time?*" Beulah screeched. "Didn't you hear what the sheriff said?"

"I heard him," Zion said. "I heard him, sure enough."

"Maybe Sweet was right," Beulah admitted. "Maybe we have made things worse for her. Maybe we should just leave them alone."

"We can't do much without Sweet's cooperation," Zion agreed. "We just have to think long and hard about what to do next."

But the question of "what to do next" took on an entirely different meaning during the middle of the night. Beulah's phone rang, shattering the peace and quiet of her bedroom. Groggily, she lifted the receiver, and what she heard next caused all the hairs to stand up on the back of her neck. She heard the judge's gravelly voice, low and harsh, and the words were the most terrible she had ever heard.

"Sweet's going to have her punishment," he growled. "And this time, I'll be smart enough to make the bruise where no one can see it." With that, he hung up.

Unable even to consider trying to go back to sleep, Beulah got up and, with shaking hands, made herself a cup of tea — and then she couldn't even take a sip of it. She sat in the dark kitchen praying, shaking, and wondering about Sweet, until the first hint of daylight came.

Beulah always had a tendency to reach out to Zion in trying times, but this time she knew what she had to do, and she knew she had to do it alone.

She sat in the still sanctuary for over two hours before she saw the judge come out onto the porch, stretch his arms wide, and go across the yard to the barn. Silently, Beulah crept across the backyard and up the steps to the back porch. But what she saw there stopped her right in her tracks. The lid was off of the trash can by the back door, and in the very top of the trash was the crumpled, broken-feathered body of the canary. Without hesitation, Beulah reached down and lifted the featherlight body into her hands. The minuscule head, with closed eyes, rolled most unnaturally. This bird had been in a cage, so how could something have happened to it?

Moreover, the tiny body was still warm! This could not have happened long ago!

As much as she was appalled by the tiny, broken body, all the hairs came up on her arms when she realized that she could hear Sweet crying inside the house.

The whole equation suddenly came together for Beulah. The judge had done this! Had crushed the life from that helpless little bird. But why? She wanted to go right inside, to comfort Sweet, but something stopped her.

Without knowing why, she simply placed the tiny, broken body of the bird back in the trash and silently, she placed the lid on the can. Then she tiptoed back down the steps, across the yard, and into the anonymity of the sanctuary. There, she sat down on the ground and wept harder than she had ever wept in her life, even counting when her beloved Paul had passed away. That had been a weeping of finality, of parting. This was a weeping for something she could only think of as a living death for her friend, Sweet.

When she finally had shed all the tears she had, she felt her emptiness filling up with an anger more terrible than any she had ever known.

"What kind of a *monster* would do something so horrible to a helpless, caged bird whose only 'crime' was that of singing?"

And the answer was even more terrible than the question: "Someone without any compassion of any kind. Someone who would destroy a helpless creature, just to intimidate, to inflict pain upon his own wife. Someone who would try everything he could to crush her spirit! To turn her into a mindless zombie to do his bidding and to have her fate — maybe even her life — in his hands and his alone."

Well, at least when she heard Sweet weeping, she knew that she was still breathing! But that poor little bird! And yes, the judge had been horribly right about one thing: he certainly did put the bruise where no one could see it!

"Father, forgive me," she said aloud, tilting her head back and looking straight up into the clear blue sky beyond the trees. "Forgive me. But I wish he would die!"

CHAPTER

— TWENTY —

When she got home, Beulah carefully composed herself before she called Zion.

"Zion, can you manage the milking without me this morning?" she asked.

"Isn't it kind of late to be asking that?" Zion sounded peeved. "Milking has already been done."

"I'm sorry," Beulah said sincerely. "I just don't feel very good this morning."

"I know that feeling." Zion's voice was softer. "After what all we went through yesterday, it's a miracle either one of us can get out of bed. You just have a good cup of tea and try to rest."

"A cup of tea," Beulah repeated senselessly. "Yes, that will do it."

For the rest of that entire day, Beulah walked around as if she had a terrible cold. She put on her bathrobe, drank cup after cup of hot tea, and intermittently broke down into tears at the thoughts of that poor little bird and the deep wound that was certainly in Sweet's heart. She moved about slowly and deliberately, often retreating to the corner of her couch, where she curled herself up as much as possible into a tight ball, all drawn in against the buffeting of the emotional winds that swirled around her.

By late afternoon, the weather itself had begun to imitate Beulah's turmoil. The wind came up, tearing the few remaining autumn leaves from the tree in her side yard and rocking the chairs on her front porch.

"Cold spell coming," she said to herself.

The next morning, she bundled up in her warmest clothes and drove out to Zion's house. Deep, dark clouds were scudding across the predawn sky, and Beulah blew on her hands as she entered the milking parlor.

Zion had already set about the tasks required, and even she was wearing wool gloves with the fingers cut out. She glanced at Beulah, smiled wanly, and said, "We'd make these poor old cows jump sky-high, what with us having such cold hands this morning!" Smiling, she reached onto a shelf and handed Beulah a pair of wool gloves with the fingers cut out.

"Just blow your breath on your fingers," Zion ordered. So they accomplished the milking and turned the cows out into a pasture where the morning dew had turned to crystal on the grass.

"Cold weather is coming," Zion said, and Beulah nodded. "Let's have us some good coffee."

Sitting at Zion's kitchen table a little later, they both cupped their warm mugs gratefully and sipped the strong, hot coffee.

"I've been thinking," Zion said. And then she stopped.

"Thinking about what?" Beulah asked, unnecessarily.

"*Him.*"

No additional information, no explanation, just that one, simple word that seemed to carry its own brand of horror in its sound.

"What about *him?*" Beulah asked, pondering whether to tell Zion about the canary and wondering, if she did start to tell her, would she be able to get the words out without weeping once again.

"I think he's more dangerous than we thought," Zion explained. "I think he's truly an evil man."

Beulah saw in her mind the sad, crumpled body of the bird, heard Sweet's pitiful crying from inside the house, and she nodded her head in agreement.

"You know," Zion started off in another tone entirely. "I've been thinking about our people and how hard they worked just to survive off the land." Beulah had been entirely unprepared for such a topic to come up, so she said nothing.

"And I've been thinking about what they would have done if somebody started beating up on his wife and threatening her and his neighbors."

Beulah tried to draw upon her imagination to formulate an answer, but her images of the ancestors were all of such quiet, kind, good-hearted people, she couldn't imagine what they would have done. Other than the story Sweet always told about her Confederate ancestor who took a piece of stovewood to that soldier, she had never heard of anything other than gentle good manners and hard work.

Beulah went back into her memory to that day when she and Sweet were just children and Sweet had showed her what was supposed to be Yankee blood on the rocks behind the barn. She shivered involuntarily.

"I think I know what they would have

done," Zion said, her eyes riveted on her cup of coffee.

"What?" Beulah finally had to ask.

Zion's eyes moved from the cup and locked into Beulah's eyes. It was long moments before she said, "I think they would have taken care of him."

"Taken care . . . how?" Beulah asked. "Back in those days, they couldn't have taken him to a clinic for anger management or anything like that!"

"That's not the kind of taking care of I meant," Zion growled.

Once Beulah settled on what Zion was saying, she heard her own voice. "I haven't told you what happened last night and this morning," Beulah whispered, attracting Zion's immediate attention.

"What?" Zion said.

"I got a phone call. From the judge," Beulah said. "He said . . ." Here, Beulah hesitated and swallowed hard. "He said he was going to punish Sweet, but in a way so that the bruise wouldn't show."

"What did he mean by that?" Zion's voice perfectly echoed the emotion that had caused the hairs to stand up on her arms.

"I didn't know, and I stayed awake all the rest of the night, worrying. So as soon as it was daylight, I went to the sanctuary and waited until I saw the judge go down to the barn. Then I sneaked onto the back porch, and that's where I saw it."

"Saw what?" Zion's brows had knitted themselves into a tight frown.

"That little canary I told you about. In the trash. With its neck broken," Sweet managed to mumble.

"With its neck broken?" Zion asked.

"Yes."

"What on earth!"

"And I could hear Sweet from inside the house, crying like her heart would break."

"How'd its neck get broken?" Zion asked.

"How do you think?" Beulah replied, trying to regain some composure.

And when it finally dawned upon Zion exactly what Beulah was saying, her face froze in a mask of disgust.

"Oh, my God!" Zion said at last. "That poor little bird. That's the bruise he said nobody would be able to see."

"Exactly. And there's something else I didn't tell you."

"Well, go on," Zion urged.

"The judge has been married twice before, and both of those wives died in accidents."

"What kind of accidents?" Zion asked.

"One was a car wreck, and the other fell and hit her head on the bathtub."

"Why didn't you tell me?" Zion asked. Then she added, "More importantly, does Sweet know about the other wives? Did you tell her?"

"No, she doesn't know, exactly. But when they went to New York, one of the judge's old aunties made some kind of remark to Sweet about being careful."

"Oh, this is lots worse than we thought," Zion pronounced. "And now, with that mean phone call to you about him punishing Sweet and that poor dead little bird . . ." Zion stumbled to a halt.

"I think Sweet doesn't see anything she doesn't *want* to see," Beulah added. "But surely, now that she saw what happened to the bird, she must have opened her eyes!"

They sat for a long while in miserable silence, and the wind picked up again, blowing something against the kitchen window — sounding like coarse sand hitting the glass. Zion got up and looked out.

"Sleet!" she said. "I need to get the cows inside."

"But what are we going to do, Zion?" Beulah asked, as if Zion would go out to bring in the cows and never come back again. Zion put on her windbreaker and gloves, and she hesitated at the door and gazed at Beulah for long moments.

"We're going to do whatever has to be done," Zion announced. "Just exactly like the people we came from. Now get on your jacket and come help me."

Once the cows were safely in the barn, Zion made another pot of coffee. They had stamped the sleet and ice from their boots and coats, and Beulah watched through the window as that strange, unaccustomed ice started coating the tree limbs, starting with the smallest twigs and few remaining fall leaves.

"I should go ahead and start for home, in case the roads get bad," Beulah said, but she made no move to leave. Zion once again put the steaming mugs on the table and sat down. Neither Beulah nor Zion said anything, but their minds were working together, nonetheless. The *whatever-we-have-to-do* sat between them in the middle of the kitchen table, invisible but very obviously present.

"We have to save her," Zion said.

"I know — but how?" Beulah answered.

Zion worried her lower lip between her teeth, and then she locked eyes with Beulah. "He likes turtle stew," Zion said, right out of the blue.

"What?" Beulah was positive that she hadn't heard Zion correctly.

"I said he likes turtle stew," Zion repeated. "When I saw Memphis the other day, she told me the judge had come into her tearoom and wanted to know if she ever served turtle stew."

"I never heard of such a thing," Beulah confessed.

"Me neither. But that's what Memphis said."

"And what does that have to do with anything?" Beulah asked.

"Well, if we mean to use something to *do what has to be done,* we have to put . . . something . . . into a dish that Sweet wouldn't touch in a million years. He's the only one we need to take care of. She's the one we want to save."

"Oh, my Lord!" Beulah moaned. "Are we talking about what I think we're talking about?"

Zion didn't answer her question directly. She simply said, "I wish there were some other way."

"I'm going home," Beulah announced suddenly. "I can't listen to this right now. And I want to get home before the roads get iced over." With that, she hurriedly put on her coat and boots and left Zion sitting at the kitchen table.

Beulah drove slowly, carefully, unlike some of the younger drivers, who whooped and laughed when their cars skidded on the light ice. Ordinarily, such foolish antics would have infuriated her, but on this day she was too deeply in thought to experience any anger. She drove methodically, slowing even more than usual before turning into her driveway.

In her living room were the vestiges of the afternoon before: her tea cup on the coffee table, her robe across the back of a chair. But unlike the afternoon before, Beulah felt little sadness and absolutely no terrible helplessness. When she noticed this change in emotions, she was surprised.

"What's different?" she asked the empty rooms. The only answer was, of course, silence, so she stood for a long time at the window, watching the unaccustomed sleet gathering on the banisters of her porch and remembering the long August afternoons of the torrid summer gone past, the blistering sun making heat waves rise up from paved roads and parking lots and everything burnished with a deep and heat-melted gold as the sun finally, finally slipped below the horizon. And Beulah was thinking that, maybe that's what she had felt like yesterday: helpless and burning and desperate with thirst. But now, standing in the same living room and looking out at the light ice coating on the leaves and hearing the soft pelting of sleet against her window, she felt cold and detached.

"Cold," she whispered aloud, clouding the window glass with her breath. And her next words surprised her: "Cold and powerful!"

But it wasn't until she reached into the closet to get a sweater that her strange feelings became actual thoughts, and they startled her completely, so that once again she spoke aloud to the empty room: "Yesterday was like the burning summers of my childhood, when nobody had any air-conditioning; all you could do was try to stay quiet and in the shade and just wait for the sun to go down. But in the winter, you put on a coat or a sweater and you could do what needed to be done to take care of yourself." She did not repeat the words, *do what needed to be done.*

By the next morning, warmer air had moved back in, and the sleet and frost of the day before had melted away. Zion and Beulah did the milking, with Beulah still mulling over the possibilities they had discussed the day before. Only now, she certainly understood much better.

"Tell you what," Beulah said, "*if* we decide to do this, it's going to look awfully strange if we just show up with a big pot of turtle stew. Especially after the events of the other day."

"So what are you thinking?" Zion asked.

"I think we should start taking food to them every few days, so it won't seem odd when we take the stew. *If* we take the stew," Beulah answered. "We can act like our offerings are something of an apology to the judge."

"Oh, that thought grates on me awful hard!" Zion said.

"But we have to do whatever it takes," Beulah argued.

"That's true," Zion agreed. "But as to turtle stew, do you know how to make it?"

"Heavens no! Never even heard of such a thing!"

"Probably make it pretty much like beef stew, I reckon," Zion mused. "Sure can't go to the library and ask Wildwood to look up a recipe now, can we?"

"Absolutely not," Beulah agreed. "And where do we get a turtle?"

"There's lots of them in the creek," Zion

advised. "But I don't know how you would go about catching one."

"Maybe we could hire someone to catch it for us?" Beulah offered.

"Have to be careful," Zion warned. "We can't leave a trail for somebody to follow!"

"I hadn't thought of that," Beulah admitted. "I've never tried to do anything secretive before. Never had to." Beulah's tone was one of bitterness.

"And we don't have to do this, either," Zion reminded her. "We could just close our eyes and our ears and let him get away with tormenting Sweet for the rest of her life."

"Which probably wouldn't be very long," Beulah added. "Not very long at all." Once again, she remembered that dead bird, with its soft gray eyelids closed over sightless eyes. And now, Sweet was in a cage as well. Beulah squared her chin. "Tonight, I'll make one of my good tuna and noodle casseroles, and we can take it out there tomorrow."

"OK," Zion agreed. And then she added, "Even if we decide not to *take care of things,* at least we will have been neighborly." And there it was again: that Southern propensity for neighborliness and good manners. How many evils could it cover up?

"Listen," Zion said. "I've got a distant cousin lives about seventy-five miles away, and I think he can get us a turtle. He's someone who knows how to keep his mouth shut, and besides, he owes me a favor."

"Why?" Beulah couldn't resist asking.

"Oh, I helped him out a little bit one time when he needed me to say that he was with me on a given date and time."

"And was he?"

"Absolutely not," Zion laughed. "But he's family!"

That night, Beulah made her famous casserole, and after the milking the next morning, she brazenly drove up to the judge and Sweet's house. Knocking on the front door was not something Beulah really wanted to do, but if she and Zion were to establish "neighborliness," she had no choice.

When the judge opened the door, she thought for sure that she was face-to-face with the evil one himself! His eyes were all puffy and his eyebrows even wilder looking than they had been when she last saw him. He was wearing the same red, silk robe over a white T-shirt and khaki pants, and he was barefoot. His yellowed toenails were split and twisted, and his feet looked absolutely obscene.

She held out the casserole. "Listen, I'm sorry about thinking there was something wrong," Beulah lied. "Zion and I wanted to bring you all something good to eat," she mumbled. "Put it in the oven at three hundred and fifty degrees for about forty-five minutes."

"That's Sweet's job," he grumbled, taking the casserole in one of his huge hands.

"May I say hello to Sweet?" Beulah asked in what she hoped was a light-sounding voice.

"You want to try and kidnap her again?" the judge sneered.

"No." Beulah tried to look contrite. "I've already said we're sorry about that. So may I please see her?"

"Uh, she's taking a nap," the judge said.

"She does that a lot, doesn't she?" Beulah couldn't keep the words from falling out. "I heard that she was taking a nap when the Reverend McKenzie came to call on you all." To that, the judge said not a word. He simply closed the door right in her face.

That afternoon, Zion and Beulah left town, according to their plan for finding a turtle for making the stew. After an hour and a half of driving, they pulled up in front of a trailer that stood in the shade of a large pecan tree. And what a circuitous journey it had been! They'd taken the interstate, and Beulah thought that was just like falling into a raging river, like going over the falls at Tallulah Gorge, high up in the North Georgia mountains. All those whizzing cars going so fast, and with signs that showed you where you could get off the interstate to get gas or food. They had taken an exit only twenty-five miles away, and then, once they passed a Waffle House restaurant, they wound up on a secondary state road that went through several small towns before they came to a junction where Zion directed Beulah to make a left-hand turn. After a while that road dead-ended, but a dirt road went off to the right, and that's the road they took. The land gently went downhill, and they crossed over a creek on a wooden bridge that groaned under the weight of Beulah's car. That's when Zion pointed out the trailer.

Zion's cousin, Andrew, answered their knock. He was an older man gone to seed. A perpetual cigarette hung from his mouth, and his ice-blue eyes bore such a reflection of misery that Beulah could hardly stand to meet his tortured gaze.

"Hi, Andrew," Zion said. "This is my friend, Beulah."

"Come on in," he murmured.

"You got that turtle I wanted?"

"Sure do. Got him back here in a washtub."

Silently the two women followed Andrew through the dark, trash-strewn living room, where beer cans littered the coffee table and the television droned, unnoticed. The kitchen he led them through was even worse, with crusted dishes piled in the sink and plates of dry dog food littering the floor. He led them through a screen door that opened to a roughly built shed. In a washtub, a creek turtle about the size of a huge watermelon paddled the rusty sides of the tub helplessly.

"He big enough?" Andrew inquired.

"I guess so." Zion sounded unsure. "Andrew, you ever make turtle stew?"

"Stew? Out of one of them things?" He seemed genuinely repulsed. "Naw — got plenty of good fish in that creek. Never ate no turtle. I seen one butchered one time though," he added. "Nasty business, that."

"Well, thanks anyway," Zion said, casting a glance at Beulah.

"You got something I can put him in for

you?" Andrew asked, reaching down and picking up the flailing turtle.

"I didn't think of that," Zion said. "Can we just put him in the trunk of the car?"

"Sure," he answered. So with Andrew grunting at the heavy weight of the turtle and Zion and Beulah following him, they went back through the dark trailer and out to the car. Beulah opened the trunk and Andrew deposited the turtle in it. When the turtle discovered that he was free enough to be able to move around, he ponderously made his way right up against the spare tire and drew in his head and legs.

"Thanks, Andrew," Zion said, putting her hand on his arm.

As the two women headed back toward the interstate, Zion noticed Beulah's questioning glance.

"Andrew came back from Korea like that," Zion offered. "Went away a bright, handsome young man with a good farm coming to him as an inheritance some day. Came back a broken ghost. Bought himself that little trailer, went inside of it, and never really came out again. Just to go to the creek and catch some fish to eat. Once in a long while, he goes into town for beer and flour, cornmeal and cigarettes. Such as that."

"That's so sad," Beulah said, and she meant it completely.

"Well, sometimes things happen," Zion said. "Sometimes things just happen."

When they got back to Beulah's house, they ran some cold water into her bathtub and then went back out to the car for the turtle. It took both of them struggling hard to carry him inside, where they dropped him noisily into the tub and stood back, watching him swimming and stroking his flippers against the smooth porcelain.

"I'll come back tomorrow and we'll butcher him," Zion said easily.

Beulah's stomach lurched in revolt of the thought. "Do we know how to make the stew?" Beulah asked.

"We'll figure it out," Zion assured her.

The next morning at the milking, Beulah and Zion didn't talk about the turtle, but Beulah said, "I made a coconut cake last night. Figured I'll take it to the judge's house, knock on the door, and leave the cake on the porch."

"At least that way you won't get a door slammed in your face," Zion added.

"That's what I figured, too," Beulah said.

Late that afternoon, Zion arrived at Beulah's house and they proceeded into the bathroom, where the turtle was still swimming around in Beulah's porcelain bathtub.

"Go get me a good, sharp knife," Zion ordered.

"Oh, my Lord!" was Beulah's response.

"Go get it!" Zion sounded rough because she, herself, didn't relish what needed to be done. "Unless you want to just throw him in the oven and cook him right in the shell!"

Such a thought drew another "Oh, my Lord!" from Beulah, but she scurried out of the bathroom, and Zion could hear her scrabbling around in her kitchen drawer. In a matter of moments, Beulah came walking slowly back into the bathroom, carrying a large butcher knife. She silently handed it to Zion, who was sitting on the edge of the tub.

"What are you going to do?" Beulah asked with her voice shaking.

"Gonna cut his throat," Zion whispered. With that, she leaned forward over the turtle and placed the knife at its throat, struggling to keep the turtle from drawing its head back into the shell.

"Here — you hold onto his head so I can get at his throat," Zion ordered. But Beulah screamed "Oh, my God!" so loudly that Zion dropped the knife into the water.

"What?" Zion yelled.

"Look at his eyes!" Beulah sobbed. "Just look at his eyes!"

"No!" Zion yelled. "Not if I'm going to have to cut his throat!" She reached under the struggling turtle and came up with the knife. Once again, she grabbed the turtle's head and placed the knife at the turtle's throat.

"NOT IN MY PORCELAIN BATHTUB!!!" Beulah shrieked.

That second scream startled Zion so much that she practically slipped into the tub herself. The turtle's head slipped out of her grasp and the poised knife jerked in her hand, nicking the turtle's throat as he drew his head back into the shell. A few drops of blood leaked out and slowly began coloring the water a deadly pink.

"Oh, my Lord!" Beulah shrieked.

"Let me finish him off!" Zion roared.

"No! No! No!" Beulah jerked open the medicine cabinet, sending bottles of cough syrup and tubes of toothpaste tumbling into the sink. She grabbed a box of Band-Aids, spilling most of them onto the floor, and with trembling hands, she held some out to Zion.

"Here!" she yelped. "Stop the bleeding!"

"You want me to put a Band-Aid on a turtle?" Zion's voice was incredulous.

"Yes! Do it now!" All the while, the drops of blood slowly leaked into the water, and Beulah reached across Zion and pulled the bathtub plug so that the water level began to go down immediately. Zion grabbed a hand towel and placed it under the turtle's throat, holding the head and trying to dry the bleeding area.

"Get him out of my tub!" Beulah yelled. "Put him on the floor so we can work on him." Zion did exactly as Beulah instructed, though lifting that heavy turtle was more of a job than any one woman could accomplish. Together, they finally got the turtle onto the bathroom floor, where Zion held its head and dried its throat, after which Beulah carefully applied a tight Band-Aid. Then she took adhesive tape and wrapped it all the way around the turtle's throat over the Band-Aid several times.

"Keep him right there," Beulah ordered, as she reached in the cabinet and brought out a bottle of bleach. This, she poured liberally into the tub, so that the fumes filled the small bathroom. As soon as she was satisfied that the tub had been sanitized, she turned to Zion.

"You need to go call Andrew," she said. "Tell him we're bringing the turtle back, and he's the one who will have to butcher it."

"You want to drive all the way over there and back?" Zion asked. "Why, it will probably be midnight before we start making the stew."

"It's what we have to do," Beulah insisted. "He said he'd seen one butchered before, so he must know how to do it."

"Ok," Zion gave in. "I'll call Andrew, but I have to take care of the milking first."

"I'll help," Beulah said.

It was almost twilight when the two women loaded the bandaged turtle back into the trunk and made the long drive back to Andrew's trailer. When they drove up, he was sitting on the steps of the trailer, puffing on the ever-present cigarette.

"I'm sorry, Andrew," Zion said, as he lifted the turtle out of the trunk. "We'll wait out here while you . . ." Andrew seemed a bit surprised when he saw the Band-Aid and the adhesive tape on the turtle's neck, and he looked at Zion questioningly.

"We tried," Zion offered. "*I* tried," she amended. "But it was too much for Beulah here."

"I understand," Andrew said, lugging the turtle into the trailer. Zion got back into the car with Beulah, and they waited, trying not to think about what was probably happening to the turtle. But when they heard Andrew's apparent digging around in his cutlery drawer — probably looking for a sharp knife — Beulah put her fingers into her ears and shut her eyes. She even started chanting "LA! LA! LA!" over and over, loudly, to drown out any sound she didn't want to hear.

Zion eyed her warily. "How're you gonna do the *real* thing that has to be done? You answer me that! When you can't stand to butcher a stinking turtle!" Zion whispered. But of course, Beulah couldn't hear her words, so Zion's question became one for Zion herself to answer.

After about half an hour, when Zion was nearly insane with Beulah's behavior, and Beulah had nearly succeeded in hyperventilating, what with the constant, loud chanting, Andrew came back out of the trailer, carrying a plastic bag of bloody meat. Zion opened the trunk and he placed the bag in it. Beulah took her fingers out of her ears.

"Don't worry, Miss Beulah," Andrew said gently. "He didn't scream none." When Beulah looked at Andrew, she saw that his face was even more haggard than it had been earlier, and his eyes were red, as if he had been crying.

"Thank you, Andrew," Zion said. "We won't be bothering you anymore."

It was well after midnight when Beulah and Zion arrived back in Tea-Olive.

"You put that turtle meat into your freezer," Zion instructed. "When we finish the milking in the morning, we'll fry up some chicken I've been thawing. Another little present for the judge. Got to keep him thinking we're just being polite."

"Yes," Beulah said absently. "By all means we must be polite."

CHAPTER
— TWENTY-ONE —

As she did nearly every morning, Beulah went straight from helping Zion to the sanctuary, where she watched the judge's house through her binoculars. And this time, Beulah's mind flashed to that horrible, bloody bag of turtle meat in her freezer.

Standing there, in that lovely, peaceful sanctuary, she could hardly fathom that she and Zion were actually plotting to end someone's life — to *do what has to be done* before he could destroy Sweet.

Just at that moment, Beulah saw the judge come out of the back door and walk rapidly across the yard, heading right for her. For a long moment, she had to fight with herself, to keep from running away just as fast as she could go. Then, she reminded herself that the King's Wood Bird Sanctuary belonged to the bird watching society, so she stood her ground, although her heart was pounding in her ears. Slowly, she turned her back on the approaching figure, swung the binoculars around, and stared through them at the treetops. She could hear his footsteps coming closer and closer, and when she thought that he was probably right behind her, she lowered the binoculars, turned around, and stared right into his eyes.

"What do you think you're doing?" he snarled.

"Why, I'm bird watching," Beulah replied, trying to sound completely unconcerned.

"You're not watching birds," he whispered. "You're spying on my house."

"Why would I do that?" she asked, hoping that her voice sounded innocent.

"Because you and that Zion woman are up to something," he accused. "First you kidnapped my wife, and now you're cooking something up to try next."

"Why, why ever would we do something like that?" she asked.

"You just remember one thing," he snarled yet again, and this time, he shook his finger right in Beulah's face. "I can still press charges against you two for kidnapping my wife. And I can press stalking charges as well."

"You can't file charges to keep us out of our own bird watching sanctuary," Beulah said. "This is *our* land you're standing on," she reminded him. "So I suggest you go on back to your own land."

"Land! Land! Land!" he yelled. "I swear, you people are just crazy! That's all you ever talk about!"

"Crazy or not, this is still our land, and we do talk about other things."

"Like what?" he asked, frowning.

"Like little birds in cages and what bad things can happen to them," she said with an even voice.

At that, the judge squinted his eyes at her. "You better be careful," he warned. "I don't know what you and your friend are up to, but I'm way too smart for the likes of you people. So you better be careful."

"And you better be careful as well," Beulah retorted. "I think you're trying to put Sweet into a cage, just like that little bird. And I don't want anything bad to happen to *her*."

For a long moment, he stared at Beulah, his incredulity clearly showing. And then, without another word, he turned on his heel and stomped out of the sanctuary. Beulah watched his broad back until he had gone back into the house, and then she turned and walked with slow deliberation across *their* land — the bird-watchers' land — back to her car.

When she got home, Beulah removed the repulsive package of turtle meat from the freezer and put it into the refrigerator so it could thaw. That afternoon, Zion came over to help make the turtle stew, and in her purse, Zion carried a small packet of rat poison and an inoculation needle she used to immunize her milk herd. When she put the rat poison and the needle on the kitchen table, Beulah put her hand over her heart and sat down at the table.

"Look." Zion raised her voice, clearly losing her temper with Beulah's repeated waffling about the task they had set for themselves. "You're either going to do this or you're not! So which one is it going to be?"

"How can you be so cold about this?" Beulah's eyes had filled with tears of fear and frustration.

"About extermination?" yelled Zion. "How many rats have I exterminated from my barn? Hundreds? Thousands?"

"This is not a rat," Beulah whispered.

"It's vermin, just the same," Zion argued. "But I still say that you're going to do this or not, so make your final decision right here and right now."

Zion sat down at the table with Beulah, crossed her arms, and waited for Beulah's final answer. Beulah looked around her familiar kitchen, a room that used to be her favorite emotional sanctuary — with the aroma of coffee early in the morning, the sweet perfume when she made fig preserves on long summer afternoons, and the quiet assurance of her own familiar aprons hanging in the pantry. She glanced over at Zion, who tilted her head and raised her eyebrows. "Zion, I don't know that this is possible for me to do," she admitted. "It's not a matter of will I or won't I; it's a matter of 'Is this possible?' "

"Well, then," Zion said, "let's just go back to the sheriff again about it and forget this ridiculous plan to *do what needs to be done* ourselves."

"The law?" Beulah yelped. "The law? I already sent the sheriff out there, and he got fooled as well! And even if the sheriff had found something, I think the judge could . . . do something to her before the law could do anything. I think perhaps he has done it before and gotten away with it."

"And I think you're right about that," Zion agreed. "The question we have to face is this: If we do it, can *we* get away with it?"

Once again, her own words came back to haunt Beulah: "I guess there are a lot of people who finally get out of prison who would like to pay him back."

"We can get away with it," Beulah finally said.

"So we're going to do it?" Zion inquired almost gently.

"Yes," Beulah answered. "We're going to do it. We're going to *do what has to be done.*"

CHAPTER
— TWENTY-TWO —

After their final agreement, Zion sent Beulah to lie down in her room, to spare her the sight of the turtle meat being injected with rat poison, and as soon as Beulah retreated to the peace and quiet of her own bedroom, she surprised herself by falling asleep and not waking up until over an hour later. The aroma of what smelled like a good chicken stew wafted down the hallway. She approached the kitchen cautiously, almost afraid to let the aroma of the stew enter her nose.

Zion was standing at the stove, one of Beulah's massive aprons wrapped twice around her skinny body.

"Is it done?" Beulah asked.

Zion turned from the stove. "It's done, and it sure does smell good!" Zion sounded surprised. "Why if those old turtles weren't so much trouble, I'd make a batch of this for myself! Well, not exactly like this batch," Zion amended. She glanced over at the used hypodermic on the table. The packet of rat poison was gone.

"How . . . how . . ." Beulah couldn't seem to get the question out.

"I injected the turtle meat before I cooked it," Zion explained, with a strange bravado in her voice. Beulah shuddered.

"I'll take it over now," Beulah decided. "I don't want it in the house any longer than possible. Thank you, Zion."

"You're entirely welcome," Zion said. "Let us just hope he likes it and has a big appetite!"

At last, Zion block-printed a label to go with the "special" stew. She clearly marked it TURTLE STEW — THE JUDGES FAVORITE! That was to assure that Sweet wouldn't be having any of that stew herself.

When Beulah drove up at the judge and Sweet's, she was grateful for all the other times she had left food for them. Carrying the stew to the front porch, she pretended that it was a high, white coconut cake. Why, she was just being neighborly! She knocked on the door and put down the pot of stew. Then she walked as casually as possible back to her car.

Perhaps Beulah's sleeplessness that night

was because she was completely unfamiliar with what it felt to have attempted to *do what has to be done* — and possibly have succeeded — or perhaps it was caused by her long afternoon nap. Regardless, sleep would not come to her, and she prowled around her own house most of the night. She scrubbed the kitchen until it was utterly spotless, and then she made herself a cup of decaffeinated tea and sat for long hours at the kitchen table, reading her Bible. When daylight began to show outside, Beulah felt almost grateful for the light. With daylight, perhaps life could return to normal. Perhaps even as the sun rose, the judge was dead in his bed and Sweet was free!

When Beulah arrived at the milking parlor an hour or so later, she and Zion said absolutely nothing about their activities of the previous day. Still, they stole glances at each other from time to time, with the question sitting there unspoken: is he dead? Had they been successful in *exterminating* him?

As soon as the milking was done, Beulah headed for the bird sanctuary, and when she walked through the woods and came to the edge of the clearing that held that little house, she halfway expected to see the coroner's car in the driveway. Or an ambulance. Or a police car. Or something!

But the driveway held only the judge's black car, with Sweet's car — still with the flat tire — parked under the shed. Nothing looked amiss. Everything looked exactly as it had the day before.

Beulah spent almost all day in the sanctuary, waiting. But then dusk began to fall and still she had seen nothing and no one — except for Jim, going from his little house and into the barn. No judge. No Sweet. Nothing!

She began thinking of some excuse for calling Jim. But nothing would prevent the judge from answering himself — if he were still alive, that is. So she finally called Wildwood at the library.

"Have you heard anything from the judge?" Beulah casually floated the question out, and it was entirely appropriate, especially since the judge had announced his plans to disapprove the Save Our Library campaign.

"He's made some phone calls to other board members, I hear," Wildwood said. "Trying to talk them into stopping the campaign. Honestly, Beulah, it was bad enough when he went against the Homework Helper Program, but then to try and stop everybody from trying our best to save our whole library? It's terrible!"

"I certainly agree with you there, but of course, we know why he's trying to get the library closed. He wants to line his own pockets with Love-Divine's money! With the library closed, that money would revert to the town, and with him on the town council, you can bet your bottom dollar he would find a nice, expensive job for that construction company he's bought into," Beulah said. Then she added, "Um . . . do you happen to know *when* he called the other members?"

"Well, he called one this morning," Wildwood answered. "Why?"

"Oh, I just wondered," Beulah said. "Just idle curiosity."

"I'm glad he called on the phone, instead of calling a full board meeting," Wildwood said. "On the phone, he's a far less intimidating man, and while I can't repeat anything that was said to me, I *can* tell you that some of the board members are beginning to see how he simply bulldozes people!"

"That's good," Beulah answered. "Good that they are really beginning to see that they heaped too much undeserved praise on him. And just for being a retired judge."

★ ★ ★

The next day, Beulah could not wait any longer to find out about the turtle stew. She dialed the phone, and when Sweet herself answered, she almost fainted with relief.

"Sweet?" Beulah tried to sound relaxed and chatty. "I was just wondering if you all got that nice container of turtle stew I left for the judge?"

"Well, yes, thank you," Sweet answered, her voice sounding bright, as if absolutely nothing was amiss in her home.

"Did he enjoy it?" Beulah asked cautiously.

"To be truthful, he said he really wasn't in the mood for it, so he had me put it in the freezer, for now."

"Oh," Beulah mumbled.

"But we really did appreciate your going to all that trouble," Sweet hastened to explain.

"Oh, it was no trouble at all," Beulah said, feeling her face getting hot.

So after all that time of wondering, Beulah knew for sure that the judge didn't eat the stew.

"We'll have to think of another way," Zion mused. "We'll have to find a way to *do what needs to be done* that looks like an accident."

"Oh, Zion, I don't know that I can go through something else," Beulah said wearily. "And maybe we don't have to. I think people are beginning to catch on that the judge isn't such a wonderful person after all."

"Oh, so if he gets unhappy enough, he'll move back to New York and take Sweet *with* him? And what on earth would happen there, where she doesn't have anyone to look out for her?"

"I didn't think of that," Beulah confessed. "That just never occurred to me at all."

"I think we should keep on trying. And we'll find a way that won't be so personal. Not like making a stew out of rat-poisoned turtle meat. Ugh!"

"You didn't let on that it bothered you so much," Beulah remarked.

"I've learned to steel myself against things that are . . . distasteful," Zion confessed. "Running a creamery isn't for the squeamish, you know."

"Let's just wait a bit, please," Beulah begged. "I'm going to sneak back into Sweet's this afternoon and check on her. So let's just wait at least until I've done that."

True to her word, Beulah waited in the bird sanctuary, watching the house with her binoculars. She had a long wait, but eventually, the judge came out of the front door and headed toward the barn. Beulah ducked down, scrambled across the backyard, and came in the back door without knocking, as she had done before.

Sweet was in the kitchen, sitting at the table and reading her Bible.

"Sweet!" Beulah shout-whispered.

Sweet jerked involuntarily, and then she glanced at the front door. "What are you doing here?" Sweet whispered. Beulah remained in the doorway, using the wall to partially conceal herself. She studied Sweet's face carefully. The bruise was almost totally gone, but there was a dullness in Sweet's eyes that Beulah had never seen there before.

"I came to see if you're OK," Beulah said. "You haven't had any more falls, have you?"

Sweet managed a wan smile. "No, I haven't had any more falls."

Beulah glanced uneasily once again toward the front door. "You don't have to worry," Sweet said. "He's likely to be gone a long time, down at the barn. Just got himself a new bull, and he's prouder of that animal than all the others put together."

"A bull?"

"Yes. A Jersey bull."

About this time, a loud noise came from the barn. Sweet and Beulah both jumped. Then they could hear the judge's faraway voice: "Calm down, you devil you!"

"That bull's awfully short-tempered," Sweet said with a smile. "Maybe the judge has met his match this time."

"Is Jim helping him?" Beulah ventured, once again hearing the judge's loud shouts and more loud noises, as if the bull were tearing down the side of the barn.

"Jim is gone," Sweet said. "He wasn't about to work around a mean bull like that!"

"So you think the judge has his mind on other things now?" Beulah asked. "That bull has kind of taken his attention off of you?"

"Yes," Sweet replied, but with a frown. "I wish I could offer you a glass of tea or something, but we'd better not take a chance on getting caught like this."

"He doesn't want you to see anyone else, even your oldest friends, does he?"

"That's right. I can't go anywhere without him, because of that flat tire. Don't guess I'd want to go away anyhow. He would just find me and bring me back." She shuddered slightly. "Might do worse."

"Listen, Sweet, just hang in there and try

not to do anything that will get the judge upset with you," Beulah advised.

"I walk on eggshells all the time," Sweet replied. "I spend every minute of my life trying to avoid making him angry."

"It's no way to live," Beulah said.

"My own fault," Sweet admitted. Then she quoted an old, old saying: "I made my bed, and now I have to lie in it."

"Not next to him, you don't," Beulah argued.

By the time Beulah crept back across the yard and into the bird sanctuary, her mind had begun to whirl. Perhaps the judge himself had provided them with the perfect means of extermination! A strong, young, evil-tempered bull! And just suppose that some morning, the judge went out to the barn and that bull wasn't where he was supposed to be. Suppose that enormous, testosterone-driven animal came bursting out of the early morning darkness inside the barn and . . . Beulah stopped herself. She and Zion had decided to wait awhile before they tried again. If Zion knew about the bull, she would figure out real fast about using him as a weapon of destruction!

The next morning, at the milking, Beulah and Zion worked silently. Beulah kept going over and over in her mind the vision of that terrible bull mauling . . . killing . . . the judge. And it would be thought of as a complete accident! No autopsy would show poison; no person could be blamed except the judge himself, for assuming he could handle such a dangerous animal. Zion glanced at Beulah a few times, but she said nothing, until the milking machines were humming rhythmically.

"Heard the judge got himself a bull," Zion said nonchalantly.

"Where'd you hear that?" Beulah was surprised.

"It seems he fired his hired man, and on his way out of town, the man stopped at the gas station. Told about the bull while he was pumping gas. Said he wasn't about to work with such an animal!"

"I was out to see Sweet yesterday," Beulah confessed. "And we could hear all kinds of banging around going on in the barn and the judge hollering at him."

"What a fool!" Zion exclaimed. "Why on earth would anybody want a bull?"

"Maybe he wanted calves," Beulah suggested.

"If he wanted calves, he should have called the county agent."

"Why?"

"Because the agent would come out to his farm with a big vial of bull semen and something that looks like a giant turkey baster . . ."

"Oh, my Lord!" Beulah turned bloodred.

"Listen, I told you that running a creamery and taking care of a herd of cows isn't for the squeamish."

"I just never thought about how you get your calves," Beulah said.

"Well, that's how I get them," Zion explained. "But I was just thinking . . ."

And before Zion could say another word, Beulah already knew that Zion had come to the same conclusion about the bull. "Maybe the judge has just given us the very thing we need to exterminate him, once and for all. Maybe he paid out lots of good money for a 'weapon.' It'll be especially easy since that handyman is gone."

"I liked Jim," Beulah murmured.

"But it will be easier with him out of the way," Zion said.

"Yes, it will be easier," Beulah agreed.

That evening was the Homework Helper Program, and as usual Beulah arrived early.

"You hear anything more from the

judge?" she asked Wildwood.

"Somebody said he's going to write a letter to the editor of the newspaper, arguing that the money spent on the library would be put to better use elsewhere," Wildwood said.

"Maybe we're lucky that he isn't from around here," Beulah was thinking out loud.

"Why?"

"Because, if he'd lived in Georgia all of his life, he would have some major connections at the state level. If he's only writing a letter to the newspaper, then he doesn't have those connections here. The ones that could really hurt our Save the Library project."

"I hadn't thought of that," Wildwood said. "Maybe you're right, but he's still on the town council."

As always, when the children in the Homework Helper Program arrived, the entire environment of the library changed from one of quiet contemplation and adult reading to one of bustling, active, healthy children who filled the room with a strange but pleasant young-animal aroma and energy.

"Those," Beulah said to Wildwood, "are the library patrons of the future!"

"Amen!" Wildwood laughed.

Again, as always, working with Tobia

provided Beulah with a wild, sweet joy. And particularly this time, because Tobia brought his report card for her to see, and his grade in spelling was much better.

"It looks as if you've won the prize!" Beulah's voice was filled with approval, and Tobia wriggled in his chair and grinned happily.

"Will you bring it next time?" Tobia asked.

"I will indeed," Beulah assured him.

For the next few days, Zion and Beulah worked side by side without saying one single word about the bull. Zion was like a tree, in that she instinctively knew when to go winter-dormant and then when her new, green leaves were ready to pop out into the gentle spring air.

"I'm going to the bird sanctuary this afternoon," she confided to Beulah. "I want to get a closer look at that barn so we can figure out how to let that bull do our work for us."

"Be careful!" Beulah urged. "You want me to go along with you?"

"No, thank you," Zion said. "This clandestine activity will be mine and mine alone. If you come along, you'll go all queasy on me and start worrying about that bull hurting his horns on the judge!"

"Well, he's got a steel stall in the barn for that bull," Zion announced the next day. "I guess he did his homework before he brought in that bull."

"So what do we do?" Beulah asked.

"We find a way to let that bull out into the barn itself. Then when the judge opens the barn door one morning, that bull will be somewhere the judge isn't expecting him to be."

"An accident," Beulah pronounced.

"If you like to think of it that way, you go right ahead," Zion laughed. "To me, it's still an extermination."

"When?"

"Couple of days, I think," Zion said.

"But how can we let that bull out of the steel stall and not get killed ourselves?"

"That's what I got to figure," Zion confessed. She frowned deeply, was silent for a few minutes, and then she said, "Can you come a little earlier for morning milking tomorrow?"

"Sure," Beulah answered. "But why?"

"I figure the best thing for us to do is drive down to South Georgia and look at a bull gate in an agricultural supply and equipment store. It will be a long drive, but we can get there and back before evening milking."

"Why all the way to South Georgia?" Beulah asked.

"Because nobody down there knows us. Sometimes I think you forget exactly what it is we're trying to do."

"Sometimes I *want* to forget."

"That's dangerous," Zion said.

"I know," Beulah answered simply.

CHAPTER
— TWENTY-THREE —

All evening long, Beulah fretted about them making a second try on the judge's life. After all, when she saw Sweet last, even though she'd had to sneak in while the judge was in the barn, Sweet seemed somewhat resigned to the judge's volatile temperament, and too, there were no additional bruises — none that Beulah could see, that is. But what if Zion was right in thinking the judge could move back to New York and take Sweet with him?

Beulah didn't dare trying to go to sleep with all of that whirling around in her mind, so she stayed up late, reading a murder mystery. That depressed her all the more. Into the middle of these troubled thoughts, the ringing of the phone made Beulah almost jump out of her chair.

"Who can be calling this time of night?" she asked aloud. When she answered, the first thing she heard was a man's voice, a clearing of his throat. The judge? Heaven forbid!

"Miss Beulah?" The voice was warm, with a soft drawl.

"Yes? Who is this, please?"

"It's Jim," he said. "I'm sorry to bother you so late."

"I wasn't asleep. What can I do for you?"

"Well, to be truthful, my conscience is nearly killing me, and I just had to talk to someone."

"Your conscience?" Beulah questioned gently.

"Yes, ma'am."

"Why is your conscience troubled, Jim? Are you sorry you left the judge's employment about the bull?"

"The bull? Oh no, ma'am. It wasn't really about the bull. That just gave me a good excuse."

"And?" Beulah waited while Jim cleared his throat again.

"Well, it's like this: I just couldn't stand seeing the way the judge was treating Miss Sweet."

"And . . . how was he treating her?" Beulah felt her heart flutter in alarm.

"He wasn't very kind to her," Jim confessed. "Did a lot of yelling at her and said some pretty bad things."

"Can you tell me what he said?"

"No, ma'am, I can't," Jim mumbled. "I

can't repeat those words to a lady."

"Well then, what *can* you tell me?"

"I can tell you that the judge 'tied one on' one night and told me some things I'd sooner not have known."

"Like what?" Beulah asked.

"Well, after he'd been drinking, he stormed out into the yard and . . . I don't know why . . . came banging on the door of my quarters. It was real late."

"And what did he tell you?"

"Seems his family up in New York made him move away. They didn't want to be around him anymore. When he took Miss Sweet up there, he thought maybe they would soften toward him, since he had married a good, Southern lady."

"Why did they make him move away?" Beulah breathed the question, but she wasn't sure she wanted to know the answer.

"I'm not really sure, but he was saying something about him being from a big, in-fluential family, and they were mad for having to get him out of some trouble."

"Did he say what kind of trouble?" She didn't add: maybe because both of his wives died in accidents? But she was cer-tainly thinking it.

"No, ma'am," Jim said. "I'm sorry to tell you all this, Miss Beulah," Jim added. "But

I just couldn't keep it to myself any longer."

"I appreciate that, Jim," she said. "I really do appreciate it. Now you just clear your conscience, because you've done the right thing in telling Miss Sweet's good friend about this."

"I'm worried about her," Jim added. "She seems like a lady who has the perfect name — she's sweet! So please let me give you my phone number, and you call me if there's ever anything I can do for you or Miss Sweet."

"Would you be willing to tell the sheriff what you've just told me?" Beulah inquired gently, and there was a long silence on the other end of the line.

"Jim?" she urged.

"Oh, ma'am, I'd really rather not do that," he mumbled. "I almost got myself into some trouble one time — I was just a foolish youngster. But I never got caught for it." His voice stumbled. "Sometimes, how the judge looks at me, I think maybe he knows about that."

"I see." Beulah sighed. "Well, give me your phone number, please, just in case things get so bad that we need your testimony desperately."

"If things get that bad, I'll talk to the

266

sheriff, no matter what happens to me," Jim promised.

The cows were not happy when the milking took place earlier than usual that next morning, so the parlor was noisy with excessive mooing and much stamping of feet. So because of the noise and the intensity of their tasks, Beulah and Zion spoke little as they went about the milking. When the milk had been strained into stainless containers and put into the cooler, Beulah sighed deeply and told Zion of Jim's late night phone call. Zion turned beet red.

"I think we're talking about something very dangerous," Beulah added. "I don't know that we should continue with our plans. It's all too dangerous."

"You want to forget our plans, *now?*" Zion shot at her angrily. And without waiting for an answer, Zion grabbed Beulah's arm and ordered, "Let's go. We've got a long way to drive and important information to gather."

CHAPTER
— TWENTY-FOUR —

Much to Beulah's alarm, Zion used the state road only long enough to get to the bypass. As she entered traffic on the wide interstate, Zion started grinning.

"I never thought I'd say this," Zion started out. "But thank the good Lord for this interstate highway!"

"How can you say such a thing?" Beulah asked. "It's ugly, and we're stupid to get on this thing!"

"You know how long it would take us on state highways?" Zion asked, accelerating yet again and reaching maximum speed while Beulah clutched the dash in alarm.

"Longer," Beulah managed to grunt between clenched teeth.

"Would take us about five hours, I figure," Zion announced. "This way, it's only around two and a half."

Beulah seemed to relax a little. "Maybe I should have been brave and used this when I took Love-Divine to the seashore."

"When was that?" Zion asked, glancing at Beulah. "I didn't know anything about such a trip. Did you tell anyone else about it?"

"No."

"Why not?"

"I'm not sure," Beulah confessed. "It just seemed like a private, special thing for Love-Divine."

"A long drive," Zion commented. "Did she enjoy it?"

"Oh yes, especially going through all the small towns. She really liked that."

"Sounds like Love-Divine, sure enough," Zion laughed. "She was the most interested person I ever knew, especially about little details nobody else would even notice."

They rode in silence for a few minutes before Beulah added, "I wonder what she would think about us using King's Wood Sanctuary mostly as a place for spying on the judge and Sweet?"

"She would probably be completely in agreement, Beulah."

Beulah sighed. "I wonder."

They both lapsed into silence, remembering Love-Divine and thinking of the task they had set before them.

Later, Beulah asked, "How are you going to find the kind of equipment store we're looking for?"

"I've got a good notion of where the agricultural centers are," Zion explained. "And when we get closer, I'll leave the interstate and we'll mosey around some of the towns. There's a lot of cattle raising going on around there. We'll find what we're looking for."

Almost an hour and a half later, Zion proved that she was right. They had exited the interstate, an event that eased Beulah considerably, and not long afterward, they saw an agricultural equipment supply store. The low, concrete building was surrounded by tractors and other farm implements, and around back were numerous pens, milking stations, and chutes.

"I'd like to see a bull pen," Zion said to the young man who sauntered outside to help them. He nodded and led them through the yard, past horse trailers, portable corrals, and cattle chutes. They approached what looked like a very heavy corral, and the young clerk pointed to it.

"That's the best bull pen we sell," he said proudly. Zion stepped forward and rubbed her fingers appreciatively on the gleaming steel and examined the gate latch.

"Is this a good latch as well?" she asked,

270

arching her eyebrows.

"Yes, ma'am," the clerk said. "See? It's a double latch." He worked the double mechanism a few times, while Zion watched with rapt attention. "Awful important to have a good latch, you know."

"I know," Zion replied. "Now, would you please show me how that latch works one more time?" Zion asked, and the young man smiled and repeated the motions that would lock or release the mechanism.

"Like this?" she asked, leaning forward and working the mechanism herself.

"Yes, ma'am," the clerk smiled. "That's the way it works."

Zion looked at Beulah and nodded her head.

"We appreciate your time," Zion said to the clerk. "Let us think it over a bit, and if you don't mind, we'll just walk around and look at some of the other things you have."

"You all help yourselves and take as long as you want," he said. And then he looked a little quizzical and added, "You got yourself a bull?"

"You could say that," Zion answered.

"Well, if I can help you all any more, just come inside and give me a holler," the clerk said, before he touched his finger to his eyebrow in a small salute and turned and walked away.

"What a charming young man," Beulah said, when the clerk was out of hearing range.

"Huh?" Zion clearly had other things on her mind. "What did you say?"

"I said he's a charming young man," Beulah repeated, but Zion had already turned her attention back to the locking mechanism. She locked and unlocked it a few more times, and then she turned to Beulah. "I think I've seen enough."

For most of the drive back, Zion was silent, and Beulah knew that her mind was working hard, trying to figure out exactly how to open the gate to the judge's bull without being in the barn herself. After they had filled up the tank at a gas station, Zion said, "Beulah, you go ahead and drive, please."

"On the interstate?" Beulah was clearly frightened.

"Just get into the right lane and stay there. It's easy. You do know how to drive a truck that has a manual transmission, don't you?"

"Of course," Beulah snorted. "All right."

As Beulah drove, watching her side and rearview mirrors carefully, Zion took a piece of paper and began making sketches that looked suspiciously to Beulah as if she were practicing geometry. After a while, Zion gave out a satisfied grunt.

"That will do it!" she said.

"What will do it?" Beulah asked.

"Open the latch on the bull pen." Zion nodded and smiled broadly. "I knew I could figure it out. Just took me a little time."

"So how does it work?" Beulah asked.

"You just tend to driving," Zion ordered. "When we get home, I'll explain it to you."

As soon as Beulah turned Zion's truck into the driveway, they could hear the cows mooing most mournfully.

"Gotta get 'em milked pronto!" Zion yelled. So they were both out of the truck almost before it came to a stop, and they ran to the milking parlor to accomplish the much-needed milking. They worked quickly, efficiently, and silently. When all was accomplished, Beulah and Zion arched their tired backs, while the cows, once again comfortable but long of memory, gazed at them reproachfully.

"They sure don't like any change in their routine," Zion commented, and that simple statement set Beulah to remembering her

273

own quiet routine, prior to the *judge mess,* as she privately thought of it.

She studied the large, liquid-brown eyes of the Jerseys, which seemed to hold the bitter glint of reproach. Their eyes seemed so different from their usual expression of gentle peacefulness.

"I know how they feel," she said, and she was surprised at the sound of her voice. She had meant only to think the words, not say them aloud.

"Yes," Zion agreed. "Sometimes, life can purely turn you upside down."

Strangely, Beulah felt tears come up in her eyes, and a bitterness deep in her chest throbbed a steady, alarming beat. Zion, busy straining the milk, didn't notice.

"I want things to go back to normal," Beulah choked out the words, drawing a startled glance from Zion. "I want to go bird watching again, not judge watching! I want to enjoy a cup of tea at the tearoom without wishing Sweet or Love-Divine could be there with me. I want things to go back to normal!" The last words were almost howled, and Zion put aside the strainer and approached Beulah. If Zion could have brought herself to hug Beulah, she would have, but that wasn't Zion's way. When Zion spotted weakness or sadness, she always got angry with it.

"Don't do this to yourself!" she ordered sternly.

"It's too much!" Beulah sobbed. "I don't want to live like this!"

"OK, then let's get this thing taken care of and out of our way." Zion's voice was wickedly calm. "Come in the kitchen and let me show you what we're gonna do about that bull pen."

On the back of an envelope, Zion drew a diagram that showed how they could release the bull into the barn itself, and in such a way that they didn't endanger themselves.

"We'll use lightweight wire, but looped, so when the latches have been released, I can pull on only one end of the wire and get it all out without going back into the barn. We'll wrap it around both elements of the latch on the bull pen, spool out the wire until we are out of the barn, release both latches, and then pull the wire out through the crack under the barn door. That way, we let out the bull, but we don't endanger ourselves. When the judge opens the barn door, he won't be expecting that bull to be loose in there, and if we are lucky, the judge will have his 'accident.' "

Beulah's head began throbbing, and she pushed away an image of the judge's mangled body being ripped to pieces on the sharp horns of an infuriated bull.

"When?" Beulah asked.

"Tomorrow night, I reckon," Zion answered. "We're both too tired tonight to try something like this."

"Tomorrow night," Beulah repeated. "And after tomorrow night, Sweet will be safe, and life can go back to normal." Then she added, "Do you think you can handle the milking by yourself in the morning?"

"Why," Zion asked. "What are you going to be doing?"

"I'm going to sit in the rocking chair on my own porch and pretend that tomorrow is just another routine day. Pretend that I am leading a perfectly normal life for a Southern lady in a small town."

When Beulah opened the door to her own house, the phone was ringing.

"Hello?" She was breathless from her dash across the living room.

"Beulah? This is Sweet," came the soft voice on the other end of the line.

"Sweet! Are you OK?"

"Yes. The judge just went down to the barn, so I thought I'd take a little minute to call and let you know that I'm all right. I know you've been worried about me."

"Yes, you're right about that." Beulah slumped into a chair and kicked off her shoes. "And may I please ask why you have to wait until the judge is out of the house before you can use the phone?" It was a blunt question, but one that simply fell out of Beulah's mouth before she could stop it.

"W-well." Sweet was stammering. "He just likes me to pay attention to him and not anybody else. It's pretty simple, actually."

"There's nothing simple about it, Sweet. He's controlling you. He's controlling every single aspect of your life! He won't let you see your friends, he won't let your friends come to see you, he won't let you out of the house unless he's with you."

"That's right," Sweet agreed.

"And he has a terrible temper. You said that yourself," Beulah reminded her.

"As long as I don't do something to set him off, everything's fine," Sweet argued.

"And if you do something to 'set him off,' as you put it, then it's *your* fault that he loses his temper?"

"Well . . . yes, I suppose," Sweet agreed.

"Oh, Sweet." Beulah felt like crying. "Can't you see what's happening? Can't you see it?"

"What's happening is that I am married to a very powerful, very sensitive man, and yes, sometimes he loses his temper. But everything is OK right now."

"And you'll settle for that?" Beulah questioned.

"This isn't what I called to talk to you about." Sweet retreated into the safety of a subject unrelated to herself.

"What did you call to talk about?" Beulah was incredulous that Sweet was speaking of that powerful, controlling, evil man as someone she was willing to put up with.

"I called to tell you that there's a library board meeting tomorrow night. Perhaps while the judge is out, you could stop by to see me. We can have a cup of tea, at least. And we can get Wildwood to call us when the meeting ends, so you can get out ahead of his coming home."

Beulah's heart was racing. Is this how they could accomplish the rigging of the bullpen? Was it possible that Beulah would be sitting with Sweet, having something as perfectly normal as a cup of tea, while Zion worked in the barn to set up the "accident"?

"I'd like that, Sweet," Beulah said, trying to sound a cheerful note. "I'll talk to Wildwood in the morning and get it set up for her to call us when the meeting's over."

"You better tell her to expect trouble from the judge," Sweet added, hesitantly. "I wish I could do something to influence him, but I don't dare say a thing about the Save Our Library project. He's still upset about that."

"I'll tell Wildwood," Beulah promised. "What time does the meeting start?"

"At seven," Sweet said. "So you can come around that time, since he will have to leave before that. Just be careful. I don't want to upset him anymore than he's already upset."

Yes, Beulah was thinking. *If he gets upset, you just might have another bad fall!*

Beulah turned right around and called Wildwood at the library, knowing as she did that Wildwood worked until 9:00 p.m that day. She told her about wanting to see Sweet without upsetting the judge, and Wildwood agreed to phone Sweet's house when the meeting ended. Then she told Beulah that some of the other board members had met in secret, to discuss how to best handle the judge.

"They aren't going to give up their library without a fight," Wildwood said, unable to keep the pride out of her voice.

"Well, glory be! It's about time!" Beulah

cheered. "How on earth we ever let that man gain such a powerful position in our community is more than I can understand."

"We were just too trusting," Wildwood said. "But judge or no judge, we mean to win this fight! The only thing I don't quite understand is why you want me to call you at Sweet's when the meeting is over."

"He's going to be pretty upset, I suspect," Beulah said. "And he doesn't like for Sweet to have company."

"That doesn't surprise me one little bit," Wildwood said. "After I gave you that information about him, I did some research on abusive personalities, and one of the primary features is *control*. Men like that isolate their spouses and then take over control of everything — what the spouse says, what she reads, how she behaves."

"Well, it's pretty sad when a woman has to be around a man like that," Beulah said, working hard to resist spilling the beans about what she and Zion were planning as a means for eliminating the problem. The words were too close to spilling out, so she said, "Well, I better go now. You have a nice evening."

The last phone call she made that night was to Zion.

"Listen, Sweet just called me and asked me to come over tomorrow evening to see her. The judge will be at a library board meeting. Can you take care of that . . . business in the barn yourself, so I can keep Sweet occupied and unaware of what you're doing?"

"Yes," Zion sounded jubilant. "It's kind of a one-man activity anyway. You keep Sweet busy, and leave the barn business to me."

CHAPTER
— TWENTY-FIVE —

Beulah tossed and turned most of the night, even getting up twice and sitting in the living room, reading her Bible in what almost seemed to be desperation. Her mind went from scripture to a replay of almost every single sermon she had ever heard on every Sunday morning of her entire life, and by the time dawn broke, she had decided that she couldn't go through with another attempt on the judge's life, not even for Sweet.

"If God wants something to happen, He will have to make it happen," she reasoned. "Vengeance is mine, saith the Lord," she quoted, followed by a long prayer for God to intervene in Sweet's predicament and another prayer for Him to help save their library.

As soon as full daylight came, she dressed and drove to the bird sanctuary. She would wait there until the judge went out to the barn, and then she would go inside and talk to Sweet, come right out and ask as many questions as she wanted to ask and make sure that Sweet would give an open, honest answer to each and every question. And if the judge came back while Beulah was still there, she would stand up to him, defy him, and threaten him with whole-community action unless he stopped treating Sweet like a prisoner!

Beulah's wait was a long one, but at last, the judge left the house and headed toward the barn. As he passed the shed where his shiny new tractor was parked, he detoured enough to run his hand over the tall wheels. Yes, he certainly did like his possessions . . . and he evidently regarded Sweet as one of them.

When Beulah crossed the backyard this time, she did not crouch down and run, as she had done in the past. Instead, she walked resolutely and with her head held high, and she knocked at the back door and called out, "Sweet? It's Beulah."

Sweet came to the door with a worried frown on her face.

"What on earth?" Sweet whispered.

"Don't whisper!" Beulah ordered, and Sweet's mouth fell open in surprise. Beulah didn't wait for an invitation, but she brushed past Sweet and went into the kitchen, where she sat down at the table.

"What are you doing here?" Sweet asked, still in a whisper.

Beulah banged her hand down on the table, making Sweet jump.

"Sweet, there are things going on that you don't know anything about," she started. "We've all tried to keep from hurting your feelings, but things have gone far enough now that you need to know."

"What are you talking about?" Sweet asked, sitting down across from Beulah.

"Did you know that the judge has been married before? Twice?" Beulah asked.

And Sweet's startled expression clearly stated that she had not known about those wives.

"Twice?" she repeated. "Well, I guess that's all right," she murmured at last.

"No, it's not all right," Beulah contradicted her. "Both of his wives died . . . accidental deaths."

Sweet thought for long moments before she said, "And?"

"We're afraid for you," Beulah said. "We're afraid that the judge may do something to hurt you."

"No," Sweet said. "I don't think he would."

"I saw the canary," Beulah said. "I saw what he did to it."

Sweet's eyes filled up, but she said nothing.

"I saw the canary!" Beulah said again. "If he would do that to a poor, helpless little bird, he would do anything! And Sweet, I hate to tell you this, but the judge called me in the middle of the night and said that he would find a way to hurt you where the bruise wouldn't show! That canary is what he meant!"

Still, Sweet said nothing. She stared down at the tablecloth and softly took her bottom lip between her teeth. When the front door opened, both women jumped. The judge came into the kitchen, and when he saw Beulah there, he stopped right in his tracks.

"What are *you* doing here?" he asked in a gruff voice.

"I am visiting my friend," Beulah said evenly, slowly rising from the chair. Sweet looked back and forth from the judge to Beulah, over and over again.

"That's it!" the judge yelled. "I'm taking out a restraining order against you and that Zion person. You will not come and go at your own wills in *my* home!"

"This is Sweet's home, too," Beulah argued. And then she looked directly at Sweet. "Do you want me to visit, Sweet?" she asked pointedly.

"I . . ." Sweet's eyes were locked on the judge's face. Her chin trembled, and finally, she said, "Maybe it's better if you don't come." There was nothing left for Beulah to do but to leave, and she did.

All afternoon, Beulah went about doing mindless, everyday things. She cleaned out the refrigerator, stripped the bed, and laundered the sheets. All those mundane chores seemed to calm her. Unimportant, everyday things to store up in her soul for the most important, dynamic thing any human being could do to another. For any doubts she may have had were now completely gone.

At five o'clock, she called Zion.

"Zion, are we all set?"

"We're set," Zion confirmed. "I've got the wire, the diagram, and a flashlight. I'll pick you up around six thirty. We can park on the other side of the bird sanctuary and wait until we see his car go down the highway. You go visit with Sweet, and I'll take care of the work in the barn. Then I'll come back to my truck and sit there until you come."

"We have to be extra careful," Beulah warned. "The judge said he was going to take out restraining orders against both of us."

"What?"

"I'll explain later. And we also have to be careful not to let Sweet catch onto what we're really doing," Beulah said, unnecessarily.

"Six thirty," Zion repeated.

By six forty-five, Beulah and Zion were parked well off the road, in between the highway and the edge of the sanctuary, with the truck lights turned off. They sat in silence, watching the end of the driveway and waiting to see the judge's black car come out and turn away from them, toward town.

Zion was mentally going over again and yet again the diagram she had developed, the diagram for wiring the bull pen gate, using a looped wire so that she could undo the latch from the safety of the big barn doors and then pull on only one end to pull the wire away, so that no trace of tampering would remain.

Beulah was remembering the crumpled, broken, feathered body of the canary in the trash can on Sweet's back porch. That, and Sweet's face when she had to agree with the judge that Beulah and Zion could not come onto the property again. Those memories burned her throat and made her relish imagining that evil beast of a man being surprised by the bull's massive muscles and the sharp horns and the murderous attitude.

"So you think he took out a restraining order?" Zion asked.

"He said he was going to do that," Beulah answered. "I don't know if he's done it . . . yet."

Just at that moment, car lights came eerily down the driveway, throwing bright beams across the dark highway and then turning, as they knew would happen, away from them and toward town. Zion waited until the taillights were out of sight, and then she flicked on her flashlight. "Six fifty-five," she announced. "Let's go."

Silently, they made their way through the sanctuary, with Beulah following Zion and the flashlight.

"You got your own flashlight, for getting back?" Zion asked.

"Right here." Beulah patted her purse.

When they arrived at the edge of the sanctuary, Zion went off toward the barn, and Beulah crept across the backyard toward the same back porch she had visited earlier. This time, she knocked on the back door, and the porch light came on immediately.

"Sweet? It's me," Beulah called, and she watched as the door opened just a crack.

Sweet's voice was almost a whisper.

"Beulah, maybe we better do this another time," she mumbled. "I'm not feeling very good right now. And you know what the judge said."

"Of course you aren't feeling good," Beulah agreed. "How could you feel good about anything, living like you're having to."

Reluctantly, Sweet opened the door. Her face was swollen and her eyes were red. As Beulah entered, Sweet's face crumpled. Beulah reached out and swept her arms around Sweet and held her, while Sweet snuffled into her shoulder.

"Come on, I'll make us some tea," Beulah said in a soothing tone. Sweet allowed herself to be led to the kitchen table, and she sat quietly while Beulah put the kettle on to boil.

At the barn, Zion carefully opened the main door and peered into the deep twilight of the interior. Moving with deliberate slowness, she entered the barn and turned on her flashlight. She shone the beam around and saw sacks of cattle feed, bales of hay, farm tools, and then the thick, shiny bars of the bullpen. At first, she thought the pen was empty, and her heart fell. If the bull was out in the pasture, all of the planning was for nothing!

But then she heard a whoosh of expelled breath and a deep snort. From between the shiny bars of the pen, a huge muzzle protruded, sniffing the air. And then the muzzle retreated, to be replaced by deep red eyes filled with a malevolent passion. The bull snorted loudly and paced around in the pen, agitated, obviously, by Zion's presence.

"Easy," Zion crooned. "I'll bother you only for a few minutes." She approached the double latch — identical in every way to the one she and Beulah had examined down in South Georgia — and began carefully looping the thin wire around the two latches. The hot smell of the bull was strong in her nostrils, and she had trouble making herself calm down enough to place the wires just so.

That accomplished, Zion began backing toward the door, unreeling the looped wires as she went and at the last, feeding them under the main door of the barn. When she closed and bolted the barn door, she breathed a deep sigh of relief. And then, ever so carefully and slowly, she began a steady pull on the wires. She felt a resistance, and she held her breath and continued to pull, hearing first one and then a second satisfying click. The pen was unlatched. She carefully began pulling only on one of the wires, feeling it unravel from the latch, as she had planned, and at the last, she pulled out the whole unlooped wire, rolled it up, and tucked it into her pocket.

Inside the barn, she could hear heavy hooves crunching in the hay, and she almost fell over backward when the steamy breath of the huge bull blew through the crack in the main door with a loud snort. Resisting the urge to run, she walked away quietly and went back to where the truck was parked on the other side of the sanctuary.

"It's done!" she whispered to herself.

In the kitchen, Beulah poured boiling water into two cups, plunked in two tea bags, and sat down at the table across from Sweet. She added cream and sugar to the tea and stirred slowly, avoiding looking directly at Sweet.

"Do you want to talk about anything?"

"No," Sweet replied. "I just can't." A long silence followed, and Beulah reached across the table and put her hand over Sweet's.

Sweet looked full into Beulah's eyes, her

own reflecting utter misery. Then Sweet looked away and slowly drew her hand from under Beulah's.

"He's got a temper," Sweet said simply. "It's my fault."

"No!" Beulah fairly shouted. "It's not your fault!"

"But I provoke him!" Sweet whined.

"It's not your fault," Beulah repeated. "You don't *cause* him to do anything! He makes his own choices!"

"But he says it's my fault!"

"Maybe in his mind, he believes that," Beulah said. "But it isn't true."

"Beulah, what am I going to do?" Sweet's question carried no resolve behind it. It was simply a soft question that Sweet believed had no answer.

"Leave him. Leave him *now!* Come home with me right now, and we'll get a restraining order against him."

"I can't," Sweet said. "No law enforcement officer is going to order such a thing against a retired *judge,* for Heaven's sake!"

"Is that what he told you?" Beulah asked.

"Yes, and I believe him."

"Listen, we can work something out. We can take you far away to where he would never find you. Start you a new life, one without him." Even as Beulah spoke those words, she was thinking that, if Sweet would come away with them now, and if Zion had been successful with the bullpen latches, the judge would be killed for absolutely no reason at all — except that Zion would have said he needed to be exterminated anyway, just for being such a monster!

"No," Sweet replied. "No." Beulah felt a bittersweet relief. The plan would go forward.

"If you change your mind at any time, you just call me, and I'll come and get you. I'll make sure you're safe," Beulah said earnestly.

For a very long time, the two friends sat together at the table, saying nothing, but sharing a deep grief. When the phone rang, they both jumped with the shock of that sudden sound. Sweet answered the ring.

"Thank you," she said, and hung up. "Meeting is over."

Beulah washed out their cups, dried them, and put them back into the kitchen cabinet. Then she gave Sweet a long hug.

"Listen, Sweet, he's probably going to be in a bad mood, after the board meeting," she said. "Why don't you meet him on the front porch and tell him you've heard some strange noises from the barn."

"But why would I do that?" Sweet asked, perplexed.

Beulah was thinking fast. "Well, I really did think I heard something out there," she lied. "And besides, maybe if he gets something else on his mind, he won't be so mad when he comes inside."

"Oh, OK," Sweet agreed, still wearing a small frown.

Beulah went out of the back door, and using her small flashlight, she made her way through the sanctuary and emerged on the other side to find Zion sitting in the truck.

"Let's go," Zion said, starting up the engine.

"How did it go?" Beulah floated the question out slowly.

"Perfect!" Zion fairly yelped. "Let's go before the judge shows back up!" Zion guided the truck onto the highway, but without turning on the lights until they had turned a curve and were beyond the line of sight from the end of the driveway.

When Zion stopped in front of Beulah's house, both women sat in silence for a few minutes.

"How's Sweet?" Zion asked.

"Not good."

"Maybe she'll be better tomorrow," Zion suggested, sending a shudder through Beulah.

Beulah opened the truck door and looked across at her own front porch.

"Yes, maybe she will," she answered.

CHAPTER
— TWENTY-SIX —

That night, Beulah's sleep was filled with strange, disturbing dreams — horns and hooves, angry bellows and blood, until she was shocked out of her nightmare by the ringing phone. She glanced at the clock — midnight! Who could be calling her at this time of day? Then her head cleared and she remembered the plan to have that bull in an unexpected place when the judge went into the barn, and goose bumps flooded across her arms.

"Hello?" She managed to breathe into the receiver.

"Beulah? It's Sweet!"

"What's wrong?"

"The judge . . ."

"The judge? *What?*"

"He's in the hospital, and I need to go over there."

"What happened?" Beulah held her breath.

"They took him in an ambulance,"

Sweet explained. "There wasn't room for me to ride with him in the ambulance, and I don't have a clue about how to drive that big car of his. I thought that I could be good and patient and wait until morning to call you, but I just can't wait any longer. Can you take me to the hospital?"

Again, Beulah asked, "What happened?"

"That bull," Sweet explained. "I guess he got out of his pen somehow, and I told the judge about hearing some strange noises — only I said that *I* heard them. Not a single mention of you or your being here. And the judge went to check, and that bull got him!"

"Got him? How is he?" Again, Beulah's heart was hammering in her ears.

"I don't know," Sweet confessed. "I didn't even know anything was wrong until he was staying at the barn for such a long time. Finally, I went to check on him, and he was just lying there. I called for an ambulance and it came and they took him to the hospital. I haven't heard anything else. And I'm sorry to call you in the middle of the night, but I just couldn't wait any longer!"

"I'll be right there," Beulah said. "Just as soon as I can throw on some clothes."

"The bull's gone. I don't know where," Sweet said in something of a dreamy voice.

"Call the sheriff and tell him the bull's gone," Beulah directed. "Be sure to do that right now. And then wait on the front porch for me. No . . . if that bull's loose, you better wait inside. I'll honk my horn for you and come up just as close as I can to the front porch."

Beulah hung up the phone and dialed Zion's number right away.

Zion sounded fully awake which, of course, she usually was. Zion operated under sleep-deprivation every day of her life. It was something she had learned to live with. Stay up late; get up early to work in the creamery.

"Zion? The judge is in the hospital, but I don't know what his condition is. I'm on my way to pick up Sweet and take her there." Beulah didn't even give Zion a chance to say a word before she hung up and headed for her bedroom.

Sweet was standing just inside her front door when Beulah's car came skidding into the yard. Beulah reached over and opened the passenger door for Sweet, who dashed across the porch and got in without a word. They roared off down the driveway and onto the highway that would take them to town.

"He was all crumpled up," Sweet said suddenly.

"Was he conscious?" Beulah asked, but she really didn't want to know. She was just trying to react to the situation as if it had truly been an accident, one in which she had no hand at all.

"No, not really," Sweet said. And then she was silent again for a few minutes before she admitted, "I felt sorry for him." Beulah glanced at her sharply but said not a word. After all, Sweet was only living up to her name!

At the hospital, the receptionist sent them to a waiting room, where they sat in silence, until finally, a doctor came out.

"How is he?" Sweet asked, and again, Beulah was surprised to hear a note of what sounded like real concern in Sweet's voice. A man like the judge didn't deserve the love of a good woman, but that didn't seem to have anything to do with it. Deserve it or not, he had Sweet's love. Or perhaps he had only her fear. One way or another, that wouldn't last.

"He's had a hard time," the doctor admitted. "Broken arm, bruised shoulder. Some scrapes. Some pretty bad internal bruising. But he will recover." In one way,

Beulah was relieved to hear that the judge wasn't in danger of imminent death, but in another way, she was deeply disappointed. Well, at least she and Zion didn't have to worry about being charged with murder. It isn't a murder until someone is dead.

And she also thought about the fact that the broken arm and internal bruises would mean that the judge would be somewhat incapacitated for a time. Sweet was going to need help, both in caring for him and in running the farm. Beulah decided right then and there that she would call Jim — she was sure he had given her his phone number — and ask him to come back to work, at least until the judge was completely healed. Beulah also dared to hope that, perhaps, this would change everything. Take the hard edge off the judge's temper. Make him a better man in some strange way. One thing was certain: with a broken right arm, he wasn't likely to be able to crush any more canaries!

Beulah and Sweet stayed at the hospital until Sweet was able to see the judge. Beulah could not bring herself to go into the room, but when Sweet pushed open the door, she could see his figure under a sheet, with his arm in a cast and sling. The thick-fingered hand extended out from the plaster cast, and all Beulah could think about was that same hand breaking the neck of a simple little bird that had never done anything against him. That he had crushed to death, just to hurt Sweet!

She felt herself filling up with tears and anger, and she went to find a pay phone so she could let Zion know that — for better or worse — probably for worse — they had failed.

The phone rang four times before Zion answered.

"It's Beulah. He's going to recover."

"Then we'll have to try something else," Zion said matter-of-factly.

"Maybe not," Beulah reasoned. "He's pretty badly hurt. Maybe this will change everything."

"That's wishful thinking, Beulah," Zion scolded.

"Maybe so, but I can tell you one thing: he's not going to be in good enough shape to do any hitting at all."

"It doesn't always have to be physical hitting that hurts," Zion added. "You can hurt someone with words just as easily. Only then, there aren't any bruises any-body can *see*."

"Well, I'm going to try to convince Sweet to stay with me the rest of tonight, and then I'm going to call Jim and see if he can come back, just until the judge gets well."

"That's a good idea," Zion said. "But don't go fooling yourself into believing any of this is going to change that blasted mean streak in that stinking vermin!"

"The only thing I can think about is that now the judge has come into contact with something bigger and stronger than himself. And maybe that will make a difference," Beulah said.

Zion said not another word, but Beulah heard her grunt of disgust as they hung up.

When Sweet came out of the judge's room, Beulah had a hard time reading her face. Perhaps what it revealed was a curious mixture of concern and justification?

"Sweet, you come stay with me tonight," Beulah said. "You don't want to stay out at the farm all by yourself. I'll call Jim and see if he will come back, just until the judge recovers."

"Oh, yes," Sweet said. "I liked Jim so much. I was sorry when he left. And thank you, Beulah. I'll take you up on your offer."

"How did the judge look?" Beulah couldn't resist asking.

"Strange," Sweet replied. "So strange. Seeing him all helpless like that!" Then Sweet managed the most unusual smile Beulah had ever seen on anyone's face.

Beulah and Sweet went by the farm to get some of Sweet's things for the night. While Sweet packed nightgown, robe, and toothbrush, Beulah noticed the judge's red silk robe hanging over the arm of a chair in the bedroom. Somehow, the vision of the bull came into her imagination — couldn't it be true that the judge was wearing a "red flag" from the beginning?

When Beulah took Sweet into her own home, it was one of the greatest pleasures Beulah had ever known. She ushered Sweet into the guest bedroom, and while Sweet was getting unpacked and settled, Beulah went into the kitchen and made them two cups of hot cocoa topped with whipped cream.

Sweet came out of the guest room wearing her nightgown and robe, and she settled at the kitchen table across from Beulah, taking the cup between her hands and sipping the creamy hot chocolate gratefully. When Sweet looked up at Beulah, something about her eyes was more relaxed. Beulah smiled at her and nodded encouragement. At least, as long as her dear friend, Sweet, was in Beulah's home, no one would hurt her. Beulah felt as if she had suddenly turned into an Amazon!

"Are you hungry?" she asked Sweet. "I can make something that will be easy on your stomach — some soft scrambled eggs and dry toast?"

"No, I'm really not hungry," Sweet answered. "The cocoa is quite enough, thanks."

"Well, when you finish, you go ahead and go to bed. I know you must be absolutely exhausted, what with the night you've had."

"That sounds good," Sweet admitted.

Sweet retreated to the guest room, and Beulah dialed Jim's phone number. She glanced at the clock — 4:00 a.m. Probably too early, but she didn't want to wait.

Jim answered on the third ring, and he sounded clear and wide awake.

"Jim? This is Beulah — Miss Sweet's friend?"

"Oh, yes, ma'am," he answered most courteously. Without even seeing him, Beulah could well imagine him sweeping off his hat, so deeply sincere and polite his voice came across.

"Jim, the judge has had an . . . accident, and Miss Sweet could really use your help. Can you consider coming back, just until the judge has recovered? Help Miss Sweet with him and also help run the farm?"

"Well," Jim hesitated. "Do I have to take care of that bull?"

"That bull is what caused the accident," Beulah said, almost believing her own words. "He's loose somewhere — we don't know where," Beulah continued. "And even if the sheriff finds him, I think Sweet should make arrangements for him to be taken care of someplace else. I don't think the judge is going to want to be around that bull, ever again."

"Is the judge going to be okay?" Jim asked.

"The doctor said he will recover," Beulah said.

"I hope you won't think badly of me if I say that I wish I could have seen that!"

"Why, Jim!" Beulah admonished, feeling completely the hypocrite — chiding Jim for his little comment, when she and Zion had been so instrumental in the accident itself.

"Yes, ma'am," Jim said. "I can come to-morrow afternoon. Will that be okay?"

"Miss Sweet is staying at my house, so please come by here to pick her up before you all go back to the farm. I'm on Andrews Street, just beyond the courthouse. And please, let the first thing you do be to fix that flat tire on her car, so she can get around — have some freedom."

"Do you remember what I told you about why I *really* left?" Jim asked.

"I do," Beulah assured him. "I think things may be quite different now."

"Maybe that's just wishful thinking," he said.

"You sound just like Zion," Beulah said.

"Maybe you should listen to us then," Jim said, with a slight edge in his voice. "I won't stay around and hear the judge say such awful things to Miss Sweet, you know."

"I know that. I still think things may be better, but if they aren't, I'm depending upon you to tell me," Beulah added.

"Well, I'll be glad to do that," Jim said. "And I hope you're right. Listen, I'll come by your house tomorrow afternoon and pick up Miss Sweet. And I'll stay as long as she needs me — or as long as I can stand being around the judge," he amended.

As soon as Beulah hung up the phone, it rang again.

"Miss Beulah?" asked a young man's voice. "This is the sheriff's department calling. I'm sorry to bother you at this hour, but you need to know that we got the judge's bull. We tried calling out at the farm, but there's no answer."

"Yes, I know. Miss Sweet is staying here with me tonight. I don't know what to do about the bull. Jim, the judge's former handyman, is coming back tomorrow so Miss Sweet won't be out at the farm all alone, and I know for a fact that he doesn't want anything to do with the bull."

"What do you want us to do with him?"

"Can't you please put him into a pasture somewhere until we find out?"

"I'll do my best, ma'am. Might be some farmer around here would keep him for his services."

"Services?" Beulah was clearly confused.

The young man from the sheriff's department cleared his throat. "Uh, I mean the bull's *services* to . . . cows." His voice stumbled to a stop.

"Oh!" Beulah exclaimed. "Oh!"

"Yes, ma'am, we'll take care of that and let you know what we've arranged." Hurriedly, the embarrassed young man hung up the phone.

"Oh!" Beulah exclaimed one last time.

★ ★ ★

Even though Beulah got up very early, as she was in the habit of doing, to get out to Zion's creamery on time, Sweet was already up and in the kitchen.

"I've made us some good biscuits," Sweet said, and Beulah could see that her face was rested and calm. The old Sweet was right there with her in the kitchen.

"And I'll fix us some scrambled eggs," Beulah added. As she broke the eggs into a bowl and beat them with a fork, she said to Sweet, "Jim will be coming this afternoon. He'll stop by here and pick you up. First thing he's going to do is fix your tire so you can come and go as you please."

"That's wonderful!" Sweet said. "That way, I can go see the judge every single day."

Beulah stopped beating the eggs. "Sweet, how *do* you feel about the judge?"

Sweet shrugged her shoulders. "He's my husband," she said simply.

"I know that," Beulah said with a hint of annoyance in her voice. "But how do you feel about him?"

"I married him," Sweet whispered. "I said 'for better or worse,' and 'until death do us part,' and I am bound by that. I know you think I should have gotten to

308

know him better before I married him, but I didn't. That was my decision, and I have to live with it."

"That sounds so sad!" Beulah was beginning to realize that Sweet was in a place in her mind where Beulah could not reach her, and when Sweet had said "until death do us part," Beulah felt goose bumps come up on her arms. "Don't you think you *deserve* to be treated with . . . respect?"

"Deserve? Well, maybe," Sweet confessed.

"You do!" Beulah fairly exploded. Sweet flinched visibly, and her eyes filled up with tears.

"I'm going to make this marriage work," Sweet whispered. "I thank you for everything you've done to help me, but this afternoon, as soon as Jim gets my flat tire fixed, I am going to the hospital to be with my *husband*."

Beulah said no more, but went back to beating the eggs. Sweet put butter inside the hot biscuits, and the two women ate a silent breakfast together.

At the creamery, Zion and Beulah went about their work silently, as was their usual way. But when the milking machines were all humming away, Zion asked Beulah,

"Did you get a look at the judge?"

"No," Beulah answered. "I didn't want to see him, but I know that he has a broken arm and some internal bruising."

"Well, Sweet's safe, for a little while at least. Until he gets well, that is," Zion growled. Then she smiled and raised her eyebrows into comical bows. "We almost did it, didn't we, Beulah?" And then Zion laughed and laughed until tears were streaming down her face.

"I think we came within a hairbreadth of being murderers!" Beulah mumbled. "Don't see anything so funny about that!"

CHAPTER
— TWENTY-SEVEN —

Once word got around town about the judge's accident and the fact that, at least for the present, he was safely sequestered in the hospital, people began to stir. Sweet's old Bible class came calling on her without hesitation, bearing food, as was their custom. Such a custom had arisen out of a common desire to provide everything someone would need to serve callers, as well as out-of-town family members. But, of course, no such family members came for the judge's accident.

And, of course, gossip in the town had been very quiet, but long filled with references to Sweet and the judge and how he was possibly mistreating her. The people pieced things together, but mostly, it was simply their imaginations. Only Beulah and Zion knew how things really were. Perhaps even Sweet herself wouldn't allow such knowledge to become real to her. When the Bible class ladies came to call, a few of them tried — quite tactfully — to bring up the subject of what they had heard about the judge, but Sweet was adamant about not saying anything negative about her new husband, so the ladies gained absolutely no insider knowledge about Sweet's life with the judge.

As for the judge himself, the town council authorized a modest flower arrangement that was sent to the hospital, but no one came to call on him. In fact, they were all scurrying around, trying to take full advantage of the judge's being temporarily restrained. They jacked up the Save Our Library project to full swing, and in response to their requests for community help, an anonymous donor put a huge envelope in the book drop, containing around a hundred dollars worth of postage stamps, writing paper, and envelopes already typed up and pre-addressed to members of the town council, which would have to approve or disapprove anything about the branch library. With the Bible class ladies calling on Sweet, and the library lovers moving as fast as possible with the project, everyone seemed to be in a flurry. They knew full well that once the judge was out of the hospital, he had the potential for roaring back to his larger-than-life self, and they knew that they all had to work hard and fast. Someone even called his doctor and asked him to please not let the judge go home too soon, but the doctor said that in all good conscience, he couldn't do that. "Well, we tried," they reasoned.

True to his word, Jim returned, and right away, he repaired Sweet's tire, so she went to the hospital almost every afternoon, often taking flowers or homemade cookies. She would sit in the judge's room in a quiet corner all afternoon, watching him as he studied all of the Court Television programs, scowling and complaining about the arguments and rulings and the sentencing. As his health improved, he took to waving his plaster-encased arm around, and during one such tirade, he swiveled his head around until he was looking right at Sweet.

"What I want to know is this: *Who* let that bull out of his pen?"

Sweet was completely taken aback by his rapid-fire question. "Why, I'm sure nothing like that happened," she sputtered.

"Yes, it did!" the judge bellowed. "That was a double-lock, and the bull couldn't have opened it himself! And where is he anyway?"

Grateful to have a question she could answer, Sweet replied, "He's at a local farm. He's staying there until you get well."

"So somebody's getting *my* bull's services — for free?" he roared even louder.

"Listen," Sweet tried to calm the judge. "I wish you'd get rid of him. He almost killed you!"

"And would you have liked that? Did *you* let him out?"

"Oh, how awful!" Sweet cried.

"Maybe you have dreams of being a rich widow," he growled. "Well, let me tell you right now that won't happen!"

"I never, *ever* thought such a thing!" Sweet was as close as she had ever come to being completely indignant. The judge raised one plaster-covered arm over his head, but the pain made him wince. "Damn!" he roared as loudly as possible. "And I'll bet you've got all your cronies coming and going in *MY* house!" he screamed at Sweet. At that moment, a nurse rushed into the room to try to calm him.

"Perhaps you better go now, Miss Sweet. We need to let the judge get his rest."

"I didn't . . ." Sweet tried to say, but finally, she just shook her head and left.

That evening, a tearful Sweet called Beulah. "He thinks I let that bull out of the pen!" she sobbed into the telephone.

"Oh, my Lord!" Beulah said. "Why would he think that?"

"He says that somebody had to open that pen," Sweet choked out the words. "But I never went near that barn! I would never have gone within a mile of that bull!"

"I know that." Beulah tried to calm Sweet.

"How on earth does he think I could go into that barn, open the pen, and be able to get out again alive?"

Beulah nodded miserably. It had taken Zion a good long time to figure out how to accomplish that very thing. "Listen, Sweet, I think he's just upset. Let him get calmed down, and then you can assure him that you never had a thing to do with that bull getting out. In the meantime, why don't you give him a day or so to cool off, before you go visiting him again," Beulah suggested.

"But I'm his wife," Sweet sobbed. "It's my job to be with him!"

"Look, Sweet, I don't know where you got all of your ideas about wifely duties, but nothing I've ever heard of requires you to put yourself in harm's way!"

To that, Sweet had nothing to say for long moments. "I think you're right, Beulah. We just need to give him some space so he can calm down."

As soon as Beulah hung up, she phoned Zion. "Listen," she started out, her voice shaking. "The judge has accused Sweet of opening the latches on the bull pen."

"How does he think she could do that?" Zion asked. "How does he think she could open the bull pen and not get herself killed in the process?"

"I don't know," Beulah said. "But something else has occurred to me: If Sweet can convince him that she didn't have anything to do with it, the judge may begin thinking the latches were faulty, and he'll probably bring a lawsuit against the manufacturer!"

"So?" Zion asked.

"So . . . if someone examines those latches, they'll find scratches on them and know that someone tampered with them. I've seen programs on television about how tiny things like that can implicate someone."

"They wouldn't find any scratches," Zion assured her.

"But how can you be so sure?" Beulah was working herself up into an emotional lather.

"Because I had the sense to use plastic-coated wire, that's why!"

"Oh, my Lord, Zion!" Beulah exclaimed.

"You're positively brilliant!"

"When I do something, I like to do it right," Zion bragged. "And when we try again, I'll be just as careful."

"Maybe we won't have to try again," Beulah said wishfully.

"So you're still trying to fool yourself?" Zion admonished. "I think he is an evil man, and I fully expect him to be even worse than he was, once he gets home. Don't you even think for a minute that Sweet is out of danger!"

"I hope you're wrong," Beulah said. "But if you aren't, at least Jim is there to kind of keep an eye on things."

Sweet stayed away from the hospital the next day, but the day after that, she tried once again. When she came into the judge's room, he looked at her with flat, almost black eyes, and Sweet caught her breath. In a flash, she could remember his eyes the way they looked when she first started meeting him at the tearoom. They had been soft and deeply brown, and slightly turned down at the corners. Those eyes had been full of love for her. These eyes were like the eyes of a snake — flat and cold and with nothing human behind them.

"Hello, dear," she tried to start out.

"Why are you out at the farm all alone with that Jim person?" the judge shot the question at her, and the eyes took on a blaze of accusation.

"What?"

"You are out there all alone, with *that man!*" the judge repeated.

"I had to have someone to help out, you know that." But Sweet's attempt to defend her decision about asking Jim to come back seemed to fall on deaf ears.

"Well, when I get out of here, I'll get everything straightened out," the judge said. Then he smiled strangely and added, "Get *you* straightened out, as well."

He crooked his finger at her, bidding her to come closer, and she did.

"What is it, dear?" Sweet asked.

"Did you know that hitting someone in the back of the head with a softball bat leaves the same kind of damage as her falling in the bathroom and hitting her head on the tub?" he whispered viciously. "Not a baseball bat — that's too small. But a softball bat is perfect!"

"What?" Sweet could hardly believe her ears!

"You heard me," the judge growled. "You heard me *right!*"

Sweet's mouth was still hanging open, but she took her usual seat in the corner of the room and waited in that terrible silence for him to speak again. He didn't. Two hours went by in silence, and then Sweet quietly left the room.

In her parked car, she wept bitterly, softly banged her head against the steering wheel, and wondered how she could have done so many things wrong! When she was able to drive, she went straight to Beulah's house.

Sitting at Beulah's kitchen table with a cup of hot tea in front of her, Sweet shared everything that had transpired that day.

"He didn't say anything else about my having released the bull," Sweet whispered miserably, "but now he's put out because I am staying out at the farm alone, with Jim there!"

"He sure has an imagination on him," Beulah agreed.

"I try so hard not to do or say anything to set him off," Sweet said. "And then he goes and imagines some infraction! I just can't seem to do anything right!"

Beulah leaned across the table and put her hands on Sweet's hands. "I'm so sorry you're having to go through all this, Sweet," she said earnestly.

"And that isn't all he said," Sweet continued. She gazed straight into Beulah's eyes and worried her bottom lip with her teeth before she spoke. "Beulah, he whispered to me that if you hit someone in the head with a softball bat, it makes the same kind of injury like they fell and hit their head on the bathtub."

"What?"

"Why would he say something like that to me?" Sweet cried. "Why?"

Beulah's face had gone paper-white, as all of the blood drained out of it. In her mind, she was back in Wildwood's office, listening to Wildwood say that the judge's second wife died from a fall in the bathroom.

"Sweet, listen to me! You've got to leave him! Leave him right now!" Beulah was fairly shouting.

"No!" Sweet whispered. "He won't hurt me." Then she amended her words, "He won't hurt me as long as Jim is around, and besides, he's pretty heavily medicated. Maybe he didn't know what he was saying."

"You don't know that for sure," Beulah warned. "Please stay here with me. We'll get a restraining order this very day!"

"I've already told you that no one is going to issue a restraining order on a retired judge!"

"No, that's what *he* said!"

"And I believe him!" Sweet argued. "Oh, I shouldn't have said anything to you about it," she wept. "I'm sure I can make things better between us. I'm sure I can!"

"Oh, Sweet," Beulah moaned. "This is a direct threat he's made against you! Please think over what I've said. And in the meantime, please be careful!"

"I will be careful," Sweet promised.

"And you remember what a softball lover the Reverend King was — so you look around in the attic and storage sheds and make sure there are no softball bats around!"

"Oh, Beulah! I think you're wrong! I can't believe he would actually do something so drastic!"

"You better at least consider such a possibility, Sweet. You *must!* Please be careful!"

As Sweet was driving back to the farm, she thought about Beulah's advice. Yes, she would need to check in the storage sheds and the attic, and if there were any softball bats around, she should get rid of them. Just in case!

Only three days after that, the judge was released from the hospital. Jim went to fetch him in the judge's big black car, and Sweet waited at home, making sure everything was ready for the judge's return. She had washed the sheets and dried them in the sweet sunshine, put a small tasteful vase of flowers on the bedside table, and had brought in extra pillows, for propping up the judge's bruised leg.

She watched through the window, nervously wondering if he had calmed down in the least. And then an awful thought went through her head. Jim himself was driving the judge back home, and nothing would prevent the judge from telling Jim his terrible suspicions! At the thought, Sweet's face burned.

Just at that moment, Sweet saw the big, black car pulling into the driveway. Jim parked as close as possible to the front door and then went around and helped the judge from the backseat. Using a cane, the judge still limped painfully, and he leaned heavily on Jim, though the scowl on his face revealed how much he hated doing that.

And Sweet could tell by Jim's haggard expression that the judge had, indeed, said something to him! When they came into the house, Jim did not meet Sweet's eyes, but the judge shot her an accusing glare.

After Jim had gotten the judge settled in his bed, he did manage one small, embarrassed glance at Sweet.

"Sorry, ma'am," he whispered to her as he left the room.

"I have a proposition for you," the judge announced suddenly.

"Proposition?" Sweet couldn't imagine what to expect next.

"Something to appease me for your indiscretion," he whispered.

"Indiscretion?" Sweet was appalled. "There has been no indiscretion!"

"Sure," the judge laughed. "Sure there hasn't! You and Jim out here all alone!"

"Please — there has been no indiscretion!"

"I say there has been," he said. "And I've been thinking about how you can make it up to me."

"There hasn't been," Sweet insisted. "But if there had been, how could I possibly have made it up to you?"

"Give me that piece of land up near Roverville."

"My great-granddaddy's old place?"

"Now listen," the judge started out. "This is a community property state, so if I were to leave you or allow you to leave me . . ." he hesitated long enough to give a short, barking laugh. "I would own half of

323

it anyway. But I want it all and in my name and mine alone."

"You want me to give you my great-granddaddy's place?" Sweet repeated, as if she couldn't believe what she was hearing.

"Yes." The judge's tone was flat and firm. "I want it!" he said, his voice rising.

"No! You can't have that! It's part of *my* heritage, not yours!" Now, Sweet allowed the full force of her emotions to surface. "My great-great grandparents farmed that land!"

The judge said nothing. He just glared at her.

"No!" Sweet repeated. "No!"

When the judge spoke again, it was in a vicious, low whisper: "Do you remember what I told you about a softball bat? Well?" he asked impatiently.

"Are you threatening me?" Sweet asked.

"Oh yes, you've got that right!"

"I can't believe this!" Sweet cried out. "I just can't believe this!"

"Well, you better believe it," cautioned the judge. "I mean to have that land."

Into Sweet's anguished mind came the vision of the story she had heard so many times, and in her imagination, she saw her ancestor dispatch a Union soldier by hitting him in the back of the head with a piece of stovewood. In her ears, she heard his laugh as the noose closed on his neck.

"No!" she repeated. "You'll have to kill me to get it!"

The judge's eyebrows went up, his mouth turned up at the corners, and at last, he laughed until he had tears in his eyes. "Well, you surprise me, Sweet! I'll have to give that much to you! I didn't think you had it in you to do that!"

Sweet watched him carefully, trying to figure out his unexpected reaction. When he finally stopped laughing, he frowned and said, "How about I just go after that nosy friend of yours . . . Beulah. Or, as you people say, Beulah-Land? And I'll bet you anything that so-called creamery that's run by Zion — Marching-to-Zion — is deficient in cleanliness. Shouldn't be too hard to get it shut down."

"What?"

"You heard me!" the judge growled.

"You wouldn't!" Sweet cried.

"Maybe you're right," he admitted. "And maybe you're not. Better not to take any chances. I mean to have that land!"

Sweet stood for long, miserable minutes, studying his face, watching his eyes and seeing the burning anger in them. "Oh, Lord," she said at last.

"Whatever," the judge answered. "Now, I'd like a good stiff drink, if you will be kind enough to pour one for me."

The uncustomary, good-mannered words surprised Sweet, and just for a moment, she felt light-headed, as if something she had been leaning against had shifted just a bit.

"I'll be glad to," she finally answered.

"And bring some writing paper," he added. "I can't write myself, because of my arm, but I can dictate to you."

CHAPTER
— TWENTY-EIGHT —

As soon as Beulah returned home from the milking parlor at Zion's her phone rang.

"Beulah? This is Wildwood," the voice said.

"Is everything OK?" Beulah asked, because she had immediately picked up a hint of alarm in Wildwood's voice.

"I just thought you would want to know that the judge called our reference desk yesterday from the hospital and asked for the mailing addresses of each town council member."

"And you gave them to him?" Beulah inquired.

"Of course I did," Wildwood sounded offended. "That's my job, you know — providing information for anyone who wants it."

"Even if he's going to use that information to try to close the library?"

"Even then," Wildwood whispered.

"Well, I guess he's moving beyond letters

to the editor of the newspaper then."

"That's right," Wildwood confirmed. "The town council meets in one week, and I'm just praying he will still be confined at home. It's bad enough for him to write the letters, but it would be even worse if he came to the council meeting."

"Thanks for letting me know, Wildwood. I'll see you at the Homework Helper Program."

On her way to the library, Beulah stopped in at the local clothing store and bought the new shirt for Tobia. She picked out one in a bright red and green plaid, and after a moment of hesitation, she asked the clerk to giftwrap it, complete with a red ribbon. For Tobia, his "prize" should look extra special, even before he opened it.

At the library, she found Wildwood right away.

"And how is the phone-in, write-in campaign for the town council going?"

"Very well," Wildwood beamed. "Someone even deposited about a hundred dollars worth of stamps and writing paper and envelopes right in the book drop. We made it available to people who were willing to write letters, and the supplies got used up right away."

"That's wonderful," Beulah responded. "Someone's heart is certainly in the right place!"

"Was it you, Beulah?" Wildwood inquired.

Beulah smiled. "No, not me. I think we both know it was Zion, though she hasn't said a word about it," Beulah replied. Just then, as usual, the children arrived, and the library fairly pulsated with the warm energy of their young minds and bodies.

Beulah's care over choosing Tobia's prize was well rewarded. He opened the package, lifted out the brand new shirt, and he fairly beamed at her. He was so pleased with it that he went right into the bathroom and came back out, proudly wearing it. When they worked together that afternoon, Beulah noticed with great satisfaction that for once, Tobia was wearing a new shirt with pristine cuffs. But another part of her heart was saddened. If the judge, somehow, managed to have their little branch library closed, what would happen to all the children like Tobia?

For the next few days, the letter-writing reached a fevered pitch, and Zion and Beulah held their breath about Sweet. For Beulah, there was some satisfaction in knowing that Jim was present on the farm, and he had promised to call her if the judge was being mean to Sweet. With all her heart, Beulah wanted to believe that the judge's accident had changed him forever. But whenever she thought like that, she always caught Zion glancing at her with a scowl on her face.

As it turned out, Zion was absolutely right. On the afternoon before the town council meeting that evening, Jim called Beulah.

"The judge is getting well in a hurry," he said. "He's asked me to drive him to the council meeting tonight, and of course, I will," Jim said. "But after that, I think I need to be going on back home."

"Have you heard anything from the judge or Sweet?" Beulah asked cautiously.

"Just some hollering on his part," Jim said. And then he added, "And some crying on her part."

"I'm sorry to hear that," Beulah confessed most sincerely.

"I'm sorry to have to tell you," Jim said. "I like Miss Sweet a lot, but he's such a hard man to be around!"

"You haven't seen any bruises, have you?"

"No, ma'am. Least while, not on the outside."

Beulah let his words sink in, and she was remembering what Zion had said about there being some bruises on a woman that you can't see.

"Well, thank you again, Jim, for coming back and helping out. And thank you for keeping an eye on . . . things."

CHAPTER
— TWENTY-NINE —

As soon as Beulah heard about the judge attending the town council meeting, she phoned Wildwood.

"He's going," she announced simply. "You better get on the phone and get as many library supporters to that meeting as you can," Beulah advised.

"And you'll be there?" Wildwood asked.

"I will, but I'll probably be a little late," she replied. "I've got something extremely important to do. But I'll say a prayer for you and the Save Our Library folks, and I'll try to get there as soon as I can."

That evening, Beulah waited in the sanctuary until she saw Jim help the judge into the car and drive away with him. With a catch in her throat, she also noticed that someone had let the air back out of the tires on Sweet's car.

Shuddering, she walked across the back-yard and let herself into Sweet's back door.

"Sweet?" she called out. Sweet was sitting at the kitchen table, snapping green beans into a bowl. The minute Beulah saw her eyes, she knew, without a single doubt, that Sweet was being abused again. Only this time, with blows that didn't leave bruises. Because Sweet's eyes were so loaded with pain, they almost seemed to turn down at the corners, such was the weight of that pain.

Beulah sat down at the table. "Are you OK?" she asked unnecessarily.

Sweet heaved a sigh and lifted her chin, which usually signaled that she would not, under any circumstances, speak against her husband. But then the chin dropped and Sweet looked down into her lap.

"He made me write letters for him," she said. "To the town council members, urging the closing of our little library." That confession brought high color to Sweet's cheeks. She looked up at Beulah, perhaps ready to see how much disappointment was registered in Beulah's face. But what Sweet saw was nothing except deep compassion.

"You had to do it, Sweet," Beulah soothed. "You didn't dare to refuse, did you?"

"No," Sweet answered. "Whatever he asks, I have to do."

"Is that out of fear?" Beulah asked. Sweet waited long minutes before she answered. "I used to think it was out of love," she said. "But yes, it *is* out of fear. And . . . there's something else."

"What?"

"I signed over my great-granddaddy's old property to him," Sweet confessed.

"What???" Beulah was incredulous. "Why on earth did you do that?"

"He . . . made me sign it over to him," Sweet confessed with deep misery in her words.

"How?" Beulah asked, frowning.

"He . . . just made me do it," Sweet whispered. She did not mention the threat to herself or to Beulah or to Zion's business.

There was a long moment of horrified silence, and then Beulah said, "Well, he's done that anyway, hasn't he? Killed you? Making you give over your great-granddaddy's land!"

Sweet sat in terrible silence, and in her mind, she watched once again as her long-ago ancestor killed a Union soldier with a thick log of stovewood and then laughed aloud as he was hanged for the deed. After a long, searching silence, Sweet whispered, "Yes! I feel as if I've lost my very soul!"

"Then you have nothing more to lose," Beulah said. "Oh, Sweet!"

The two women sat for a long time in mutual misery, and at the last, Beulah simply patted Sweet's arm and went out of the back door.

Beulah had trouble finding a parking space anywhere near the town hall. Cars were parked all over the place, even up on the grass, and when Beulah entered the courthouse, people were lined two deep along the entire corridor. Some of them carried signs that read SAVE OUR LIBRARY! As the proceedings went along, people close to the door would pass along the information about what was going on in the chambers. But Beulah wasn't too worried about getting inside. She had only to look at the multitude of people jamming the hallways to realize what the room itself must look like!

"Did the judge talk?" Beulah asked someone closer to the door.

"Did he ever! Ranted like a crazy man!"

"Good!" Beulah said. "I think enough people are onto him now that he won't have that much influence." And the people in the hallway, noticing that Beulah had arrived, parted themselves so that she could be closer to the door. She wasn't sure why they had accorded her such a courtesy, but she accepted it gratefully.

And she could hardly believe it when the moderator announced, "And now, we will hear from Tobia Johnston." Everyone standing near Beulah turned and grinned at her.

"What on earth!" Beulah whispered, placing her hand over her heart as she saw Tobia . . . *her* Tobia . . . approaching the front of the crowded room. At first, he moved hesitantly, but then he seemed to gain control of his situation and moved more confidently, finally even giving off a tiny swagger, and he was wearing the new shirt Beulah had bought for him. The lectern was far too tall for him, and someone fetched a wooden chair for him to stand on. He had no notes. He simply began speaking.

"Members of the town council, ladies and gentlemen, library patrons, and students of the Tea-Olive Library Homework Helper Program." Here, Tobia hesitated for a moment and grinned, as if the words had tickled his tongue. He wore that same grin the entire time he spoke. "I been . . . *I've* been in the Homework Helper Program for two years, and it's made me a better student. I get good grades!" he chortled happily, drawing a murmur of approval from the crowd for his Chanticleer pronouncement. At that unexpected sound from the audience, Tobia's eyebrows shot straight up and he glanced toward the side of the room. Beulah stretched her neck and saw the venerable Miss Dabney, of the Homework Helper Program, smiling and nodding her head at Tobia.

Reassured, Tobia went ahead: "Miss Beulah helps me, and she makes me want to make her proud of me." Again, he hesitated. "My mama's proud of me, too," he announced, looking into the crowd and smiling. "But she has to be proud of me, 'cause she's my mama." A murmur again went through the crowd, and Tobia waggled his shoulders in a gesture of delight. Then he suddenly went very sober. "But Miss Beulah doesn't have to be proud of me; I have to earn that! So I'm here to ask the town council members not to vote away our library. I know there's another library not too far away, and maybe some people who have cars wouldn't mind driving their children over there. But some of our mamas don't have cars, and we wouldn't have a way to get to another library. And besides, that other library wouldn't have Miss Beulah in it! We need our library here." Tobia hesitated, and he started to hop down from the chair. But then he turned once more toward the people gathered and whispered, *"Please!"*

A roar of applause followed him from the front of the room, and Beulah was surprised to find her eyes filled with tears. Several people standing near Beulah patted her shoulder and smiled.

"Shhh!!" someone whispered. "They're voting!"

In the hallway behind Beulah, people were dead silent, leaning forward, straining to hear the results of the votes. But they didn't have to wait long. Word was whispered along the line about how the council members were voting. So that before the head of the council could announce the vote, a rousing cheer went up from inside the meeting room and outside in the hallway.

The library was saved!

But Beulah knew that the judge would be in a terrible mood when he got home, so she went to find a pay phone so she could call Sweet and tell her about the vote, and about the importance of her keeping an extremely low profile once the judge got home.

As she came back to the hallway, people were cheering and Wildwood and the Friends of the Library folks were making victory signs with their fingers. Into the middle of all that celebration, Beulah was surprised to see Tobia coming toward her. He was holding the hand of a dark-complexioned, smiling woman, but he dropped her hand and ran to Beulah.

"I talked to the council members!" Tobia said, as if he couldn't quite believe it himself. "I told them not to close the library!"

"I know!" Beulah laughed. "I heard you! You were wonderful!"

A lady close by patted Tobia's shoulder. "What a beautiful job you did!" she added, smiling at Tobia and Beulah. "Why, with his speaking ability and his personality, I wouldn't be surprised to see him become the governor of this whole state one of these days!"

As the lady continued congratulating Tobia, Beulah saw the woman who had been holding Tobia's hand approaching her.

"This is my mama!" Tobia said proudly.

"Miss Beulah?" the woman asked. "Are you the Miss Beulah who helps Tobia?"

"Yes, I have that honor," Beulah said, gazing at Tobia and wondering how on earth he had found the courage to speak before the council and all those people crowded into the room.

"Thank you so much!" the woman said. "You have made a big difference in Tobia."

"I think we have to credit Tobia himself with that," Beulah said. And in her spinning head, all she could picture was the judge, all gruff and grumpy and angry at the world, faced with the simple testimony of a single child in the Homework Helper Program!

"I'm very proud of you, Tobia," Beulah said. "And I know your mama is proud of you, too."

"Oh, I am!" the woman exclaimed. "I always knew my Tobia here was a very special person, and tonight, he showed that to everybody!"

"Look, Miss Beulah," Tobia shouted. "I'm wearing my prize!"

"In more ways than you know, Tobia," Beulah answered him. "In more ways than you know."

As Beulah turned to leave, she was confronted with other joyous library supporters and patrons, who were shaking her hand and expressing their happiness.

"But I didn't do anything!" Beulah tried to protest.

"You tutored that blessed little boy!" they exclaimed. "And I think he's the one who convinced the council members that our library is doing something very important for our community!"

In the midst of all the congratulations, Zion's scowling face appeared.

"Zion!" Beulah exclaimed. "I didn't know you were here."

"Had to park all the way down at the end of the street, right by the hardware store," Zion fumed. "Had to walk a country mile to get to this meeting."

"Well, come on," Beulah said. "I'll give you a ride back to your truck. There's something I have to talk about with you anyway." She grabbed Zion's arm, and they made their way through the crowded hall and out to Beulah's car.

"Get in," Beulah ordered. "We've got something private to talk about." Beulah started the car, reminded Zion to fasten her seat belt, and as she drove down the main street, she said, "The judge made Sweet sign over her great-granddaddy's old property to him!"

"What?" Zion was as incredulous as Beulah had been at hearing this news. And then she asked the question that so surprised Beulah: "Why?"

Beulah sputtered, "I . . . I don't know." Those were her words, but her heart told her another truth: that sometimes, he did things just to be cruel . . . unbelievably cruel! So Beulah had just assumed that it was yet one more way to hurt Sweet, to diminish her as a human being.

Then Zion fairly yelped, "Wait a minute! Isn't that land adjacent to the old Maxson place? The one the developer has been snooping around about?"

Beulah was horrified. Such a thing had never entered her mind! "Sweet didn't say anything about that," Beulah exclaimed.

To which Zion replied, "Maybe she doesn't know!"

Beulah thought as fast as she could. "I'll call Wanda, Sweet's old friend. See if she knows anything about the possibility of a sale."

Zion, ever practical, asked: "You know her phone number?"

"No," Beulah admitted, "but I'll bet Wildwood can find it out for us."

"Well, it was bad enough for him to take the land away from Sweet, but if he's selling it to developers, it's even worse. And I do wonder how on earth he got Sweet to give it up?"

"I shudder to think," Beulah said. And

then she actually shuddered.

"I don't think he knows about how important ancestral land is to folks like us," Zion muttered.

"Or maybe he *does!*" Beulah countered.

Beulah took Zion to where her truck was parked, and then Beulah started right for Sweet's house. Surely, with Jim around, the judge would not vent his fury onto Sweet! But Beulah was worried enough that she parked on the roadside near the sanctuary, flicked on her flashlight, and headed off through the woods.

She was just in time to see the judge's car pull into the driveway and Jim get out to help the judge. The judge, visibly agitated, jerked his arm away from Jim and struggled across the yard, unaided. Jim followed close behind him, with one hand held out to catch the judge if he started to fall. At the steps, the judge begrudgingly allowed Jim to take his arm, but when he had gotten up on the porch, he pulled his arm away again, shouting something that Beulah couldn't make out. She watched as Sweet came to the door. She, too, tried to take the judge's arm, but he jerked away from her and shouted something unintelligible once again.

As the judge entered the house, Jim

made a small salute to Sweet and headed off to his own small house. When Jim was gone and the door to the judge's house closed, Beulah crept out of the anonymity of the sanctuary and across the backyard until she crouched down beside the back porch. From inside the house, she could hear voices — mostly the judge's, but sometimes Sweet's. His tone loud and agitated, hers soft and soothing. But while she listened, Sweet's kind voice seemed to dominate the conversation, and whenever he spoke, Beulah could hear in his voice that she had diffused his agitation. Gratefully, Beulah crept back across the yard and into the sanctuary.

As soon as she got into her house, Beulah called Wildwood at home.

"I'm so glad you called," Wildwood exclaimed. "I'm so excited about the town council meeting, I can hardly stand it!"

"I'm thrilled about that too," Beulah answered. "But that isn't why I'm calling."

"Oh?"

"First thing in the morning, when you get to the library, could you please try to find a phone number for that friend of Sweet's — Wanda something?"

"That's not much to go on," Wildwood said.

"Well, she lived in Tea-Olive for a short while a few years ago. Went to the Presbyterian Church. Lives in Augusta and is in the real estate business."

"That's good," Wildwood replied, obviously jotting down notes. "I'll call the church and find a last name and then go from there."

"Will you let me know as soon as possible?" Beulah asked.

"Of course!" Now that she was chasing down the answer to a reference question, Wildwood was all business. "I'll call you tomorrow. This shouldn't be too hard."

"Thanks, Wildwood," Beulah breathed.

At 4:15 a.m., Beulah's phone rang. She had been dreaming that she, Wildwood, Zion, and Sweet were in the sanctuary together, with nothing more to worry about than being able to spot a pine warbler or a brown-headed nuthatch. The phone dissolved that happy dream completely.

"Hello?" Beulah couldn't keep the deep concern out of her voice.

"Miss Beulah? This is Jim."

"Is anything wrong?" she pressed.

"Well, yes, ma'am, something is wrong. I'm in jail, and I've made my one phone call to you."

"In *jail?*" Beulah yelped, trying to make the pieces fit. "What for?"

"The judge has charged me with assault," Jim said, with misery in his voice.

"Assault?"

Jim cleared his throat. "Assault on . . . Miss Sweet," he confessed. "She's in the hospital, but I swear to you, Miss Beulah, I never laid a hand on her." Jim's voice choked.

"In the hospital? What on earth happened? Is she OK?" Beulah pressed.

Jim hesitated and then she heard a male voice in the background, saying something unintelligible.

"I've gotta go now," he said. "Please go to the hospital and see about Miss Sweet."

"And what about you?" Beulah asked.

"If you want to come see me, I'll be happy to explain everything."

"Of course, I'll come," Beulah assured him. "Don't say anything to anyone until we talk. I'll call John Anderson — he's Love-Divine's old attorney — and get him to come, too. Are you sure Sweet's OK?"

"Yes, ma'am, I think so. But I'll feel better when we know for sure," Jim muttered, and then he hung up. She could easily imagine a sheriff's deputy standing beside him, waiting to take the phone once

Jim had made his one phone call.

With shaking hands, Beulah looked up the attorney's number. She hadn't had the occasion to speak with him since he had read Love-Divine's will, but she knew that, like most small-town lawyers, he handled almost every kind of problem a person could run into. He answered on the third ring, and Beulah explained about Jim and asked Mr. Anderson to meet her at the jail in about an hour. That would give her time to go to the hospital and see about Sweet.

As Beulah was driving to the hospital in that predawn darkness, the full implications of what she had heard began to come home to her. She knew with all her heart that Jim had not hurt Sweet. That he would never, ever hurt anyone or anything. But what was he doing that could result in those charges against him?

At the hospital, a receptionist directed Beulah to Sweet's room, but when Beulah entered, the very first thing she saw was the judge, asleep in a chair in the corner. His face was bloated and maliciously soft in his sleep, and that always-determined chin was buried in his shoulder. Across from him, Sweet was lying in a bed quietly and with her eyes closed. One hand was

347

bandaged, and she had an evil-looking, purple bruise across her left temple. While Beulah stood there, Sweet stirred, and the instant her eyes opened, she glanced over to where the judge was crumpled in the chair. Then she spotted Beulah and slowly lifted her good hand to place a finger on her lips. So Beulah said not a word, simply came forward quietly, leaned down, and kissed Sweet on the side of her face that wasn't bruised.

"Are you OK?" Beulah whispered. Again, Sweet glanced at the judge, and then she gave a small, hesitant nod. In the chair, the judge stirred, smacked his lips, and opened his eyes. When he saw Beulah, he sat up straighter and smoothed the front of his shirt.

"Good morning, judge," Beulah said, though the words were bitter gall in her mouth.

"Not such a good morning," he responded. "Just look what that common farm helper has done to Sweet! Broke right into my house, he did, and assaulted my wife!"

At that very moment everything became crystal clear to Beulah — the judge had hit Sweet, done God-knows-what to her hand, and then managed to blame Jim for it.

Beulah tried to keep her face from revealing what she believed to have happened. Turning to Sweet, Beulah asked softly, "Sweet, what happened?" And the way Sweet's frightened eyes searched out the judge gave Beulah all the confirmation she needed.

"I *told* you what happened!" the judge growled. "I already told you!"

"Yes, you did," Beulah answered. "You certainly did. And now, I'd like to hear it from Sweet." But the look of horror on Sweet's face melted Beulah's heart. So that Beulah realized that this was not the time or place to hear what Sweet had to say.

"Is there anything I can get you?" Beulah asked Sweet.

"She's got everything she needs," the judge answered. "Absolutely everything she needs."

"Something's not right here," Beulah said, meeting the judge's glare. "Something's definitely not right!"

"It's none of your business," the judge growled.

"Oh, yes it is," Beulah insisted. The judge continued to glare at her, but he said not another word. Beulah patted Sweet's good hand and slowly backed out of the room, the judge's horrible eyes following her every step of the way.

When Beulah parked in front of the county jail, John Anderson was already standing at the steps, waiting for her.

"Thank you for coming," Beulah murmured. "I don't know what's going on, but I do know that Jim is one of the most gentle men I've ever known. He would never hurt anyone, much less Sweet."

"Let's go inside and hear what he has to say," John said.

They met alone with Jim in a private office. His eyes were haggard, and he had a plaster bandage across one eyebrow. A dark bruise had come up just under his eye. While they talked, a uniformed deputy stood outside of the door.

"What happened?" John asked, with his pen poised over a legal pad.

"Is Miss Sweet OK?" was Jim's primary question.

"She seems to be," Beulah assured him.

"Well, as long as she's all right," Jim breathed. Then he took a deep breath and continued: "I knew the judge was upset, after the council meeting, so I just tried to keep my mouth shut when I drove him home. And when I went to my cottage, I left my window open, so if he started in to screaming at Miss Sweet, I could hear him and go over to stop him if I thought it got too rough-sounding," Jim said in a low voice.

"Go on," John urged.

"I fell right to sleep, but sometime or other during the night, I heard the judge shouting at the top of his lungs and then I heard glass breaking. The very first thing I did was to call the police, because I didn't know if maybe a burglar had broken in or whether . . ." His voice trailed off. "And then I ran over to the house and went right in the front door, without knocking. I could already hear the siren of the police car far off down the highway, but getting closer every second."

He paused, watching the attorney's pencil. "Go on," John said again.

"Well, I'm really not sure of what happened after that," Jim admitted.

"Why?" the attorney asked, with the pencil poised.

"Everything happened so fast! I heard Miss Sweet scream, and I ran into the bedroom, and the judge came after me like a wild man!"

"Tell me about Miss Sweet," the attorney said.

"I never even saw her," Jim said. "And that's the honest-to-God truth!"

"Go on."

"The judge punched me twice," he said, reaching up and touching the bandage tenderly. "He's strong as a bull, even though he's still in bad shape from encountering a real bull."

John glanced at Beulah, but he said nothing.

"I didn't want to punch him back," Jim said. "So I was just trying to look around and see to Miss Sweet when he punched me again, and then the police came and the judge roared, 'Arrest that man! He's guilty of assault, as well as breaking and entering!' And the police dragged me away, but not before I could shout over and over for them to find Miss Sweet and see if she was OK."

"How did you know she's in the hospital?" John asked Jim.

"While I was being booked, an ambulance went right by the jail, coming from Miss Sweet's direction," he explained. "It had to be Miss Sweet or the judge, one or the other, and since I never laid a hand on the judge, I figured it was Miss Sweet." Jim paused and looked at Beulah. "I'm glad to hear she's OK," he added.

"So tell me again about the sounds that woke you up," John Anderson said.

"Well, I heard the judge yelling," Jim repeated. "And then I heard glass breaking. That's when I called the police. And when I got inside the house, I heard Miss Sweet scream, but I never did see her, and that's the truth!"

"The judge says you broke into his home and assaulted Miss Sweet," John said in a calm voice.

"I know," Jim whispered miserably. "But I didn't break into anything. The front door was unlocked, just as it always is. I only went in because I was worried about Miss Sweet, but once I got inside, I never saw her."

"That's not what the judge says," John Anderson pressed gently.

Jim studied the attorney's face carefully. "And who is the law going to believe?" Jim finally asked. "A retired judge or a . . . farmhand?"

Beulah sat quietly, listening carefully, and remembering the look of terror on Sweet's face when Beulah asked her, in the judge's presence, what had really happened.

"I need to talk with Miss Sweet," the attorney said.

"I don't think that will do any good," Beulah said.

"Why?" Oh, the simplicity of that one question! And Beulah understood right away that she had to be careful. Sweet's life might depend upon her handling of this touchy subject. Or, at the least, when she and Zion could finally accomplish their extermination task, they would become highly suspect.

"I think she will agree with anything her husband says," Beulah finally said, glancing meaningfully at Jim.

The attorney waited a few moments before he said to Beulah, "I've heard all the rumors that are going around town. Are they true?"

"I believe that they are," Beulah confirmed.

Then to Jim, the attorney said: "You know, I heard that you had stopped working for the judge some time ago."

"I had," Jim agreed. "But after the judge's accident, I agreed to come back to help out, just until he got his strength back." At that, Jim gave a brief, bitter laugh. "Guess he's gotten it back now," he said, again rubbing the plaster on his eyebrow.

"Well, let's see about getting you out on bond, and we'll figure what to do later."

"Thank you," Jim whispered.

"Jim," Beulah said. "When you get out, you won't be able to go back to the judge's house or anywhere near it."

"I know."

"So maybe it's best if you go on back to your own home. I'll keep you informed about everything. And when the hearing comes, you can stay at my house."

Once the bond papers were carried through, Jim thanked John Anderson and Beulah profusely, and he said: "I'd like to go on home right away, but I'm afraid my truck is still out at the judge's house."

Beulah stepped right in: "You don't want to go anywhere near that place," she announced. "So if John will give me a ride out there, I'll bring your truck to you."

"You know how to drive a stick-shift truck?" Jim inquired.

"I've driven Zion's plenty of times. I can do it," Beulah announced.

So that was how Mr. Anderson and Beulah got Jim's truck, and Jim — deeply appreciative as always — left town right away.

Beulah knew that she needed to talk to Zion. When they had last talked, they were concerned not only about Sweet's safety but about the need for keeping Sweet's great-granddaddy's land out of the hands of developers. But now, the fate of an innocent man was also in the picture. Surely Sweet wouldn't let an innocent man go to prison for "assaulting" her? Beulah knew beyond any doubt that it was the judge himself who had assaulted Sweet, and she wondered why was that called "domestic violence" when the same act, committed by someone NOT married to a woman was called "assault"?

Beulah dialed Zion's number.

"I heard all about it," Zion said right away. "Things are piling up on us, and we have to make some solid plans as soon as possible."

"I can't imagine that Sweet would let an innocent man go to prison for something he didn't do," Beulah said.

"But if she goes against what the judge told the police, I believe that her life will be in jeopardy," Zion added. Then she said, "Poor Sweet — she's in one of those 'damned if you do and damned if you don't' quagmires!"

Wildwood called Beulah about an hour after the library opened the next morning.

"I've got a phone number for you," she announced.

"I'm ready to write it down," Beulah answered.

"Wanda?" Beulah said into the receiver. "I'm a friend of Sweet's; you know, in Tea-Olive."

"Oh yes," Wanda said.

"Well, I was wondering if you would please find out something for me. It's about the potential sale of a parcel of land adjacent to the Maxson property, just north of Tea-Olive? It's probably being handled by a realtor who deals in commercial property."

"Sure," Wanda said. "I'll snoop around a bit for you."

"Thank you ever so much," Beulah replied, and then she gave Wanda her phone number.

"And how is Sweet?" Wanda asked, just as Beulah was ready to hang up.

"She's . . . OK," Beulah sputtered.

"Well, tell her I said hi," Wanda said. "And I'll call you back as soon as I find out what you need."

For most of the afternoon, Zion and Beulah sat at Zion's kitchen table, staring at glasses of iced tea that they weren't drinking.

"Now that Jim's gone, I'm even more worried," Beulah confessed.

"Did you go see Sweet this morning?" Zion asked.

"No," Beulah confessed. "I just can't stand being anywhere near that man!"

"I'm going to see her this afternoon," Zion announced. "This is just getting ridiculous. Him sitting there like a big old puffed-up frog and us tippy-toeing around him all the time!"

"Be careful, Zion," Beulah warned her. "He's truly an evil person."

"I know that," Zion answered. "I know that full well." She hesitated for a few minutes and then she added, "I wonder if the *L* in his name stands for Lucifer?"

Beulah's mouth fell open. "Who on earth would give a poor little baby a name like *that?*" she exclaimed.

"A long time ago, some lady here in Tea-Olive was going to name her son Judas, to punish her husband, who'd been running around on her," Zion announced. "But I guess someone explained that the child would suffer much more than her sorry husband, so she named him Joseph instead."

"Did you hear about that Hispanic couple living north of here who named their son Jesus?" Beulah asked.

"Yes, I heard about that, only they pronounce it 'hey-soos,'" Zion answered.

Then Beulah and Zion locked eyes and both of them smiled. "Isn't it fun to forget, even for just a little minute, the terrible thing we've been planning on doing?"

"I guess so," Zion answered. "But now I think it's probably time to get back to the planning. And I don't think the *L* stands for Lucifer at all. That just seems to fit, is all."

Later that afternoon, Beulah received a phone call from Wanda.

"Beulah? I have some information for you," Wanda announced. "The sale of that land is pending. Seems that the buyer wants both properties, so he's holding off on signing for the Maxson property. The agent thinks the paperwork is all going to go through in about two weeks."

"So technically, the land hasn't been sold yet?" Beulah asked hopefully.

"Technically, that's right," Wanda answered. "But when we last spoke, and I asked about Sweet, you sounded kind of . . . evasive," Wanda added.

"She's had a fall, but she's going to be OK," Beulah assured her.

"I'm sorry to hear that. Please give her

my best wishes, and you let me know if there's anything more I can do for you all. Anything at all," Wanda said.

When Beulah hung up the phone, she muttered to herself, "Two weeks! If we can stop this whole thing, I'll bet Sweet could even get her land back. Surely, someone can't be *forced* to turn over something if they don't want to!"

Right at that moment, Beulah heard Zion coming up onto her porch. She always knew when it was Zion because her friend always stomped on the porch, as if dislodging barn dust from her boots.

"I went to see Sweet, but she's already been released," Zion announced.

"Then she's back out there alone with him."

"That's right."

"I heard from that Wanda person Sweet knows, and she says the signing for the land will be in about two weeks," Beulah said.

Zion narrowed her eyes. "Then we have that long to get the job done," she announced.

"I can't see any other way," Beulah said miserably.

Beulah fixed some iced tea for them, and they sat down at Beulah's dining table, while myriad attempts at murder traipsed through their minds. Zion imagined a shotgun accident, while Beulah envisioned that bull finishing up what he started. Then Zion thought about the judge's shiny, new tractor. In her mind, she walked across the fields near the judge's house, noticing the "tractor path," which was the dirt road around the perimeter of any field. Maybe, just maybe those "sweet rolling hills" — as Miss Love-Divine used to call them — could help! The vision that came to her mind next was of an overturned tractor, with the judge's lifeless body crushed by that heavy machine.

"I think I've got it," Zion said. "You remember that day we were out there, and I noticed the judge's tractor didn't have a safety roll-bar on it?"

"I think I remember," Beulah commented.

"That's what we'll use."

"How?"

"We gotta make sure that tractor rolls over on him, next time he drives it," Zion announced.

"How?" Beulah repeated.

"Well, I was just thinking that the tractor road goes along a stretch where there's a pretty steep incline, with a ravine at the bottom." Zion sounded as if she were simply thinking out loud. "Mmm . . . let me think."

Beulah sat in silence, watching Zion's forehead, as if she could see tiny, brass wheels and cogs turning and clicking. Suddenly, Zion's face lit up. "I've got it!" she yelped, and then in rapid-fire words, she said: "If we dig a trench in one of the ruts and conceal it, the tractor tire would go into it, and combined with the natural incline, it would be enough to tip the tractor over and send it all the way into the ravine!"

Beulah imagined such a thing, and she could almost smell the oil on the hot engine and see the monstrous tires slowly spinning after the crash. It was an altogether pleasant imagining.

"Dig a trench," Beulah repeated, mindlessly.

"That'll do it!" Zion yelped again.

"But what if he doesn't use the tractor road?" Beulah asked.

"He has to use it to get to the pasture," Zion repeated. "And now that Jim's not around to haul the hay bales, the judge will have to do it himself."

"So what do we do now?" Beulah inquired.

"Pray for rain," Zion answered simply, and seeing Beulah's furrowed brow, she added, "to make the ground easier to dig in. And in the meantime, we'll just pray for Sweet to be OK."

After the milking the next morning, Beulah went to the sanctuary and studied the house through her binoculars. All seemed quiet and peaceful, but then it had seemed very much like that just before the judge assaulted Sweet and found a way to blame Jim for it! While Beulah watched, the judge came out of the house, wearing overalls and with his arm still in a sling. He went into the shed and climbed into the high seat of the tractor. Watching his agility, she remembered what Jim had said about the judge making such a speedy recovery. He certainly seemed unencumbered by the sling. She watched as he started the engine, saw the belch of black smoke from the stack, and followed his movements through the binoculars. He drove as far as the barn, stopped the tractor, went inside, and came back out carrying a bale of hay in one hand. With a little difficulty, he swung the bale onto the back of the tractor, and then he drove off toward the pasture. Beulah moved through the sanctuary until she reached a location from which she could watch his drive all the way. Sure enough, Zion had been right!

About halfway, the tractor road tilted sharply, but not quite sharply enough to cause an overturn. The trench Zion wanted to dig would be just enough to tip the weight of the tractor over. Best of all, the place where Beulah and Zion would dig was completely out of sight of the house. They could work unseen! Beulah looked down into the ravine through the binoculars and shuddered. She knew that she was looking literally into the jaws of death!

Inside of the house, Sweet sat in the living room, her bandaged hand in her lap and a cold compress on her forehead. She stared through the window toward the sanctuary, thinking hard about Love-Divine and her gracious gift to the bird watching society. To give *land!* To give something that would always be there, no matter what. Sweet's mind immediately flew to the land the judge had taken away from her, and hot tears formed in her eyes. "My land!" she screamed silently. "My land and my people's land!" The land . . . lost! So far beyond any pain or humiliation her husband could inflict!

She wiped away the tears viciously, an-grily, and suddenly, she felt compelled to find the box of old photographs she had brought with her when she married the judge — old, yellowed photographs of her people, the old house they had lived in, and especially, the land.

She walked into the hallway, pulled down the fold-down stairs, and slowly and carefully, she went up into the attic. When she switched on the light, her eyes fell right upon the very box of photographs she was looking for, and she sat down on the floor, opened the box, and began looking through the photos. There was her great-grandmother, wearing an apron and leaning against the banister of the porch, as if she were looking down the road for someone to come.

And the photo of her great-grandfather, standing so proudly behind his new team of mules, with his plow already planted firmly into the good rich earth.

"How could I lose it?" Sweet asked herself, feeling such a pain in her heart that she pressed her hand against the place in her chest where that heart grieved and bled. She looked up from the box, and her eyes fell upon a huge, old softball bat standing in the corner. For a moment, it almost didn't register.

"Reverend King and his love of softball!"

she said aloud. She should hide that, even though the judge had surely killed her and in a more painful way than crushing her skull. Sweet closed the box of photos, reached over, and picked up the bat. She was completely surprised to feel a sense of power wash over her, with the weight of the bat in her hand! Carefully, she took the bat and made her way down the ladder.

"Where can I hide it so that he won't find it?" she whispered to herself. And then she put it into the pantry. The judge never went in there. "A woman's place," he would grumble early on in their marriage, whenever Sweet innocently asked him to hand something to her out of the pantry. Now, of course, she knew better than to ask anything of him. Anything at all.

CHAPTER
— THIRTY —

Perhaps God heard Zion and Beulah's prayers for rain, and perhaps not. Would God even listen to a prayer that would help them to commit a murder?

Regardless of the answer to that question, the rain started around midnight and fell steadily until dawn, leaving the earth of Tea-Olive, Georgia, soft and sweet and pliable. Zion awakened when she heard the rain start, and she reached over and set her alarm clock before she smiled and turned over in bed, pulling the covers up over her shoulder.

Beulah heard someone tapping on her bedroom window, and at first, she was startled. She turned on the bedside light and saw Zion's rain-drenched face in the window.

"What on earth?" Beulah muttered, throwing on her robe and opening the window. "What's wrong?" Beulah demanded in a startled voice.

"We have to go take care of business. Get yourself dressed."

"Why didn't you call on the phone or come to the door?" Beulah fussed. "You scared me half to death!"

Zion grinned. "It's more fun this way," she pronounced. "More dangerous!" With that, the grinning face disappeared. Within only a couple of minutes, Beulah dressed, grabbed her flashlight, and went out to climb into the passenger's seat of Zion's truck. "I was out at the sanctuary last afternoon," Beulah said to Zion. "And I see exactly what you mean about that steep incline. I think we'll do it this time!"

"Have to!" Zion shouted. "Haven't you ever heard the old saying about the third time being the charm?" Zion laughed and revved the engine before they drove off into the darkness, the shovels in the bed of the pickup truck rattling ominously.

They were most careful going through the sanctuary, because if the judge were awake, he could easily see their flashlights. And they were also careful that they each carried only one shovel, to avoid the clanking sound that would surely attract his attention. As they came out the other end of the sanctuary and out of sight of the house, Zion sighed in relief.

"We're almost there," she said. "And we're lucky the judge doesn't like dogs!"

When they reached the area of the incline, Zion whispered to Beulah: "I'll start digging, and you go find lots of long twigs so we can conceal the alterations to the tractor road." So there in the pouring rain, Zion started digging what would turn out to be a trench about two feet deep, exactly enough, she had calculated, to throw the tractor into an overturn down the ravine. Beulah gathered twigs and leaves, stuffing them into her shirt and with the rain dripping off of her nose.

For almost two hours they labored, and when the trench was finished, they spent long minutes placing the concealing twigs and dead leaves over the trench. At last, Zion stood up and pushed her dripping hair out of her face.

"It's done!" she said to Beulah.

"Yes, God forgive us!" Beulah answered.

When Zion reached the crossroads where she should have turned right to take Beulah back home, she turned left instead.

"Where are we going?" Beulah asked. "I want to go home and get into dry clothes!"

"We've got the milking to do," Zion

answered. "Cows won't care if we're wet!"

At Zion's house, Beulah took off her soaked clothes and tried to fit herself into some clothes that Zion provided. However, Zion stayed thin and lean, what with the hard work of the dairy herd and the creamery, so that Beulah struggled mightily to fasten the button on the slacks Zion had provided. Finally, feeling bloated and simply plain *fat,* Beulah left the slacks unbuttoned and wore the oversized shirt with the shirttails out, to cover the waistband. She had towel-dried her hair, as had Zion, and they set about the milking, as if this were a morning like any other.

Beulah felt that there was something strangely soothing about the *thrum-thrum* of the milking machines, the sweet mixture of milk-aroma and clean hay, and especially, the beautiful brown eyes of the gentle Jerseys seemed to calm her.

How lucky you all are, Beulah thought. *Your lives are perfectly ordered, and you know what to expect of every single day. You don't have to make hard decisions, and you trust Zion to provide for you. You are fortunate creatures! So unlike human beings! And you sweet cows don't even have to worry about free will! That terrible choice God gave us, to obey or not to obey! To believe or not to believe! And if we have succeeded this time and the judge dies, Zion and I will both go to hell!*

All through Beulah's milking-parlor thinking, Zion glanced at her from time to time. Now, Beulah was a good church-goer, but Zion wasn't. Zion always maintained that she could feel closer to God out in the middle of a pasture full of cows than she could in any confined building, no matter what a great organ a church had. In Zion's own internal cathedral, the chirping of birds and the thrumming of milking machines made a music more heady than gospel songs. And even though Zion's mother had followed the town's tradition of naming her daughter out of the Baptist Hymnal, Zion had always marched to the beat of that proverbial different drummer. Still, Zion could well imagine the pangs of severe guilt that were tearing through her good friend, Beulah. She felt them as surely as if they were passing through Zion's own body and soul.

"You gonna be OK?" Zion finally asked Beulah, over the humming of the milking machines.

At the question, Beulah turned shining eyes toward Zion. "It's hard!" Beulah admitted. "Maybe even harder than trying to button these stinking, skinny slacks of yours!!"

Zion laughed. *Yes, Beulah would be OK, no matter what!*

But would Sweet be OK, as well?

CHAPTER
— THIRTY-ONE —

After the milking was done, Zion drove Beulah back home. As Beulah got out of the truck, Zion leaned across the seat and took Beulah's hand.

"It's all gonna be OK," Zion said again, and she added a force to the words that almost sounded as if she were willing them to be true.

"Who would have thought that we could ever stoop so low?" Beulah asked.

"We never know," Zion assured her. "I suppose any good person, under certain circumstances, could be driven to do the same thing."

"I hate to think that," Beulah reluctantly agreed. "But perhaps you're right. Damned free will!"

In the house, Beulah got into her own clean, dry clothes, but she felt a restlessness unlike anything she had ever experienced. She tried to distract herself with a fresh tomato sandwich, but the food was bitter in her mouth.

"What a way to diet!" she chided herself.

Finally, she picked up her car keys and left the house, knowing where she was going.

It was a strange, compelling attraction she had for the King's Wood Bird Sanctuary, not because she could spy on Sweet's house from it, but simply for the pure desire for something more simple than plotting a man's death. The first vestiges of a restless spring were in the sanctuary, with the bare, gray trees beginning to show a mist of green among their branches. Beulah tilted down the limb of a young dogwood tree, studied the minuscule brilliant-green buds of new leaves, and, as always, marveled at the miracle of new life. A new season beginning, and a new season for Beulah as well. For if Zion's plan succeeded, Beulah would forever see herself as a murderess. A new season, but not a good one. She stayed in the sanctuary for several hours, letting the breeze stir her hair and inhaling the earthy aroma of last year's leaves on the ground.

Beulah thought about Love-Divine and her gift of this sanctuary, and she wondered what Love-Divine would think about someone using it as a place to spy on Sweet and the judge. It seemed like a terrible departure from what Love-Divine intended. At the last, Beulah tried to pray, but that felt as if she were affronting God Almighty Himself! At the last, she sat down on the dead, wet leaves, covered her face with her hands, and wept long and hard.

As Beulah was opening her door, the phone was ringing.

"Beulah? This is Wildwood."

"Wildwood?"

"Did you forget Homework Helper time today?"

"Oh!" Beulah slapped her forehead with the palm of her hand. "Oh! Yes, I simply forgot! Is Tobia still there? Is he terribly upset with me?"

"Of course he was disappointed, but Thankful Broderick took him under her wing, and he did very well. And no, he's gone home now."

"Oh, I just feel terrible!" Beulah wailed. "And after that wonderful job he did of standing up and speaking to the council members!"

"Well, I was looking forward to your

coming by as well. You should see the new banner we have on the front of the building! It says: 'We Saved Our Library! Thanks to the whole community, especially the Friends of the Library and our own Tobia!' "

"That's wonderful!" Beulah shouted, and she felt as if she should give Wildwood some kind of an excuse for missing her session with Tobia, but for the life of her, she couldn't think of what to say. *I was busy plotting a murder* would have been accurate! And she was horrified to realize that those very words were trying to come roaring out of her mouth! So she clamped her jaw and said nothing.

In Love-Divine's old house, sleep would not come to Sweet, even though she longed for its oblivion. She was lying as still as possible, listening to the judge's raucous snoring, hoping against hope that she wouldn't move around and awaken *him*. Deprived of the oblivion of sleep herself, she took comfort in knowing that he was not awake, not "in the world with her," was the way she thought about it.

So for long hours, she was just as still as she could be, trying to control the sobs that begged to wrack through her body. Instead, she kept her breathing as steady as possible and did not lift a hand to wipe away the tears that ran from the outer corners of her eyes and into her ears. Warm, very wet tears. Liquid grief!

Finally, just as she could see the first light of dawn around the edges of the drapes in the bedroom, she fell into a light, lovely sleep where the aromas of the land awaited her, and she felt her heart reaching down and entwining itself in the land of her great-grandfather, just as surely as an oak would put its roots deep into the soil.

But just as she fell into a deeper sleep, the judge's snoring stopped, and Sweet was awakened by his great bulk pressing against her.

"Wake up, wife," he growled into her startled ear. "Wake up and *cleave* — you like all that Bible talk so much! Wake up and cleave to your husband!" Even though her mind was swirling, she managed to speak somewhat coherently. She fought hard against the revulsion that arose in her, like a hot, bubbling pot of bile!

"Oh, don't you worry," he laughed into her ear. "I'm not interested in you this morning. Not interested at all!"

"Why did you marry me?" Sweet was surprised at her own words. She had not even thought them at all.

He paused and gazed at her with his flat, cold eyes. No love in them, no passion, just cruel power.

"I guess you reminded me of my second wife," he said. And then he smiled cruelly and added, "Before I stopped loving her."

In all Sweet's life, she had never felt such a horrible wrath as the one that began filling her heart and soul at that moment. And it only increased and flowed over her like molten lava as the judge swung his legs off of the bed and stood up.

As soon as he had gone into the bathroom, Sweet's mind detached itself from his cruel words, and when it slowly came back, she felt as if her very soul had been rent asunder. She had thought there was no greater defilement than the loss of her land, but she knew, instinctively, that here was the final and complete defilement, for now, the judge had taken her sense of individuality, her self-value, and her honor. Such was her devastation that even tears would not come, just a terrible trembling, the aftermath of having been so defiled.

Somehow a liberating thought entered her addled mind: that wasn't about passion! That was about *power!* He had taken her heart and broken it into two bloody pieces with his own words. And worse, he had taken her land and her honor; he had even had a good man thrown into prison for his own atrocities!

From what seemed like a very far away place, she listened to the sound of water running in the bathroom and imagined him running a razor across his bulbous chin. Suddenly, the shaking stopped and she felt almost as if she were beginning to fall asleep. But it was like no sleep she had ever known. She simply began falling in upon her own self, everything going so low and slow, that for a moment, she wondered if she were dying! And if that had been the case, she was ready for the physical death that would mirror the emotional one she had just suffered. But she finally realized that she was neither falling asleep nor was she dying. Whatever was the absolute core of Sweet was simply folding inward, and her last truly conscious thought was of how good that softball bat had felt in her hands. If it had been within her reach, she was absolutely certain that she would have used it to defend herself . . . defend her land!

In that strange, sleeplike but sleepless state, she began dreaming, and in her dream, she was on the land her great-grandfather had handed down to her. She could smell the rich perfume of newly turned soil, and she could feel the cool earth under her feet. She was standing by the front door of the house, looking beyond the sweet fields and out over the rolling hills. In the distance, she could see the first rounded peaks of the mountains. And something else in the valley: smoke, as if a house were burning. While she stood there wondering, a strange shadow-creature came up to her, and without even asking, she knew that it was her ancestor, coming out of the shadows both of time and of place. He wore a wide-brimmed hat pulled down over his face, so that she could not see him clearly, but she felt no fear — only the security and protection of his strange presence. But then she felt a shudder come over her, as if an errant, icy wind had slipped down out of the northern mountains, and her breathing of it made her mind as clear as a pristine stream. The shadow-figure reached out to her, and she thought at first that it wanted to take her hand. But when she held out her own hand to it, the eerie figure handed her a thick piece of firewood and pointed toward a Union soldier who had suddenly appeared in the dream. He was bending down, perhaps drinking from a stream, as she could hear the running of the water.

When she looked back, the shadow-figure was gone, leaving only his rich, brittle laugh in the air.

"Don't you bury him on *my land!*" she heard herself shout.

And then, in what would have been the most horrible and yet magnificent moment of her life — *if she had ever remembered it, but she did not!* — she awakened herself hearing her own raucous laughter.

The next morning, Beulah was just leaving for the milking parlor when her phone rang. When she heard that sound, all of the hairs came up on the back of her neck. It was Sweet.

"Oh, Beulah!" Sweet's words were garbled.

"Sweet? What's wrong?" And that very innocent-sounding question was like bile in Beulah's mouth. "What's wrong?" she repeated.

"The judge . . ."

"What about him?" Now Beulah's heart was pounding so hard that she could feel the beats in her temples.

"He's . . . dead!" Sweet half-spoke and half-screamed the words.

"Oh, my Lord!" Beulah said, but she was thinking: *That's a good one, Beulah! Call upon the Lord, you stinking murderess!*

"Listen," Sweet's voice took on a note of slightly calmer resolve. "I'll tell you all about it later. I just wanted you to know, and right now, I have to call the sheriff!"

With those words, Sweet hung up the phone.

"Sweet!!!" Beulah fairly screamed into the receiver. "Sweet!!!" But there was no answer.

Beulah dropped the phone, grabbed her car keys, and left for Zion's.

By the time Beulah burst into the milking parlor, she was in the throes of full hysteria. Zion had just brought in the cows, and when Beulah burst in and threw herself on Zion, the cows scattered around the confines of the milking parlor, mooing, running into one another, and throwing frightened glances toward the women.

"What on earth!!!" Zion managed to say, reeling under Beulah's forceful hug.

Beulah couldn't answer. She could only sob in great tearing breaths.

The cows quieted and stared at the two women from the far corner of the milking parlor. Under their curious gazes, Zion suddenly realized that only their success in exterminating the judge could have affected Beulah in this manner. Zion said nothing, just held the sobbing Beulah and started rocking her gently back and forth. Over Beulah's shoulder, Zion winked at the staring cows and smiled.

It took a long time for Beulah to start calming down, and when she did, she pulled away from Zion and, without saying a thing, she started guiding the cows into their individual holders. Zion, also without speaking, did the same, and then the two women started washing and drying udders as if nothing else in the whole world mattered.

Once the machines were purring away, Zion put her hand on Beulah's arm. Beulah still had tears in her eyes, but she was strangely calm, as if the hysterics had left her completely exhausted.

"When?" was Zion's only question.

"I'm not sure. Sweet called me about half an hour ago."

"Sweet is safe," Zion pronounced, as if to remind Beulah of why they had embarked upon the dastardly attempts on the judge's life.

"Yes, Sweet is safe," Beulah repeated. "But Sweet suspects foul play!" The last words came out in a soft yelp.

"Why do you say that?"

"Because she said she had to call the sheriff," Beulah moaned.

Zion frowned, and once again, Beulah could almost see the wheels and cogs moving in perfect precision. Finally, she said, "I wonder why?"

"Maybe she found that trench we dug. Maybe she put two and two together after the tractor went into the ravine!"

Again, Zion thought for long moments. "That hardly seems plausible," she said. "That's why we wanted it to rain. The rain would have washed away any shovel marks or anything like that. That rain was hard enough and long enough that the trench could have been the result of a gully-washer."

"Do you really think so?" Beulah asked, wanting with all her heart to believe that. Then she hesitated. "Well, even if nobody can prove foul play, we've still . . . killed a man!"

"Exterminated him," Zion reminded Beulah gently.

"Exterminated him," Beulah repeated.

They looked into each other's eyes for long, silent moments.

Beulah nodded. "We're going to hell," she added in a whimper.

When the cows were let out of the parlor and the milk was strained and in the cooler, Beulah said, "I think we ought to go out to Sweet's and see about her."

"You think so?" Zion asked.

"It's what we would do . . . under ordinary circumstances," Beulah said.

"Should we call anybody else and let them know?"

"Listen, Zion, with Memphis's cousin working at the sheriff's office and with Memphis's large breakfast crowd, you can bet that everybody in town knows about it by now. So let's square our shoulders and go out there and see what's up."

"What if the sheriff is waiting for us?" Zion asked.

"Even if anyone expects that someone helped the judge along to his . . . reward . . . it would be too soon for them to have gathered any clues."

"I hope you're right! Now, what do we have that we can take out there?"

Zion thought for a moment and said, "I made a big banana pudding last night. We can take that."

"So you had trouble sleeping, too?" Beulah asked.

"A little. But it's because I was worried about you."

Beulah had been right about Memphis's tearoom being a community communications center, because when they got to Sweet's, eight or ten cars were lining the driveway. Women from the town were coming and going, bringing in covered dishes and a feigned sympathy. Because Southern women of that generation knew only to carry on as if everything were normal; they certainly didn't have any idea of how to treat a grieving widow who wouldn't be grieving one little bit! And they didn't know how to be in a community where anyone would come right out and say that they were glad the judge was dead and hoped he was sizzling in hell!

So they were all quiet and polite, murmuring noncommittal statements, such as "Everything will be OK" and "You just get plenty of rest now," where customarily they said, "He's with Jesus now," or "He's walking streets of gold!" And the customary food delivered to regular bereaved widows began piling up in the kitchen — platters of fried chicken, deviled eggs, potato salad, blackberry cobbler, pecan pies. How the women of the town were able to prepare that much food so quickly led to some silent speculation that perhaps it had been prepared earlier, in hopeful expectation of the judge's demise.

As Zion and Beulah came across the front yard, Zion happened to look at the tractor shed, and what she saw almost made her drop the banana pudding right in the middle of Sweet's yard.

"What's wrong?" Beulah asked.

But Zion's mouth was hanging open, and she could only balance the pudding in one hand and to feebly point with the other. Beulah looked. The shiny new tractor was in the shed, looking just as pristine as it had the day before. No dents! No scratches!

"What on earth?" Beulah breathed.

"Well, we sure didn't get him with the tractor," Zion whispered. "I just wonder if he thawed that turtle stew and had it for his supper?"

"Oh, my Lord!" Beulah breathed.

"We've got to go on in, no matter what," Zion said.

"Yes, you're right. But oh, my Lord!"

When Zion and Beulah came into the living room, Sweet was sitting in a chair, surrounded by hand-patting hypocrites, all of whom were glad the judge was gone.

Sweet, herself, was a perfect parody of a grieving widow. In such a strange atmosphere, Beulah halfway expected everyone to break into a riotous line dance at any moment!

"Beulah! Zion!" Sweet called to them. And Zion and Beulah exchanged brief glances with each other before they went to Sweet. They each kissed her cheek, and Beulah noticed a strange smile on Sweet's face. Not the usual smile of the old Sweet, but a stronger smile that lifted her chin and flared her nostrils. The volume of the chatter in the room was increasing, indicating a complete absence of any real grief, and whatever had happened, Sweet was like a brand new lady — no, a brand new woman!

Zion and Beulah went into the kitchen, where Wildwood was rearranging things in the refrigerator, trying to make room for dishes that needed to be kept cool. Zion handed over the banana pudding and glanced meaningfully at Beulah before she asked, "Wildwood, how did it happen?"

"What?" Wildwood called from the depths of the refrigerator.

"I said, 'how did it happen?'" Zion raised her voice over the clattering of dishes as Wildwood shifted things around.

"I'm sorry?" Wildwood said.

Zion's eyes were growing wide as she almost yelled, "How did it happen????"

"Oh," Wildwood backed her head out of the refrigerator. "How did it happen?" she repeated.

"Yes!" an exasperated Zion shot back at her.

"Oh, in the bathroom," Wildwood said. Zion and Beulah looked at each other incredulously.

"In the bathroom?" Beulah asked.

"Yes, he must have fallen and hit his head on the bathtub."

Beulah's mouth dropped open, and suddenly, she seemed to be able to hear Sweet's tearful relating of what the judge had said to her when he was in the hospital. *He whispered to me that if you hit someone in the head with a softball bat, it makes the same kind of injury like they fell and hit their head on the bathtub.* Still openmouthed, Beulah glanced back into the living room, where Sweet was accepting false condolences, and for only an instant, Sweet's eyes met Beulah's. Sweet's eyes were totally clear and completely innocent, and neither of the women ever knew what strange thing had almost passed between them at that moment.

Wildwood left the kitchen, and Zion and Beulah stood in silence. Then, without a word, Zion opened the freezer and looked inside.

There, in full view, was the turtle stew just as they had marked and delivered it, unopened and frozen as solid as a brick.

"An accident!" Zion almost yelped. "A real accident!"

Beulah felt her head spinning and the room tilting, and the last thing she remembered was Zion reaching out to catch her. "Hold on there!" Zion had yelled.

CHAPTER
— THIRTY-TWO —

It was late afternoon before Beulah really had a chance to speak at length in private with Sweet.

"Sweet," Beulah asked. "Why did you have to call the sheriff so fast?"

Sweet blushed. "Because the first thing I thought when I saw . . . him . . . dead as a doornail on the bathroom floor was, 'I've got to call the sheriff and corroborate Jim's story!' Just think — an innocent man was charged with a crime because I didn't have the courage to speak up. To defy the judge. To tell the whole world that it was my very own husband who had assaulted me, and that Jim had come only to try to help me!"

"But you would have," Beulah assured her. "If he'd gone to trial and been found guilty, you would have spoken up. I know it!"

Sweet shrugged her shoulders. "I guess I'll never know now, but I certainly hope I would have spoken up, no matter the price I would have paid."

"It would have been a dear price," Beulah whispered.

"Yes, I know."

Of course, Beulah had another question quivering on her lips, but she managed to hold it back. No one would gain anything by the asking of it, or by the answering. So that for all the many years left of their beautiful friendship, Beulah never asked, and Sweet never answered. Over the years, Beulah came to realize that Sweet would not have known the answer at all.

Arrangements for the judge's funeral were hard to make. John Anderson had taken the responsibility for contacting the judge's family in New York, asking them how they wanted things done. He was almost certain they had a family cemetery there in which they would have liked to bury the judge. John spoke with the judge's brother and learned that the judge had alienated everyone in his whole family to the point where they wanted nothing to do with him, even his final resting place.

"Just put him in the ground down there," the brother said. "His first two wives are buried here, and if they thought he was coming back — even dead — they would probably rise from their graves and run like hell!"

The day before the funeral, the attorney called Beulah. He knew that Sweet had been staying with Beulah because neither Beulah nor Sweet thought that Sweet should stay out at the farm alone at night.

"Miss Beulah, would you and Miss Sweet please stop by my office sometime this afternoon?"

"Certainly," Beulah answered. "But what's it about?"

"It's good," he said. "Around two o'clock?"

"We'll be there," Beulah promised.

When the two women were seated across the large mahogany desk from the attorney, he cleared his throat and gazed at them without blinking.

"Miss Sweet, I heard about your great-granddaddy's land, and when I heard about the judge's . . . uh, demise . . . I took it upon myself to go to the courthouse and check on the status of the paperwork for shifting the title on the land."

That said, the attorney opened his desk drawer and withdrew a folder.

"The exchange had not yet been officially

recorded," the attorney explained. "So I got the papers back for you." Sweet reached out with both hands and took the folder from him. Her chin trembled and she closed her eyes and pressed the folder against her heart. For a long moment, she looked hard at the papers, and she seemed to be trying to remember something. But then she shook her head and smiled.

"I hope I did the right thing," John whispered.

"Yes!" Sweet yelped. "My great-granddaddy's land! *My* land! Oh, thank you!"

Beulah was thinking hard: without the additional land, the developers' interest in the old Maxson place would probably be severely limited. She was visualizing the beautiful, natural rolling hills of the land, the magnificent trees and fresh-running streams. Perhaps John Anderson had been right in saying that development would not stay away from Tea-Olive forever, but for the time being, at least, Tea-Olive was saved!

The next day, the judge's funeral was held in the old, venerable Tea-Olive cemetery. A large crowd of "mourners" showed up, out of support and respect for Miss

Sweet. Three standing flower arrangements flanked the grave site. One was white carnations with a banner across the front saying "husband." But if you looked closely, you could see a slight discoloration where the word "beloved" had been scraped off ahead of the word "husband." A few people noticed, but of course said nothing. Wildwood had to cover her mouth for a moment, but she soon regained her dignified composure. The second standing spray was made of yellow carnations and had a banner across the front that said "Friends of the Tea-Olive Library." The third spray was the smallest of all, a dozen gladioli with a crooked, hand-printed banner that read, "Tea-Olive Library Homework Helper Program."

The service itself was awkward, because the minister was clearly uncomfortable, basing his remarks solely upon the scriptures that dealt with Christ's admonition to let whoever is without sin cast the first stone. At that moment, Beulah was thinking: *Well, of course I am a sinner. We all are. But at least — thank you, Father — I'm not guilty of the sin of murder!* Then Beulah glanced quickly at Sweet, who was sitting with her hands in her lap. Sweet did not look back at Beulah and Beulah silently admonished herself: *No, I mustn't think that way!*

The minister then asked if anyone had anything they wanted to say, and the moment was awkward, for there was no one to come forward and say anything good about the judge. The minister cleared his throat and said a final prayer.

The crowd dispersed quickly after the service was over, mostly because no one knew what to say to a grieving widow who, clearly, had nothing to grieve about.

Zion, Beulah, Wildwood, and Memphis clustered around Sweet, touching her shoulder, patting her hands, and saying nothing.

From the back of the cemetery, Jim stepped forward and approached the women.

"Jim!" Sweet exclaimed. "I didn't know you were here!"

"Well," he murmured to Sweet, "I didn't come for the judge's sake; I came because of you." To the others, he commented, "I just wanted to thank Miss Sweet, for calling the sheriff and telling him the truth."

"Oh, Jim, I was such a coward!" Sweet apologized. "I did it only after I . . . found the judge dead on the bathroom floor!"

"But you would have stepped forward to help me, in the long run."

"I'll never know for sure," Sweet confessed.

"*I* know for sure," Jim said easily. "And I think that's enough, isn't it?"

"It will have to be enough," Sweet answered.

Throughout this exchange, Zion, Beulah, Wildwood, and Memphis stepped back and tried not to eavesdrop. But then, Jim motioned them to come closer.

"I just wanted to say, right here in front of your good friends, that I ask your permission to move back into the cottage, to help you with the farm."

Sweet glanced at her friends. "Well, I don't know how that would look," she protested.

"Miss Sweet," Jim began. "I am a gentleman. I would never, ever make any advances or do anything to spoil your good name in this town."

Zion started nodding vigorously, and soon, the others joined in.

Beulah spoke up, "Sweet, that's wonderful! I was worried about your having to be out there all by yourself."

Sweet glanced around at her friends, at their smiles and nodding heads. "Your offer is gratefully accepted," Sweet said, blushing.

"Thank you," Jim whispered. He tipped his hat to the ladies, and walked away, humming. When they had all finished tittering about the return of Sweet's great-granddaddy's land and her acceptance of Jim's offer, Zion and Beulah started walking away toward where they had parked their cars.

But at the edge of the cemetery, Jim was waiting for them. As they approached, he lifted off his hat.

"Miss Beulah, I just wanted to thank you for helping me when I was arrested," he said.

"Think nothing of it," Beulah said.

Jim cleared his throat and started turning his hat around and around by the brim. "After a respectful amount of time, I wanted you to know that I would like to keep company with Miss Sweet — honorable company, of course — if she will allow that," he said.

"Oh, I don't know, Jim," Beulah protested. "She's certainly had a bad experience in that department, as you well know. I can't imagine what the future will hold for her."

"Well, we'll just have to wait and see,"

Jim offered, and he seemed relieved that he had shared that information with Beulah and Zion. Then he said, "And I wanted to ask both you ladies about something that's pretty much a mystery to me." They gazed at him questioningly.

"Just before coming to the funeral, I went out to the judge's . . . I mean Sweet's farm, just to see if there was anything I should do for her. She had already left for the funeral, but I figured that I could at least take a load of hay to the cows in the pasture."

"That was nice of you, I'm sure," Zion said, glancing uneasily at Beulah.

"Well, a funny thing happened," Jim continued. "I was driving down the tractor road and I noticed something strange-looking in the road. I stopped the tractor and went and inspected it, and sure enough, there was a kind of trench dug out in the road. Looked about in the right place that, if I hadn't seen it, might have been deep enough to flip the tractor over."

"Well, it rained awfully hard the other night. Perhaps it was a gully-wash," Zion offered, resisting the temptation to glance once again at Beulah.

"No, ma'am," Jim continued. "If it had been a gully-wash, it would have kept going all the way to the edge of the ravine. This trench just *stopped,* and I was wondering if either of you good ladies could help me to figure it out."

Beulah and Zion were now standing as if they were at attention, staring unsmilingly at Jim. He gave a short laugh and smiled. "Well, I just wondered if you ladies knew anything about it," he added. "Just curious, I suppose. Anyway, I filled it in so it won't ever cause any trouble."

With that, he smiled, lifted his hat to them, and slowly walked away.

Beulah and Zion stood as if they were carved out of stone.

"He suspects!" Beulah whispered.

"He can suspect all he wants," Zion whispered back. "Remember, Beulah, that it *didn't* work. We didn't kill him!"

Until Jim could move back into the cottage, the members of the Tea-Olive Bird Watching Society took turns spending the night out at the farm with Sweet. And Sweet was certainly good company! With Wildwood, she discussed the latest book she had read and what she thought about it; with Memphis, she discussed various recipes for canapés her mother had made. Zion insisted on taking a turn, even though that meant that Beulah had to spend the night at Zion's own house, because of the possibility that the cows could need attention, and with Zion, Sweet talked about the stories she had heard about her great-grandparents and their own farm in those beautiful rolling hills. But with Beulah, Sweet spoke of Jim and his impending move back into the cottage.

"He's such a good man, Beulah," Sweet admitted. "And I don't know why, but I think he wants to be . . . closer to me."

"He certainly is a good man, Sweet," Beulah agreed. "But he will never pressure you for anything other than friendship, if friendship's all you want."

"I don't know that I would ever be able to have more than a friendship," Sweet admitted. "I've been through too much."

"It's all up to you, Sweet. You are the one in control of anything you and Jim might possibly come to mean to each other," Beulah reminded her.

Sweet smiled a long and genuine smile. "Yes," she finally said, "It's all up to me."

For the last time, Beulah tried to picture kind, gentle Sweet wielding a softball bat and dispatching the man who had so belittled and dishonored her. It was a picture that just wouldn't come together in her mind. So, once and for all, Beulah dismissed the whole idea.

A few days later, Jim moved back into the cottage, and one afternoon not long afterward, Beulah was in the bird sanctuary, waiting for Sweet to join her for a long, peaceful morning of bird watching. She had already spotted a towhee and a pine warbler, so she was already happy enough. But when she saw Sweet coming across the backyard toward the sanctuary, she couldn't help but grin at Sweet's easy stride and her ready smile. Just as Sweet was coming across the yard, Jim was driving the tractor out from under the shed. He shaded his eyes and spotted Beulah at the edge of the sanctuary. He threw up his arm in greeting, and then, with a grin on his face, he waggled his finger at her, as if to say "shame on you!" The grin, of course, belied his gesture, and Beulah waved back at him.

As Sweet approached the bird sanctuary, Beulah felt Love-Divine's spirit all around her, stirring the leaves and causing the sunlight to stream through the trees in a shade of gold too unbelievable to be real. From high above Beulah's head, the raucous call of a blue jay punctuated Sweet's steps as she came ever closer and closer to the King's Wood Bird Sanctuary. The mélange of sounds and images melted into Beulah's mind, and the feeling of Love-Divine's spirit was so strong that she actually spoke aloud to Love-Divine:

"Just look at Sweet, Love-Divine," Beulah whispered. "Doesn't she make the most beautiful widow you've ever seen?"

ACKNOWLEDGMENTS

Christy, Alexa, Valerie, and Cindy, who, years ago, tossed my initial idea for this story around with me;

Betty Belanger, bird watcher extraordinaire and cherished friend;

My best friend, Beverly, for helping me with Tobia's speech; the Tea Leaves 'n' Thyme Tea Shop in Woodstock, Georgia, for inspiration; Friends of the Woodstock Library for interest and support; Kathie for helping me understand "library business."

Harvey Klinger, my agent; Carole Baron and Julie Doughty, my editors.

And at last, the proverbial question: "Did I tell this story right, Mama?"

ABOUT THE AUTHOR

Augusta Trobaugh is the author of the novels *River Jordan, Swan Place, Sophie and the Rising Sun, Resting in the Bosom of the Lamb,* and *Praise Jerusalem!,* which was a semifinalist in the Pirate's Alley Faulkner Competition. She earned a master's degree in English from the University of Georgia and has been awarded several grants from the Georgia Council of the Arts. She lives in Georgia.